*Everyman, I will go with thee,
and be thy guide*

GW00657438

THE BEST OF
O. HENRY

Edited by
IAN F. A. BELL
University of Keele

Consultant Editor for this volume
CHRISTOPHER BIGSBY
University of East Anglia

EVERYMAN
J. M. DENT · LONDON
CHARLES E. TUTTLE
VERMONT

First published as an Everyman Classic, 1989
Reissued 1992
Reprinted 1992

This edition first published in Everyman in 1993

J. M. Dent
Orion Publishing Group
Orion House, 5 Upper St Martin's Lane,
London WC2H 9EA
and
Charles E. Tuttle Co. Inc.
28 South Main Street, Rutland, Vermont
05701, USA

Typeset by ROM-Data Corporation, Falmouth, Cornwall
Printed in Great Britain by
The Guernsey Press Co. Ltd, Guernsey, C.I.

British Library Cataloguing-in-Publication Data is available
upon request.

ISBN 0 460 87339 3

CONTENTS

NOTE ON THE AUTHOR AND EDITOR

O. HENRY is the pseudonym of William Sidney Porter. He was born the son of a doctor in Greenboro, North Carolina, on 11 September 1862. His mother died when he was three. Porter attended school in Greenboro until the age of fifteen when he left to work for five years in his uncle's drugstore. In 1882 he moved to Texas, where a variety of jobs included ranching, bookkeeping, draftsmanship and journalism for his own, short-lived newspaper, the weekly *Rolling Stone* and the Houston *Daily Post*. Always in need of funds, he also sought the security of regular employment as a teller at the First National Bank in Austin. In 1896, following the discovery of discrepancies in the bank's books, Porter fled the country, ending up in Honduras. The critical condition of his wife's health forced him to return in 1897, when he stood trial for embezzlement, was convicted and sentenced to five years' imprisonment. In the event, he served only three years in the Ohio State Penitentiary, years which confirmed his resolve to adopt a writing career as his means of livelihood. After a brief spell in Pittsburgh, Porter moved to New York in 1902, the city which was to sustain him materially and imaginatively for the rest of his life. He had already tried his hand at short-story writing, but it was not until his incarceration that the form began to flourish, reaching its apotheosis during his period in New York. This final decade of his life was extraordinarily productive, yielding over six hundred stories – a productivity matched in size by popular acclaim. His first volume was *Cabbages and Kings*, published in 1904. Its topics were mainly tales of revolution and adventure in South America, but with the publication of *The Four Million* in 1906, Porter established what many regard as his true and finest subject – tales of New York itself. His popularity and fame were enhanced by *The Trimmed Lamp* and *Heart of The West* (1907), *The Gentle Grafter* and *The Voice of the City* (1908). In 1909 came *Options* and *Roads of Destiny*, followed by *Whirligigs, Let Me Feel Your Pulse*, and *Strictly Business* in 1910, the year of his death. Posthumously, three further volumes appeared: *Sixes and Sevens, Rolling Stones*, and *Waifs and Strays*. Diabetes, cirrhosis of the liver, and dilation of the heart contributed to Porter's death on 5 June 1910.

IAN F. A. BELL is Professor of American Literature at the University of Keele. He received his BA in English and Philosophy from the University of Reading, where he also gained his PhD for research into the works of Ezra Pound. He is the author of *Critic as Scientist: The Modernist Poetics of Ezra Pound, Henry James and the Past: Readings Into Time, Washington Square: Styles Of Money*. He has written articles and essays on Pound, James, Emerson, Yeats, Eliot and Cather. He has edited *Ezra Pound: Tactics For Reading, Henry James: Fiction as History* and (with D. K. Adams) *American Literary Landscapes: The Fiction and the Fact*.

INTRODUCTION

'The time has come,' the Walrus said,
'To talk of many things;
Of shoes and ships and sealing-wax,
And cabbages and kings.'

Lewis Carroll's rhyme provided both the epigraph and the title for O. Henry's first volume of stories, *Cabbages and Kings*, in 1904. The whimsical conjunction of the incongruous prepares us for a weaving of the ordinary and the extravagant that is characteristic of the writer who has been variously, and accurately, called both 'the Henry Ford of the short story' and 'the prose laureate of Manhattan Island'. To this mixture, we may add the element of literary seriousness: O. Henry tells us that his work is addressed 'to the man who sits smoking with his Sabbath-slippered feet on another chair, and to the woman who snatches the paper for a moment while boiling greens or a narcotized baby leaves her free. With these I love to sit upon the ground and tell sad stories of the death of kings'. His audience is imagined not only as a literal version of 'cabbages and kings', but his own role carries Shakespearean echoes, recalling Mamillius's pronouncement in *The Winter's Tale* that 'a sad tale's best for winter'. But, at the same time, O. Henry does not want us to take his seriousness too seriously – he will later invoke another character from this play, the comic rogue Autolycus, in referring to Jeff Peters, a central figure in three of the stories collected here, as an 'Autolycan adventurer'. In the preamble to *Cabbages and Kings*, 'The Proem. By the Carpenter', O. Henry defines the kind of fiction he wishes to pursue. His *persona*, the Carpenter, wants 'a little tale to tell of many things. Perhaps to the promiscuous ear of the Walrus it shall come with most avail; for in it there are indeed shoes and ships and sealing-wax and cabbage-palms and presidents instead of kings'. If the writer, in a reversal of Carroll's model, is envisaged as the adventurous Carpenter, his audience is imagined as the open-eared Walrus. O. Henry continues: 'Add to these a little love and counterplotting, and scatter everywhere throughout the maze a trail of tropical dollars – dollars warmed no more by the torrid sun than by the hot palms of the scouts of Fortune – and, after all, here seems to be Life, itself, with talk enough to weary the most garrulous of Walruses.'

It is 'talk', above all else, that distinguishes O. Henry's tales, 'talk' which registers the flexibility of the tongue itself in a manoeuvring of the commonplace and the idiosyncratic. It is 'talk' which uses what one critic has defined as the traditional devices of American humour (exaggeration, incongruous comparisons, malapropisms and misquotations, irreverence and inflated circumlocution) to re-invent the great strain of the oral in American literature. It is 'talk' which enables O. Henry to achieve that most difficult of literary tasks – a capturing of the ordinariness in ordinary life which, through his stylized and baroque comedy, manages to avoid the feel of literariness. It is 'talk', perhaps, which has established his place as the most prolific and popular of American short story writers. He produced over six hundred stories in the last decade of his life, years which also marked the bulk of his writing career. As his best critic, Gerald Langford, has noted, 'in the decade following his death no other writer's stories, except Kipling's, sold more widely and were more highly esteemed than O. Henry's'. By 1920, sales in the United States alone numbered five million volumes, and by 1923 he had been translated into French, Spanish, German, Swedish, Danish, Norwegian, and Japanese.

What we have in O. Henry is the strain of the talker that has been persistent throughout nineteenth-century American writing from the stories of Washington Irving and Nathaniel Hawthorne during the early and middle years of the century through to, most famously, Mark Twain's invention of Huckleberry Finn at its end. Frequently the stories involve the telling of stories, and frequently the position of the oral is emphasized, as is the site of the telling – the store-front, the porch of a house, or simply a gathering of friends. Such foregrounding emphasizes the dialogical nature of story-telling, that it is an act of exchange and sharing: 'The Shamrock and the Palm' begins on a moment of collectivity, when 'five men were grouped about the door of the photograph establishment of Keogh and Clancy'. Ben Granger in 'The Moment of

Victory' rallies 'his corporal's guard of cronies in the shade of his well-whittled porch' before commencing his tale-telling, while more intimately the narration of 'Telemachus, Friend' begins 'I sat on the porch of the Summit House and discussed the functions of life with Telemachus Hicks'. Where O. Henry uses a first-person narrative, it is usually there from the very start – 'I saw a light in Jeff Peters's room over the Red Front Drug Store' ('The Atavism of John Tom Little Bear'), or 'I never got inside of the legitimate line of graft but once' ('Hostages to Momus') – and so the reader enters directly and immediately into the action. It is an entry facilitated by this pervasive sense of the speaking voice, taking us instantly into the scene as we see in O. Henry's other style of beginning: 'If you do not know Bogle's Chop House and Family Restaurant it is your loss' ('The Brief Debut of Tildy'); 'Ben Granger is a war veteran aged twenty-nine – which should enable you to guess the war' ('The Moment of Victory'); 'Miss Lynnette D'Armande turned her back on Broadway. This was but tit for tat, because Broadway had often done the same thing to Miss D'Armande' ('The Memento'); 'Across our two dishes of spaghetti, in a corner of Provenzano's restaurant, Jeff Peters was explaining to me the three kinds of graft' ('The Man Higher Up').

This immediacy of the speaking voice is amongst O. Henry's most important innovations on behalf of the short story form, as we can see by comparison with more customary opening strategies: 'In the bosom of one of those spacious coves which indent the eastern shore of the Hudson ...' (Irving's 'The Legend of Sleepy Hollow'); 'During the whole of a dull, dark, and soundless day in the autumn of the year ...' (Poe's 'The Fall of the House of Usher'); 'It was many years ago. Hadleyburg was the most honest and upright town in all the region round about ...' (Twain's 'The Man That Corrupted Hadleyburg'). O. Henry, of course, was not the first to rely on the speaking voice – the most famous American novel of the nineteenth century, Melville's *Moby Dick*, begins its story proper with 'Call me Ishmael' – but he was the first to develop so fully and so richly its narrative possibilities for the short story. The oral had always been a potent resource for the American literary imagination, but it is not until we arrive at O. Henry that it is realized as more than an artistic or ideological device and made manifest as a new and marvellously comic realism. In 1920, H. L. Mencken commented on how his characters 'talk the same highly ornate Broadwayese', and this is absolutely right, laying the ground that would be mined later to even greater extravagance and humour by the stylized laconicism of W. C. Fields and Damon Runyon. All literary beginnings are important, but usually in the sense that they set a scene – physical, psychological, social, or temporal. With O. Henry they establish a new form of fiction – one that wishes to enter into dialogue with the reader straightaway. He is very serious about this tactic; so much so that he can treat it comically, as in 'The Princess and the Puma' where we enter a story of mock-heroic Texan chivalry *via*, 'There had to be a king and queen, of course', or in 'The Passing of Black Eagle' where the opening sentence plays upon the potential reductiveness of standard novelistic beginnings with, 'For some months of a certain year, a grim bandit infested the Texas border along the Rio Grande'. (Note how the adjectival 'grim' and the metaphoric 'infested' effect a wonderful deflation that will turn out to be one of the story's main thrusts.) Such is O. Henry's mastery that he can make his point against unnecessary literariness by means of a single adjective: one of his most important stories, 'The Last of the Troubadours', begins 'Inexorably Sam Galloway saddled his pony'. Nobody saddles anything 'inexorably' (it is repeated in the next paragraph), and O. Henry's comic economy secures the whole range of feelings experienced by a character whose sense of sorrow is 'deepened with regret and slightly tempered by the patient forgiveness of a connoisseur who cannot be understood'.

Such adjectives are indeed comic *and* economical, and they point to the core of O. Henry's humour which, thoroughly within the tradition of the speaking voice, tends to be the humour of words and utterance rather than of situation. Most obviously, we have the inflations of what Mencken has termed his 'ornate Broadwayese', the factitious elegance of the partially educated, whereby the eye becomes the 'optic nerve', stories become 'oral constructions', a waitress's 'pulchritude might season and make ambrosia of their bacon and eggs', where a tale-teller may announce 'I had a friend once, of the entitlement of Paisley Fish' (the extent to which the names of characters share this linguistic cornucopia is striking), and where 'labial dabs' may take the place of kisses. Closely allied here is the propensity for malapropisms: a character is given 'the name by which he denounced himself', another asked 'to denominate the terms by which his country is called', and yet another 'to inoculate the occasion with a few well-timed trivialities' in a world where 'about a dozen people permeated along the sidewalks'. This special linguistic 'elegance' manifests itself also in a vocabulary which strongly declares its origin in a thesaurus or dictionary – 'hegira', 'eleemosynary', 'cinctured', 'transudations'. Such words shriek their distance from naturalistic discourse and the language of the tongue, however designed that language otherwise remains. In one sense they alienate the reader from even O. Henry's customary burlesque, but they also point to his pervasive efforts to record the ordinary and the actual without resorting to any commonplace of representation. In fact he makes a point of this very issue in 'A Municipal Report' where, in striving for 'an approximate conception of a Nashville drizzle', he informs us that 'having searched the thesaurus in vain for adjectives, I must, as a substitution, hie me to comparison in the form of a recipe'. The 'recipe' is as follows: 'Take of London fog 30 parts; malaria 10 parts; gas leaks 20 parts; dewdrops, gathered in a brickyard at sunrise, 25 parts; odour of honeysuckle 15 parts. Mix.'

If this is a 'substitution', then it is all the better for it in terms of figurability (giving a far more vivid picture than the feeble simile which follows – 'not so fragrant as a mothball nor as thick as pea-soup'), and it approaches one of O. Henry's signal successes: his quasi-literal use of highly expressive and usually comic metaphors. Here, his linguistic playfulness engenders words made flesh. While his similes are visually resonant (a waiter has 'a voice like butter cakes and an eye like the cherry in a Manhattan cocktail', a man rises up from the pavement 'joint by joint, as a carpenter's rule opens'), his metaphors have a more important task which contributes substantially to the complex of the writer/story-teller/talker which, I am suggesting, is his importance for the history of the American short story. Customarily, metaphors operate 'as if' dissimilar things may be conjoined by a previously undiscerned similarity, but O. Henry turns this operation around by making the conjoining a literal event. The 'debut' of the waitress Tildy in 'The Brief Debut of Tildy' refers to a kiss bestowed upon her by a young man named Seeders and to its subsequent effect upon her social standing. Seeders works in a laundry, and the kiss 'performed for her a miraculous piece of one-day laundry-work' whereby 'He had taken the sackcloth of her uncomeliness, had washed, dried, starched and ironed it, and returned it to her sheer embroidered lawn – the robe of Venus herself'. (Comparable is the extended sheep metaphor applied to Willie Robbins in 'The Moment of Victory'.) Here we have a gesture of linguistic primitivism in which O. Henry draws upon the Adamic strain of American writing where words are imagined to have a realistic rather than arbitrary relation to their objects (similarly, 'Chicken' Ruggles in 'The Passing of Black Eagle' is so named because of his physiognomy and his eating habits), but on other occasions metaphor creates a sharable world of its own which establishes a community of feeling between two people that would otherwise be difficult (or merely commonplace) to express. In 'Telemachus, Friend', Paisley Fish and Telemachus Hicks debate the threat to friendship posed by their pursuit of the same woman, Mrs Jessup. When Fish, with appropriate malapropism, ventures that, 'The smiles of woman is the whirl-pool of Squills and Chalybeates, into which vortex the good ship Friendship is often drawn and dismembered', Hicks is later able to return with a solution which he expresses as 'With that arrangement I don't see why our steamboat of friendship should fall overboard in the medicinal whirlpools you speak of, which-ever of us wins out'. The comradeship established by the sharing of metaphor persists throughout the trials of the subsequent courtships and marriage, and the sharing avoids, economically and figuratively, any of the sentimentality that can accrue to male intimacy (central not only to the themes of O. Henry's stories but to the structure of story-telling itself) in the face of perceived female threat.

O. Henry's pleasure in making metaphors literal is a principal project in the linguistic adventurousness that preoccupies his stories. When we encounter the following description of the hotel in 'The Memento', we recognize the extent to which such adven-turousness takes the mechanics of syntax itself as freshly real:

> The indeterminate hum of life in the Thalia is enlivened by the discreet popping – at reasonable and salubrious intervals – of beer-bottle corks. Thus punctuated, life in the genial hostel scans easily – the comma being the favourite mark, semicolons frowned upon, and periods barred.

The metaphor here might suggest a view of language as a disci-plinary exercise whereby randomness may be ordered. But words are not so easily controlled, as we see in a comparable moment from 'The Shamrock and the Palm' where the story-teller, Clancy, who is always getting the names of Kamchatka and Guatemala confused, offers this description of the latter:

> Ye'll find that country on the map. 'Tis in the district known as the tropics. By the foresight of Providence, it lies on the coast so the geography man could run the names of the towns off into the water. They're an inch long, small type, composed of Spanish dialects, and, 'tis my opinion, of the same system of syntax that blew up the *Maine*.

The convenience of the coastal location for the cartographer may initially stress the comedy of the metaphor, but its inherent ambition for order is then undermined radically by the 'syntax' of an event, the sinking of the battleship *Maine* in Havana harbour in 1898, which played a large part in precipitating America's declaration of war with Spain. Through the metaphor, landscapes and nations become maps and words which turn out to be destroyers. (A substantial element of O. Henry's point here is to imply the role of the yellow press in whipping up jingoistic fervour after the sinking of the *Maine*, a fervour which in its turn contributed to the impulse towards war.)

The gravity of O. Henry's argument should not be suppressed by the humourousness of the narrative voice. Words have material effects, and they are frequently comic, as in Chicken Ruggles's move from St Louis to San Antonio ('The Passing of Black Eagle') where prolixity helps him to scrounge free meals:

> The bartenders there would not kick him. If he should eat too long or too often at one place they would swear at him as if by rote and without heat. They swore so drawlingly, and they rarely paused short of their full vocabulary, which was copious, so that Chicken had often gulped a good meal during the process of the vituperative prohibition.

We need to retain, certainly, this comedy, not only for its intrinsic delight, but for its revitalizing of worn phrases which abounds throughout these stories – 'discretion was the better part of filibusterin' ', 'a woman that would have tempted an anchovy to forget his vows', 'There was no fear of the extemporaneous, of variety spicing her infinite custom', 'that land of bilk and money' – and for its neological wit. Kansas Bill, in 'A Ruler of Men', is offended by the native naming processes of South America and claims that the town of Guayaquerita presents 'a clear case where spelling reform ought to butt in and disenvowel it'. These revitalizations express O. Henry's abiding distrust of literariness, rhetoric, and commonplace expression. He has one of his main characters, Jeff Peters, inveigh against the 'educated' voice which 'adorns the atmosphere with the various idioms into which education can fracture the wind of speech' and employs 'the science of making three words do the work of one'.

Jeff Peters, with all his naturalistic primitivism where language is concerned, may stand as the type for the story-teller. O. Henry observed that 'You have to be a cad before you can be an artist', and in the figures of Peters and the other story-tellers in his tales, we can see how the artistry of the 'cad' brings together the strands of the inquiry into words that I have been identifying and so provides a new notion of writing itself – writing as trickery and criminality. Crime, it would seem, sometimes does pay – literally so, for O. Henry's period in prison not only animated a new career as a short story writer but also provided the name under which he published (William Sydney Porter took his pseudonym from one of the prison guards, Orrin Henry). The three stories where Jeff Peters appears in this collection ('The Atavism of John Tom Little Bear', 'Jeff Peters as a Personal Magnet', and 'The Man Higher Up') confirm the elements of the type that go to make up the figure of the confidence trickster, the figure which allows O. Henry to pursue his arguments about artistry and language. Like O. Henry himself, Peters is a man of many experiences and jobs, a man 'of a hundred occupations, with a story to tell (when he will) of each one'. This variousness is shared by O. Henry's other story-tellers exemplified in Telemachus Hicks (in 'Telemachus, Friend') and, more tellingly, Clancy (in 'The Shamrock and the Palm'), 'an American with an Irish diathesis and cosmopolitan proclivities' whose 'mood was the gossip's'.

This wide experiential base is essential to both story-telling and confidence trickery, and is matched in its necessity by a capacity for rhetoric and exaggeration (seen at its best in 'Jeff Peters as a Personal Magnet') that is effectively transformative. Again, this is given a particular literalness – not only the concrete results of swindling based on persuasion (usually money) but by a kind of shape-changing. Chicken Ruggles (in 'The Passing of Black Eagle'), for example, is a small-time con-man who transforms himself into Black Eagle, the 'Terror of the Border', by means of the tall tales he tells, gaining advancement in a gang of outlaws precisely through the exotic adventurousness of those tales. Stories are to be understood as fundamentally protean, changing their tales according to differences in circumstances and audience (seen most clearly in 'The Princess and the Puma'), and their capacity for self-invention draws the reader into their trickery. We experience this not only in the twist or surprise endings that are characteristic of so many of O. Henry's stories (and a considerable contribution to his development of the form), but in stories such as 'A Ramble in Aphasia' where a perfectly respectable lawyer (not a con-man), Elwyn Bellford, assumes a completely different identity as a druggist, Edward Pinkhammer, to seek release from the pressures of business. Here we have the trickster in a different and more radical form, and the reader is as completely deceived by the invention as the other characters in the story: there is no hint, until the very end, that Bellford is not suffering from amnesia.

O. Henry's stories are largely populated by tricksters ('Hostages to Momus' is another example), and the author is careful to distinguish them from the character who also appears frequently – the adventurer or soldier of fortune. The latter is usually presented as a predominantly literary creation (in 'A Ruler of Men' and, to a lesser extent, in 'The Shamrock and the Palm') and so occupies a fairly menial place in the scheme of things. He may share the trickster's capacity for experience and the tall tale, but he is invariably the duped rather than the duper, one who is the victim of others' tricks precisely through the tallness of the tales he invents for himself. The trickster as swindler or confidence man assumes a variety of forms, as does the story-teller, but we should note, parenthetically, that there remains a strain of idealism in O. Henry's conception of the writer. Sam Galloway, for example, is 'The Last of the Troubadours', and the honourable literary cloak is donned in order to present an essentially non-materialistic image of the wandering story-teller, one whose living is for 'Art's sake' and for 'entertainment and pleasure'. Inevitably such idealism serves principally to make us aware of the trickery of writing by its very distance from it: Jeff Peters, the 'Autolycan adventurer' whose 'profession' is 'an incorporated, uncapitalized, unlimited asylum for the reception of the restless and unwise dollars of his fellow-men', remains as our type for the writer as confidence man. He is a figure whose logic is distorted but compelling:

> I never yet drew upon honest toil for its hard-earned pittance. The dollars I get are surplus ones that are burning the pockets of damfools and greenhorns. When I stand on a street corner and sell a solid gold diamond ring to a yap for $3.00, I make just $2.60. And I know he's going to give it to a girl in return for all the benefits accruing from a

$125.00 ring. His profits are $122.00. Which of us is the biggest faker?

Beyond the sophistic reasoning, Peters's final question is a meaningful one, and it asks us to move beyond the simplistic dichotomy of trickster and tricked in order to question the notion of confidence itself and the extent to which writing and words may be trusted. It is here that O. Henry joins the scepticism about language so characteristic of American literary thought – a scepticism about the referentiality and reliability of words. Most notably in Emerson's essay on *Nature* and Melville's *The Confidence Man*, the capacity of words for truthfulness and stability is interrogated rigorously to suggest that language is duplicitous more often than it is honest – serving the interests of power rather than those of accurate representation. Words are recognized to be as various as stories, chameleons which both extend language's referential schemes and distort its ambitions for truthfulness. But it would be a mistake to see such questioning as a negative activity, as leaving the reader confined by a universal scepticism. Melville's great lesson about confidence is to see it as both trick and liberator, and the latter is frequently possible mainly as a result of the former, as a result of a continual questioning and a willingness to open the self up to being tricked. Words can be, and frequently are, tyrannical if left uninterrogated, and it is precisely the lesson of O. Henry's incessant linguistic playfulness to alert us to that tyranny. It would exaggerate his importance to see this playfulness as carrying the weight of, say, Thoreau's punning in *Walden*, or the radicalism of Melville (although it is surely not accidental that one of the characters in the *Cabbages and Kings* volume, Frank Goodwin, has a name that echoes Frank Goodman, one of the aliases of *The Confidence Man*) who went so far as to see writing as a form of murder (in 'The Bell-Tower') and of rape (in 'The Tartarus of Maids'), but his exuberant lexical tactics lead powerfully to the conception of the writer as trickster. Despite his antipathy to literariness, it is on this very literary point of linguistic scepticism that O. Henry's stories of story-telling and trickery most firmly belong *In the American Grain* (to borrow a title from William Carlos Williams), and most generatively extend the range of the short story form. It is O. Henry's trickery, like Oscar Wilde's lying, which places him at the beginning of literary modernism.

IAN F. A. BELL

NOTE ON THE TEXT

The stories in this edition have been selected to display the best of O. Henry's vast output (even his kindest critic would admit to the inevitable uneven quality of that output) and its diversity. O. Henry was an intensely local writer (one of the principal sources for his success) and this selection draws upon the three main locales which fascinated his tales – the American southwest, Latin America, and New York. They were originally published in the following volumes:

'The Passing of Black Eagle' (*Roads of Destiny*, 1909)

'The Shamrock and the Palm' (*Cabbages and Kings*, 1904)

'The Princess and the Puma' and 'Telemachus, Friend' (*Heart of the West*, 1907)

'The Atavism of John Tom Little Bear' and 'A Ruler of Men' (*Rolling Stones*, 1912)

'The Brief Debut of Tildy', 'The Cop and the Anthem' and 'The Gift of the Magi' (*The Four Million*, 1906)

'Hostages to Momus', 'Jeff Peters as a Personal Magnet' and 'The Man Higher Up' (*The Gentle Grafter*, 1908)

'A Ramble in Aphasia', 'Past One at Rooney's' and 'A Municipal Report' (*Strictly Business*, 1910)

'The Moment of Victory' (*Options*, 1909)

'The Last of the Troubadours' (*Sixes and Sevens*, 1911)

'The Memento' (*The Voice of the City*, 1908)

THE BEST OF
O. HENRY

THE PASSING OF BLACK EAGLE

For some months of a certain year a grim bandit infested the Texas border along the Rio Grande. Peculiarly striking to the optic nerve was this notorious marauder. His personality secured him the title of 'Black Eagle, the Terror of the Border.' Many fearsome tales are on record concerning the doings of him and his followers. Suddenly, in the space of a single minute, Black Eagle vanished from earth. He was never heard of again. His own band never even guessed the mystery of his disappearance. The border ranches and settlements feared he would come again to ride and ravage the mesquite flats. He never will. It is to disclose the fate of Black Eagle that this narrative is written.

The initial movement of the story is furnished by the foot of a bartender in St Louis. His discerning eye fell upon the form of Chicken Ruggles as he pecked with avidity at the free lunch. Chicken was a 'hobo.' He had a long nose like the bill of a fowl, an inordinate appetite for poultry, and a habit of gratifying it without expense, which accounts for the name given him by his fellow-vagrants.

Physicians agree that the partaking of liquids at meal times is not a healthy practice. The hygiene of the saloon promulgates the opposite. Chicken had neglected to purchase a drink to accompany his meal. The bartender rounded the counter, caught the injudicious diner by the ear with a lemon squeezer, led him to the door and kicked him into the street.

Thus the mind of Chicken was brought to realize the signs of coming winter. The night was cold; the stars shone with unkindly brilliance; people were hurrying along the streets in two egotistic, jostling streams. Men had donned their overcoats, and Chicken knew to an exact percentage the increased difficulty of coaxing dimes from those buttoned-in vest pockets. The time had come for his annual exodus to the south.

A little boy, five or six years old, stood looking with covetous eyes in a confectioner's window. In one small hand he held an empty two-ounce vial; in the other he grasped tightly something flat and round, with a shining milled edge. The scene presented a field of operations commensurate to Chicken's talents and daring. After sweeping the horizon to make sure that no official tug was cruising near, he insidiously accosted his prey. The boy, having been early taught by his household to regard altruistic advances with extreme suspicion, received the overtures coldly.

Then Chicken knew that he must make one of those desperate, nerve-shattering plunges into speculation that fortune sometimes requires of those who would win her favour. Five cents was his capital, and this he must risk against the chance of winning what lay within the close grasp of the youngster's chubby hand. It was a fearful lottery, Chicken knew. But he must accomplish his end by strategy, since he had a wholesome terror of plundering infants by force. Once, in a park, driven by hunger, he had committed an onslaught upon a bottle of peptonized infant's food in the possession of an occupant of a baby carriage. The outraged infant had so promptly opened its mouth and pressed the button that communicated with the welkin that help arrived, and Chicken did his thirty days in a snug coop. Wherefore he was, as he said, 'leary of kids.'

Beginning artfully to question the boy concerning his choice of sweets, he gradually drew out the information he wanted. Mamma said he was to ask the drug store man for ten cents' worth of paregoric in the bottle; he was to keep his hand shut tight over the dollar; he must not stop to talk to anyone in the street; he must ask the drug store man to wrap up the change and put it in the pocket of his trousers. Indeed, they had pockets – two of them! And he liked chocolate creams best.

Chicken went into the store and turned plunger. He invested his entire capital in C.A.N.D.Y. stocks, simply to pave the way to the greater risk following.

He gave the sweets to the youngster, and had the satisfaction of perceiving that confidence was established. After that it was easy to obtain leadership of the expedition; to take the investment by the hand and lead it to a nice drug store he knew of in the same block. There Chicken, with a parental air, passed over the dollar and called for the medicine, while the boy crunched his candy, glad to be relieved of the responsibility of the purchase. And then the successful investor, searching his pockets, found an overcoat button – the extent of his winter trousseau – and, wrapping it carefully, placed the ostensible change in the pocket of confiding juvenility. Setting the youngster's face homeward and patting him benevolently on the back – for Chicken's heart was as soft as those of his feathered namesakes – the speculator quit the market with a profit of 1,700 per cent. on his invested capital.

Two hours later an Iron Mountain freight engine pulled out of the railroad yards, Texas bound, with a string of empties. In one of the cattle cars, half buried in excelsior, Chicken lay at ease. Beside him in his nest was a quart bottle of very poor whisky and a paper bag of bread and cheese. Mr Ruggles, in his private car, was on his trip south for the winter season.

For a week that car was trundled southward, shifted, laid over, and manipulated after the manner of rolling stock, but Chicken stuck to it, leaving it only at necessary times to satisfy his hunger and thirst. He knew it must go down to the cattle country, and San Antonio, in the heart of it, was his goal. There the air was salubrious and mild; the people indulgent and long-suffering. The bartenders there would not kick him. If he should eat too long or too often at one place they would swear at him as if by rote and without heat. They swore so drawlingly, and they rarely paused short of their full vocabulary, which was copious, so that Chicken had often gulped a good meal during the process of the vituperative prohibition. The season there was always spring-like; the plazas were pleasant at night, with music and gaiety; except during the slight and infrequent cold snaps one could sleep comfortably out of doors in case the interiors should develop inhospitality.

At Texarkana his car was switched to the I. and G.N. Then still southward it trailed until, at length, it crawled across the Colorado bridge at Austin, and lined out, straight as an arrow, for the run to San Antonio.

When the freight halted at that town Chicken was fast asleep. In ten minutes the train was off again for Laredo, the end of the road. Those empty cattle cars were for distribution along the line at points from which the ranches shipped their stock.

When Chicken awoke his car was stationary. Looking out between the slats he saw it was a bright, moonlit night. Scrambling out, he saw his car with three others abandoned on a little siding in a wild and lonesome country. A cattle pen and chute stood on one side of the track. The railroad bisected a vast, dim ocean of prairie, in the midst of which Chicken, with his futile rolling stock, was as completely stranded as was Robinson with his land-locked boat.

A white post stood near the rails. Going up to it, Chicken read the letters at the top, S. A. 90. Laredo was nearly as far to the south. He was almost a hundred miles from any town. Coyotes began to yelp in the mysterious sea around him. Chicken felt lonesome. He had lived in Boston without an education, in Chicago without nerve, in Philadelphia without a sleeping-place, in New York without a pull, and in Pittsburg sober, and yet he had never felt so lonely as now.

Suddenly through the intense silence he heard the whicker of a horse. The sound came from the side of the track toward the east, and Chicken began to explore timorously in that direction. He stepped high along the mat of curly mesquite grass, for he was afraid of everything there might be in this wilderness – snakes, rats, brigands, centipedes, mirages, cowboys, fandangoes, tarantulas, tamales – he had read of them in the story-papers. Rounding a clump of prickly pear that reared high its fantastic and menacing array of rounded heads, he was struck to shivering terror by a snort and a thunderous plunge, as the horse, himself startled, bounded away some fifty yards, and then resumed his grazing. But here was the one thing in the desert that Chicken did not fear. He had been reared on a farm; he had handled horses, understood them, and could ride.

Approaching slowly and speaking soothingly, he followed the animal, which, after its first flight, seemed gentle enough, and secured the end of the twenty-foot lariat that dragged after him in the grass. It required him but a few moments to contrive the rope into an ingenious nose-bridle, after the style of the Mexican *borsal*. In another he was upon the horse's back and off at a splendid lope, giving the animal free choice of direction. 'He will take me somewhere,' said Chicken to himself.

It would have been a thing of joy, that untrammelled gallop over the moonlit prairie, even to Chicken, who loathed exertion, but that his mood was not for it. His head ached; a growing thirst was upon him; the 'somewhere' whither his lucky mount might convey him was full of dismal peradventure.

And now he noted that the horse moved to a definite goal. Where the prairie lay smooth he kept his course straight as an arrow's toward the east. Deflected by hill or arroyo or impracticable spinous brakes, he quickly flowed again into the current, charted by his unerring instinct. At last, upon the side of a gentle rise, he suddenly subsided to a complacent walk. A stone's cast away stood a little mott of coma trees; beneath it a *jacal* such as the Mexicans erect – a one-room house of upright poles daubed with clay and roofed with grass or tule reeds. An experienced eye would have estimated the spot as the headquarters of a small sheep ranch. In the moonlight the ground in the near-by corral showed pulverized to a level smoothness by the hoofs of the sheep. Everywhere was carelessly distributed the paraphernalia of the place – ropes, bridles, saddles, sheep pelts, wool sacks, feed troughs, and camp litter. The barrel of drinking water stood in the end of the two-horse wagon near the door. The harness was piled, promiscuous, upon the wagon tongue, soaking up the dew.

Chicken slipped to earth, and tied the horse to a tree. He halloed again and again, but the house remained quiet. The door stood open, and he entered cautiously. The light was sufficient for him to see that no one was at home. He struck a match and lighted a lamp that stood on a table. The room was that of a bachelor ranch-man who was content with the necessaries of life. Chicken rummaged intelligently until he found what he had hardly dared hope for – a small, brown jug that still contained something near a quart of his desire.

Half an hour later, Chicken – now a gamecock of hostile aspect – emerged from the house with unsteady steps. He had drawn upon the absent ranchman's equipment to replace his own ragged attire. He wore a suit of coarse brown ducking, the coat being a sort of rakish bolero, jaunty to a degree. Boots he had donned, and spurs that whirred with every lurching step. Buckled around him was a belt full of cartridges with a big six-shooter in each of its two holsters.

Prowling about, he found blankets, a saddle and bridle with which he caparisoned his steed. Again mounting, he rode swiftly away, singing a loud and tuneless song.

Bud King's band of desperadoes, outlaws and horse and cattle thieves, were in camp at a secluded spot on the bank of the Frio. Their depredations in the Rio Grande country, while no bolder than usual, had been advertised more extensively, and Captain Kinney's company of rangers had been ordered down to look after them. Consequently, Bud King, who was a wise general, instead of cutting out a hot trail for the upholders of the law, as his men wished to do, retired for the time to the prickly fastnesses of the Frio valley.

Though the move was a prudent one, and not incompatible

with Bud's well-known courage, it raised dissension among the members of the band. In fact, while they thus lay ingloriously *perdu* in the brush, the question of Bud King's fitness for the leadership was argued, with closed doors, as it were, by his followers. Never before had Bud's skill or efficiency been brought to criticism; but his glory was waning (and such is glory's fate) in the light of a newer star. The sentiment of the band was crystallizing into the opinion that Black Eagle could lead them with more lustre, profit and distinction.

This Black Eagle – sub-titled the 'Terror of the Border' – had been a member of the gang about three months.

One night while they were in camp on the San Miguel waterhole a solitary horseman on the regulation fiery steed dashed in among them. The new-comer was of a portentous and devastating aspect. A beak-like nose with a predatory curve projected above a mass of bristling, blue-black whiskers. His eye was cavernous and fierce. He was spurred, sombreroed, booted, garnished with revolvers, abundantly drunk, and very much unafraid. Few people in the country drained by the Rio Bravo would have cared thus to invade alone the camp of Bud King. But this fell bird swooped fearlessly upon them and demanded to be fed.

Hospitality in the prairie country is not limited. Even if your enemy pass your way you must feed him before you shoot him. You must empty your larder into him before you empty your lead. So the stranger of undeclared intentions was set down to a mighty feast.

A talkative bird he was, full of most marvellous loud tales and exploits, and speaking a language at times obscure but never colourless. He was a new sensation to Bud King's men, who rarely encountered new types. They hung, delighted, upon his vainglorious boasting, the spicy strangeness of his lingo, his contemptuous familiarity with life, the world, and remote places, and the extravagant frankness with which he conveyed his sentiments.

To their guest the band of outlaws seemed to be nothing more than a congregation of country bumpkins whom he was 'stringing for grub' just as he would have told his stories at the back door of a farmhouse to wheedle a meal. And, indeed, his ignorance was not without excuse, for the 'bad man' of the South-west does not run to extremes. Those brigands might justly have been taken for a little party of peaceable rustics assembled for a fish-fry or pecan gathering. Gentle of manner, slouching of gait, soft-voiced, un-picturesquely clothed; not one of them presented to the eye any witness of the desperate records they had earned.

For two days the glittering stranger within the camp was feasted. Then, by common consent, he was invited to become a member of the band. He consented, presenting for enrolment the prodigious name of 'Captain Montressor.' This name was immediately overruled by the band, and 'Piggy' substituted as a compliment to the awful and insatiate appetite of its owner.

Thus did the Texas border receive the most spectacular brigand that ever rode its chaparral.

For the next three months Bud King conducted business as usual, escaping encounters with law officers and being content with reasonable profits. The band ran off some very good companies of horses from the ranges, and a few bunches of fine cattle which they got safely across the Rio Grande and disposed of to fair advantage. Often the band would ride into the little villages and Mexican settlements, terrorizing the inhabitants and plundering for the provisions and ammunition they needed. It was during these bloodless raids that Piggy's ferocious aspect and frightful voice gained him a renown more widespread and glorious than those other gentle-voiced and sad-faced desperadoes could have acquired in a lifetime.

The Mexicans, most apt in nomenclature, first called him The Black Eagle, and used to frighten the babes by threatening them with tales of the dreadful robber who carried off little children in his great beak. Soon the name extended, and Black Eagle, the Terror of the Border, became a recognized factor in exaggerated newspaper reports and ranch gossip.

The country from the Nueces to the Rio Grande was a wild but fertile stretch, given over to the sheep and cattle ranches. Range was free; the inhabitants were few; the law was mainly a letter, and the pirates met with little opposition until the flaunting and garish Piggy gave the band undue advertisement. Then Kinney's ranger company headed for those precincts, and Bud King knew that it meant grim and sudden war or else temporary retirement. Regarding the risk to be unnecessary, he drew off his band to an almost inaccessible spot on the bank of the Frio. Wherefore, as has been said, dissatisfaction arose among the members, and impeachment proceedings against Bud were premeditated with Black Eagle in high favour for the succession. Bud King was not unaware of the sentiment, and he called aside Cactus Taylor, his trusted lieutenant, to discuss it.

'If the boys,' said Bud, 'ain't satisfied with me, I'm willin' to step out. They're buckin' against my way of handlin' 'em. And 'specially because I concludes to hit the brush while Sam Kinney is ridin' the line. I saves 'em from bein' shot or sent up on a state contract, and they up and says I'm no good.'

'It ain't so much that,' explained Cactus, 'as it is they're plum locoed about Piggy. They want them whiskers and that nose of his to split the wind at the head of the column.'

'There's somethin' mighty seldom about Piggy,' declared Bud, musingly. 'I never yet see anything on the hoof that he exactly grades up with. He can shore holler a plenty, and he straddles a hoss from where you laid the chunk. But he ain't never been smoked yet. You know, Cactus, we ain't had a row since he's been with us. Piggy's all right for skearin' the greaser kids and layin' waste a cross-roads store. I reckon he's the finest canned oyster buccaneer and cheese pirate that ever was, but how's his appetite for fightin'? I've knowed some citizens you'd think was starvin' for trouble get a bad case of dyspepsy the first dose of lead they had to take.'

'He talks all spraddled out,' said Cactus, ''bout the rookuses he's been in. He claims to have saw the elephant and hearn the owl.'

'I know,' replied Bud, using the cow-puncher's expressive phrase of scepticism, 'but it sounds to me!'

This conversation was held one night in camp while the other members of the band – eight in number – were sprawling around the fire, lingering over their supper. When Bud and Cactus ceased talking they heard Piggy's formidable voice holding forth to the others as usual while he was engaged in checking, though never satisfying, his ravening appetite.

'Wat's de use,' he was saying, 'of chasin' little red cowses and hosses 'round for t'ousands of miles? Dere ain't nuttin' in it. Gallopin' t'rough dese bushes and briers, and gettin' a t'irst dat a brewery couldn't put out, and missin' meals! Say! You know what I'd do if I was main finger of dis bunch? I'd stick up a train. I'd blow de express car and make hard dollars where you guys gets wind. Youse makes me tired. Dis sook-cow kind of cheap sport gives me a pain.'

Later on, a deputation waited on Bud. They stood on one leg, chewed mesquite twigs and circumlocuted, for they hated to hurt his feelings. Bud foresaw their business, and made it easy for them. Bigger risks and larger profits was what they wanted.

The suggestion of Piggy's about holding up a train had fired their imagination and increased their admiration for the dash and boldness of the instigator. They were such simple, artless, and custom-bound bushrangers that they had never before thought of extending their habits beyond the running off of live-stock and the shooting of such of their acquaintances as ventured to interfere.

Bud acted 'on the level,' agreeing to take a subordinate place in the gang until Black Eagle should have been given a trial as leader.

After a great deal of consultation, studying of time-tables, and discussion of the country's topography, the time and place for carrying out their new enterprise was decided upon. At that time there was a feedstuff famine in Mexico and a cattle famine in certain parts of the United States, and there was a brisk international trade. Much money was being shipped along the railroads that connected the two republics. It was agreed that the most promising place for the contemplated robbery was at Espina, a little station on the I. and G.N., about forty miles north of Laredo. The train stopped there one minute; the country around was wild and unsettled; the station consisted of but one house in which the agent lived.

Black Eagle's band set out, riding by night. Arriving in the vicinity of Espina, they rested their horses all day in a thicket a few miles distant.

The train was due at Espina at 10.30 p.m. They could rob the train and be well over the Mexican border with their booty by daylight the next morning.

To do Black Eagle justice, he exhibited no signs of flinching from the responsible honours that had been conferred upon him.

He assigned his men to their respective posts with discretion, and coached them carefully as to their duties. On each side of the track four of the band were to lie concealed in the chaparral. Gotch-Ear Rodgers was to stick up the station agent. Bronco Charlie was to remain with the horses, holding them in readiness. At a spot where it was calculated the engine would be when the train stopped, Bud King was to lie hidden on one side, Black Eagle himself on the other. The two would get the drop on the engineer and fireman, force them to descend and proceed to the rear. Then the express car would be looted, and the escape made. No one was to move until Black Eagle gave the signal by firing his revolver. The plan was perfect.

At ten minutes to train time every man was at his post, effectually concealed by the thick chaparral that grew almost to the rails. The night was dark and lowering, with a fine drizzle falling from the flying gulf clouds. Black Eagle crouched behind a bush within five yards of the track. Two six-shooters were belted around him. Occasionally he drew a large black bottle from his pocket and raised it to his mouth.

A star appeared far down the track which soon waxed into the headlight of the approaching train. It came on with an increasing roar; the engine bore down upon the ambushing desperadoes with a glare and a shriek like some avenging monster come to deliver them to justice. Black Eagle flattened himself upon the ground. The engine, contrary to their calculations, instead of stopping between him and Bud King's place of concealment, passed fully forty yards farther before it came to a stand.

The bandit leader rose to his feet and peered around the bush. His men all lay quiet, awaiting the signal. Immediately opposite Black Eagle was a thing that drew his attention. Instead of being a regular passenger train it was a mixed one. Before him stood a box car, the door of which, by some means, had been left slightly open. Black Eagle went up to it and pushed the door farther open. An odour came forth – a damp, rancid, familiar, musty, intoxicating, beloved odour stirring strongly at old memories of happy days and travels. Black Eagle sniffed at the witching smell as the returned wanderer smells of the rose that twines his boyhood's cottage home. Nostalgia seized him. He put his hand inside. Excelsior – dry, springy, curly, soft, enticing, covered the floor. Outside the drizzle had turned to a chilling rain.

The train bell clanged. The bandit chief unbuckled his belt and cast it, with its revolvers, upon the ground. His spurs followed quickly, and his broad sombrero. Black Eagle was moulting. The train started with a rattling jerk. The ex-Terror of the Border scrambled into the box car and closed the door. Stretched luxuriously upon the excelsior, with the black bottle clasped closely to his breast, his eyes closed, and a foolish, happy smile upon his terrible features, Chicken Ruggles started upon his return trip.

Undisturbed, with the band of desperate bandits lying motionless, waiting the signal to attack, the train pulled out from Espina. As its speed increased and the black masses of chaparral went whizzing past on either side, the express messenger, lighting his pipe, looked through his window and remarked, feelingly:

'What a jim-dandy place for a hold-up!'

THE SHAMROCK AND THE PALM

One night when there was no breeze, and Coralio seemed closer than ever to the gratings of Avernus, five men were grouped about the door of the photograph establishment of Keogh and Clancy. Thus, in all the scorched and exotic places of the earth, Caucasians meet when the day's work is done to preserve the fullness of their heritage by the aspersion of alien things.

Johnny Atwood lay stretched upon the grass in the undress uniform of a Carib, and prated feebly of cool water to be had in the cucumber-wood pumps of Dalesburg. Dr Gregg, through the prestige of his whiskers and as a bribe against the relation of his imminent professional tales, was conceded the hammock that was swung between the door jamb and a calabash-tree. Keogh had moved out upon the grass a little table that held the instrument for burnishing completed photographs. He was the only busy one of the group. Industriously from between the cylinders of the burnisher rolled the finished depictments of Coralio's citizens. Blanchard, the French mining engineer, in his cool linen viewed the smoke of his cigarette through his calm glasses, impervious to the heat. Clancy sat on the steps, smoking his short pipe. His mood was the gossip's; the others were reduced, by the humidity, to the state of disability desirable in an audience.

Clancy was an American with an Irish diathesis and cosmopolitan proclivities. Many businesses had claimed him, but not for long. The roadster's blood was in his veins. The voice of the tin-type was but one of the many callings that had wooed him upon so many roads. Sometimes he could be persuaded to oral construction of his voyages into the informal and egregious. To-night there were symptoms of divulgement in him.

''Tis elegant weather for filibusterin',' he volunteered. 'It reminds me of the time I struggled to liberate a nation from the poisonous breath of a tyrant's clutch. 'Twas hard work. 'Tis strainin' to the back and makes corns on the hands.'

'I didn't know you had ever lent your sword to an oppressed people,' murmured Atwood, from the grass.

'I did,' said Clancy; 'and they turned it into a ploughshare.'

'What country was so fortunate as to secure your aid?' airily inquired Blanchard.

'Where's Kamchatka?' asked Clancy, with seeming irrelevance.

'Why, off Siberia somewhere in the Arctic regions,' somebody answered, doubtfully.

'I thought that was the cold one,' said Clancy, with a satisfied nod. 'I'm always gettin' the two names mixed. 'Twas Guatemala, then – the hot one – I've been filibusterin' with. Ye'll find that country on the map. 'Tis in the district known as the tropics. By the foresight of Providence, it lies on the coast so the geography man could run the names of the towns off into the water. They're an inch long, small type, composed of Spanish dialects, and, 'tis my opinion, of the same system of syntax that blew up the *Maine*. Yes, 'twas that country I sailed against, single-handed, and endeavoured to liberate it from a tyrannical government with a single-barrelled pickaxe, unloaded at that. Ye don't understand, of course. 'Tis a statement demandin' elucidation and apologies.

''Twas in New Orleans one morning about the first of June; I was standin' down on the wharf, lookin' about at the ships in the river. There was a little steamer moored right opposite me that seemed about ready to sail. The funnels of it were throwin' out smoke, and a gang of roustabouts were carryin' aboard a pile of boxes that was stacked up on the wharf. The boxes were about two feet square, and somethin' like four feet long, and they seemed to be pretty heavy.

'I walked over, careless, to the stack of boxes. I saw one of them had been broken in handlin'. 'Twas curiosity made me pull up the loose top and look inside. The box was packed full of Winchester rifles. "So, so," says I to myself; "somebody's gettin' a twist on the neutrality laws. Somebody's aidin' with munitions of war. I wonder where the popguns are goin'?"

'I heard somebody cough, and I turned around. There stood a little, round, fat man with a brown face and white clothes, a first-class-looking little man, with a four-carat diamond on his finger and his eye full of interrogations and respects. I judged he was a kind of foreigner – maybe from Russia or Japan or the archipelagoes.

'"Hist!" says the round man, full of concealments and confidences. "Will the señor respect the discoveryments he has made, that the mans on the ship shall not be acquaint? The señor will be a gentleman that shall not expose one thing that by accident occur."

'"Monseer," says I – for I judged him to be a kind of Frenchman – "receive my most exasperated assurances that your secret is safe with James Clancy. Furthermore, I will go so far as to remark, Veev la Liberty – veev it good and strong. Whenever you hear of a Clancy obstructin' the abolishment of existin' governments you may notify me by return mail."

'"The señor is good," says the dark, fat man, smilin' under his black mustache. "Wish you to come aboard my ship and drink of wine a glass."

'Bein' a Clancy, in two minutes me and the foreign man were seated at a table in the cabin of the steamer, with a bottle between us. I could hear the heavy boxes bein' dumped into the hold. I judged that cargo must consist of at least 2,000 Winchesters. Me and the brown man drank the bottle of stuff, and he called the steward to bring another. When you amalgamate a Clancy with the contents of a bottle you practically instigate secession. I had heard a good deal about these revolutions in them tropical localities, and I begun to want a hand in it.

'"You goin' to stir things up in your country, ain't you, monseer?" says I, with a wink to let him know I was on.

'"Yes, yes," said the little man, pounding his fist on the table. "A change of the greatest will occur. Too long have the people been oppressed with the promises and the never-to-happen things to become. The great work it shall be carry on. Yes. Our forces shall in the capital city strike of the soonest. *Carrambos!*"

'"*Carrambos* is the word," says I, beginning to invest myself with enthusiasm and more wine, "likewise veeva, as I said before. May the shamrock of old – I mean the banana-vine or the pieplant, or whatever the imperial emblem may be of your downtrodden country, wave for ever."

'"A thousand thank-yous," says the round man, "for your emission of amicable utterances. What our cause needs of the very most is mans who will the work do, to lift it along. Oh, for one thousands strong, good mans to aid the General De Vega that he shall to his country bring those success and glory! It is hard – oh, so hard to find good mans to help in the work."

'"Monseer," says I, leanin' over the table and graspin' his hand,

"I don't know where your country is, but me heart bleeds for it. The heart of a Clancy was never deaf to the sight of an oppressed people. The family is filibusterers by birth, and foreigners by trade. If you can use James Clancy's arm and his blood in denudin' your shores of the tyrant's yoke they're yours to command."

'General De Vega was overcome with joy to confiscate my condolence of his conspiracies and predicaments. He tried to embrace me across the table, but his fatness, and the wine that had been in the bottles, prevented. Thus was I welcomed into the ranks of filibustery. Then the general man told me his country had the name of Guatemala, and was the greatest nation laved by any ocean whatever anywhere. He looked at me with tears in his eyes, and from time to time he would emit the remark, "Ah! big, strong, brave mans! That is what my country need."

'General De Vega, as was the name by which he denounced himself, brought out a document for me to sign, which I did, makin' a fine flourish and curlycue with the tail of the "y".

'"Your passage-money," says the general, businesslike, "shall from your pay be deduct."

'"'Twill not," says I, haughty. "I'll pay my own passage." A hundred and eighty dollars I had in my inside pocket, and 'twas no common filibuster I was goin' to be, filibusterin' for me board and clothes.

'The steamer was to sail in two hours, and I went ashore to get some things together I'd need. When I came aboard I showed the general with pride the outfit. 'Twas a fine Chinchilla overcoat, Arctic overshoes, fur cap and earmuffs, with elegant fleece-lined gloves and woollen muffler.

'"*Carrambos!*" says the little general. "What clothes are these that shall go to the tropic?" And then the little spalpeen laughs, and he calls the captain, and the captain calls the purser, and they pipe up the chief engineer, and the whole gang leans against the cabin and laughs at Clancy's wardrobe for Guatemala.

'I reflects a bit, serious, and asks the general again to denominate the terms by which his country is called. He tells me, and I see then that 'twas the t'other one, Kamchatka, I had in mind. Since then I've had difficulty in separatin' the two nations in name, climate and geographic disposition.

'I paid my passage – twenty-four dollars, first cabin – and ate at table with the officer crowd. Down on the lower deck was a gang of second-class passengers, about forty of them, seemin' to be Dagoes and the like. I wondered what so many of them were goin' along for.

'Well, then, in three days we sailed alongside that Guatemala. 'Twas a blue country, and not yellow – as 'tis miscoloured on the map. We landed at a town on the coast, where a train of cars was waitin' for us on a dinky little railroad. The boxes on the steamer were brought ashore and loaded on the cars. The gang of Dagoes got aboard, too, the general and me in the front car. Yes, me and General De Vega headed the revolution, as it pulled out of the seaport town. That train travelled about as fast as a policeman goin' to a riot. It penetrated the most conspicuous lot of fuzzy scenery ever seen outside a geography. We run some forty miles in seven hours, and the train stopped. There was no more railroad. 'Twas a sort of camp in a damp gorge full of wildness and melancholies. They was gradin' and choppin' out the forests ahead to continue the road. "Here," says I to myself, "is the romantic haunt of the revolutionists. Here will Clancy, by the virtue that is in a superior race and the inculcation of Fenian tactics, strike a tremendous blow for liberty."

'They unloaded the boxes from the train and begun to knock the tops off. From the first one that was open I saw General De Vega take the Winchester rifles and pass them around to a squad of morbid soldiery. The other boxes was opened next, and, believe me or not, divil another gun was to be seen. Every other box in the load was full of pickaxes and spades.

'And then – sorrow be upon them tropics – the proud Clancy and the dishonoured Dagoes, each one of them, had to shoulder a pick or a spade, and march away to work on that dirty little railroad. Yes; 'twas that the Dagoes shipped for, and 'twas that the filibusterin' Clancy signed for, though unbeknownst to himself at the time. In after days I found out about it. It seems 'twas hard to get hands to work on that road. The intelligent natives of the country was too lazy to work. Indeed, the saints know, 'twas unnecessary. By stretchin' out one hand, they could seize the most delicate and costly fruits of the earth, and, by stretchin' out the other, they could sleep for days at a time without hearin' a seven-o'clock whistle or the footsteps of the rent man upon the stairs. So, regular, the steamers travelled to the United States to seduce labour. Usually the imported spade-slingers died in two or three months from eatin' the over-ripe water and breathin' the violent tropical scenery. Wherefore they made them sign contracts for a year, when they hired them, and put an armed guard over the poor divils to keep them from runnin' away.

"Twas thus I was double-crossed by the tropics through a family failin' of goin' out of the way to hunt disturbances.

'They gave me a pick, and I took it, meditatin' an insurrection on the spot; but there was the guards handlin' the Winchesters careless, and I come to the conclusion that discretion was the best part of filibusterin'. There was about a hundred of us in the gang startin' out to work, and the word was given to move. I steps out of the ranks and goes up to that General De Vega man, who was smokin' a cigar and gazin' upon the scene with satisfactions and glory. He smiles at me polite and devilish. "Plenty work," says he, "for big, strong mans in Guatemala. Yes. T'irty dollars in the month. Good pay. Ah, yes. You strong, brave man. Bimeby we push those railroad in the capital very quick. They want you go work now. *Adios*, strong mans."

"'Monseer," says I, lingerin', "will you tell a poor little Irishman this: When I set foot on your cockroachy steamer, and breathed liberal and revolutionary sentiments into your sour wine, did you think I was conspirin' to sling a pick on your contemptuous little railroad? And when you answered me with patriotic recitations, humping up the star-spangled cause of liberty, did you have meditations of reducin' me to the ranks of the stump-grubbin' Dagoes in the chain-gangs of your vile and grovellin' country?"

'The general man expanded his rotundity and laughed considerable. Yes, he laughed very long and loud, and I, Clancy, stood and waited.

"'Comical mans!" he shouts, at last. "So you will kill me from the laughing. Yes; it is hard to find the brave, strong mans to aid my country. Revolutions? Did I speak of r-r-revolutions? Not one word. I say, big, strong mans is need in Guatemala. So. The mistake is of you. You have looked in those one box containing those gun for the guard. You think all boxes is contain gun? No.

"'There is not war in Guatemala. But work? Yes. Good. T'irty dollar in the month. You shall shoulder one pickaxe, señor, and dig for the liberty and prosperity of Guatemala. Off to your work. The guard waits for you."

"'Little, fat, poodle dog of a brown man," says I, quiet, but full of indignations and discomforts, "things shall happen to you.

Maybe not right away, but as soon as J. Clancy can formulate somethin' in the way of repartee."

'The boss of the gang orders us to work. I tramps off with the Dagoes, and I hears the distinguished patriot and kidnapper laughin' hearty as we go.

"'Tis a sorrowful fact, for eight weeks I built railroads for that misbehavin' country. I filibustered twelve hours a day with a heavy pick and a spade, choppin' away the luxurious landscape that grew upon the right of way. We worked in swamps that smelled like there was a leak in the gas mains, trampin' down a fine assortment of the most expensive hothouse plants and vegetables. The scene was tropical beyond the wildest imagination of the geography man. The trees was all sky-scrapers; the underbrush was full of needles and pins; there was monkeys jumpin' around and crocodiles and pink-tailed mockin'-birds, and ye stood knee-deep in the rotten water and grabbled roots for the liberation of Guatemala. Of nights we would build smudges in camp to discourage the mosquitoes, and sit in the smoke, with the guards pacin' all around us. There was two hundred men workin' on the road – mostly Dagoes, nigger-men, Spanish-men and Swedes. Three or four were Irish.

'One old man named Halloran – a man of Hibernian entitlements and discretions, explained it to me. He had been workin' on the road a year. Most of them died in less than six months. He was dried up to gristle and bone, and shook with chills every third night.

'"When you first come," says he, "ye think ye'll leave right away. But they hold out your first month's pay for your passage over, and by that time the tropics has its grip on ye. Ye're surrounded by a ragin' forest full of disreputable beasts – lions and baboons and anacondas – waitin' to devour ye. The sun strikes ye hard, and melts the marrow in your bones. Ye get similar to the lettuce-eaters the poetry-book speaks about. Ye forget the elevated sintiments of life, such as patriotism, revenge, disturbances of the peace and the dacint love of a clane shirt. Ye do your work, and ye swallow the kerosene ile and rubber pipestems dished up to ye by the Dago cook for food. Ye light your pipeful, and say to yoursilf, 'Nixt week I'll break away,' and ye go to sleep and call yersilf a liar, for ye know ye'll never do it."

'"Who is this general man," asks I, "that calls himself De Vega?"

'"'Tis the man," says Halloran, "who is tryin' to complete the finishin' of the railroad. 'Twas the project of a private corporation, but it busted, and then the government took it up. De Vegy is a big politician, and wants to be prisident. The people want the railroad completed, as they're taxed mighty on account of it. The De Vegy man is pushin' it along as a campaign move."

"'Tis not my way," says I, "to make threats against any man, but there's an account to be settled between the railroad man and James O'Dowd Clancy."

"'Twas that way I thought mesilf, at first," Halloran says, with a big sigh, "until I got to be a lettuce-eater. The fault's wid these tropics. They rejuices a man's system. 'Tis a land, as the poet says, 'Where it always seems to be after dinner.' I does me work and smokes me pipe and sleeps. There's little else in life, anyway. Ye'll get that way yersilf, mighty soon. Don't be harbourin' any sintiments at all, Clancy."

"'I can't help it," says I; "I'm full of 'em. I enlisted in the revolutionary army of this dark country in good faith to fight for its liberty, honours and silver candlesticks; instead of which I am set to amputatin' its scenery and grubbin' its roots. 'Tis the general man will have to pay for it."

'Two months I worked on that railroad before I found a chance to get away. One day a gang of us was sent back to the end of the completed line to fetch some picks that had been sent down to Port Barrios to be sharpened. They were brought on a hand-car, and I noticed, when I started away, that the car was left there on the track.

'That night, about twelve, I woke up Halloran and told him my scheme.

"'Run away?" says Halloran. "Good Lord, Clancy, do ye mean it? Why, I ain't got the nerve. It's too chilly, and I ain't slept enough. Run away? I told you, Clancy, I've eat the lettuce. I've lost my grip. 'Tis the tropics that's done it. 'Tis like the poet says: 'Forgotten are our friends that we have left behind; in the hollow lettuce-land we will live and lay reclined.' You better go on, Clancy. I'll stay, I guess. It's too early and cold, and I'm sleepy."

'So I had to leave Halloran. I dressed quiet, and slipped out of the tent we were in. When the guard came along I knocked him over, like a ninepin, with a green coco-nut I had, and made for the railroad. I got on that hand-car and made it fly. 'Twas yet a while before daybreak when I saw the lights of Port Barrios about a mile away. I stopped the hand-car there and walked to the town.

I stepped inside the corporations of that town with care and hesitations. I was not afraid of the army of Guatemala, but me soul quaked at the prospect of a hand-to-hand struggle with its employment bureau. 'Tis a country that hires its help easy and keeps 'em long. Sure I can fancy Missis America and Missis Guatemala passin' a bit of gossip some fine, still night across the mountains. "Oh, dear," says Missis America, "and it's a lot of trouble I'm havin' ag'in with the help, señora, ma'am." "Laws, now!" says Missis Guatemala, "you don't say so, ma'am! Now, mine never think of leavin' me – te-he! ma'am," snickers Missis Guatemala.

'I was wonderin' how I was goin' to move away from them tropics without bein' hired again. Dark as it was, I could see a steamer ridin' in the harbour, with smoke emergin' from her stacks. I turned down a little grass street that run down to the water. On the beach I found a little brown nigger-man just about to shove off in a skiff.

'"Hold on, Sambo," says I, "savve English?"

'"Heap plenty, yes," says he, with a pleasant grin.

'"What steamer is that?" I asks him, "and where is it going? And what's the news, and the good word and the time of day?"

'"That steamer the *Conchita*," said the brown man, affable and easy, rollin' a cigarette. "Him come from New Orleans for load banana. Him got load last night. I think him sail in one, two hour. Verree nice day we shall be goin' have. You hear some talkee 'bout big battle, maybe so? You think catchee General De Vega, señor? Yes? No?"

'"How's that, Sambo?" says I. "Big battle? What battle? Who wants catchee General De Vega? I've been up at my gold mines in the interior for a couple of months, and haven't heard any news."

'"Oh," says the nigger-man, proud to speak the English, "veree great revolution in Guatemala one week ago. General De Vega, him try be president. Him raise armee – one – five – ten thousand mans for fight at the government. Those one government send five – forty – hundred thousand soldier to suppress revolution. They fight big battle yesterday at Lomagrande – that about nineteen or fifty mile in the mountain. That government soldier wheep General De Vega – oh, most bad. Five hundred – nine hundred – two thousand of his mans is kill. That revolution is smash suppress – bust – very quick. General De Vega, him r-r-run away fast on one big mule. Yes, *carrambos!* The general, him r-r-run away, and his armee is kill. That government soldier, they try find General De Vega verree much. They want catchee him for shoot. You think they catchee that general, señor?"

'"Saints grant it!" says I. "'Twould be the judgment of Providence for settin' the warlike talent of a Clancy to gradin' the tropics with a pick and shovel. But 'tis not so much a question of insurrections now, me little man, as 'tis of the hired-man problem. 'Tis anxious I am to resign a situation of responsibility and trust with the white wings department of your great and degraded country. Row me in your little boat out to that steamer, and I'll give ye five dollars – sinker pacers – sinker pacers," says I, reducin' the offer to the language and denomination of the tropic dialects.

'"*Cinco pesos*," repeats the little man. "Five dollee, you give?"

'Twas not such a bad little man. He had hesitations at first, sayin' that passengers leavin' the country had to have papers and passports, but at last he took me out alongside the steamer.

'Day was just breakin' as we struck her, and there wasn't a soul to be seen on board. The water was very still, and the nigger-man gave me a lift from the boat, and I climbed on to the steamer where her side was sliced to the deck for loadin' fruit. The hatches was open, and I looked down and saw the cargo of bananas that filled the hold to within six feet of the top. I thinks to myself, "Clancy, you better go as a stowaway. It's safer. The steamer men might hand you back to the employment bureau. The tropics'll get you, Clancy, if you don't watch out."

'So I jumps down easy among the bananas, and digs out a hole to hide in among the bunches. In an hour or so I could hear the engines goin', and feel the steamer rockin', and I knew we were off to sea. They left the hatches open for ventilation, and pretty soon it was light enough in the hold to see fairly well. I got to feelin' a bit hungry, and thought I'd have a light fruit lunch, by way of refreshment. I creeped out of the hole I'd made and stood up straight. Just then I saw another man crawl up about ten feet away and reach out and skin a banana and stuff it into his mouth. 'Twas a dirty man, black-faced and ragged and disgraceful of aspect. Yes, the man was a ringer for the pictures of the fat Weary Willie in the funny papers. I looked again, and saw it was my general man – De Vega, the great revolutionist, mule-rider and pickaxe importer. When he saw me the general hesitated with his mouth filled with banana and his eyes the size of coco-nuts.

'"Hist!" I says. "Not a word, or they'll put us off and make us walk. 'Veev la Liberty!'" I adds, copperin' the sentiment by shovin' a banana into the source of it. I was certain the general wouldn't recognize me. The nefarious work of the tropics had left me lookin' different. There was half an inch of roan whiskers coverin' me face, and me costume was a pair of blue overalls and a red shirt.

'"How you come in the ship, señor?" asked the general as soon as he could speak.

'"By the back door – whist!" says I. "'Twas a glorious blow for liberty we struck," I continues: "but we was overpowered by numbers. Let us accept our defeat like brave men and eat another banana."

'"Were you in the cause of liberty fightin', señor?" says the general, sheddin' tears on the cargo.

'"To the last," says I. "'Twas I led the last desperate charge against the minions of the tyrant. But it made them mad, and we was forced to retreat. 'Twas I, general, procured the mule upon which you escaped. Could you give that ripe bunch a little boost this way, general? It's a bit out of my reach. Thanks."

'"Say you so, brave patriot?" said the general, again weepin'.

"Ah, *Dios!* And I have not the means to reward your devotion. Barely did I my life bring away. *Carrambos!* what a devil's animal was that mule, señor! Like ships in one storm was I dashed about. The skin on myself was ripped away with the thorns and vines. Upon the bark of a hundred trees did that beast of the infernal bump, and cause outrage to the legs of mine. In the night to Port Barrios I came. I dispossess myself of that mountain of mule and hasten along the water shore. I find a little boat to be tied. I launch myself and row to the steamer. I cannot see any mans on board, so I climbed one rope which hang at the side. I then myself hide in the bananas. Surely, I say, if the ship captains view me, they shall throw me again to those Guatemala. Those things are not good. Guatemala will shoot General De Vega. Therefore, I am hide and remain silent. Life itself is glorious. Liberty, it is pretty good; but so good as life I do not think."

'Three days, as I said, was the trip to New Orleans. The general man and me got to be cronies of the deepest dye. Bananas we ate until they were distasteful to the sight and an eyesore to the palate, but to bananas alone was the bill of fare reduced. At night I crawls out, careful, on the lower deck, and gets a bucket of fresh water.

'That General De Vega was a man inhabited by an engorge-
ment of words and sentences. He added to the monotony of the
voyage by divestin' himself of conversation. He believed I was a
revolutionist of his own party, there bein', as he told me, a good
many Americans and other foreigners in its ranks. 'Twas a
braggart and a conceited little gabbler it was, though he considered himself a hero. 'Twas on himself he wasted all his regrets at
the failin' of his plot. Not a word did the little balloon have to say
about the other misbehavin' idiots that had been shot, or run
themselves to death in his revolution.

'The second day out he was feelin' pretty braggy and uppish
for a stowed-away conspirator that owed his existence to a mule
and stolen bananas. He was tellin' me about the great railroad he
had been buildin', and he relates what he calls a comic incident
about a fool Irishman he inveigled from New Orleans to sling a
pick on his little morgue of a narrow-gauge line. 'Twas sorrowful
to hear the little, dirty general tell the opprobrious story of how
he put salt upon the tail of that reckless and silly bird, Clancy.
Laugh, he did, hearty and long. He shook with laughin', the
black-faced rebel and outcast, standin' neck-deep in bananas,
without friends or country.

'"Ah, señor," he snickers, "to the death you would have
laughed at that drollest Irish. I say to him: 'Strong, big mans is
need very much in Guatemala.' 'I will blows strike for your
down-pressed country,' he say. 'That shall you do,' I tell him.
Ah! it was an Irish so comic. He sees one box break upon the
wharf that contain for the guard a few gun. He think there is gun
in all the box. But that is all pickaxe. Yes. Ah! señor could you
the face of that Irish have seen when they set him to the work!"

''Twas thus the ex-boss of the employment bureau contributed
to the tedium of the trip with merry jests and anecdote. But now
and then he would weep upon the bananas and make oration
about the lost cause of liberty and the mule.

''Twas a pleasant sound when the steamer bumped against the
pier in New Orleans. Pretty soon we heard the pat-a-pat of
hundreds of bare feet, and the Dago gang that unloads the fruit
jumped on the deck and down into the hold. Me and the general
worked a while at passin' up the bunches, and they thought we
were part of the gang. After about an hour we managed to slip
off the steamer on to the wharf.

''Twas a great honour on the hands of an obscure Clancy,

havin' the entertainment of the representative of a great foreign filibusterin' power. I first bought for the general and myself many long drinks and things to eat that were not bananas. The general man trotted along at my side, leavin' all the arrangements to me. I led him up to Lafayette Square and set him on a bench in the little park. Cigarettes I had bought for him, and he humped himself down on the seat like a little, fat, contented hobo. I look him over as he sets there, and what I see pleases me. Brown by nature and instinct, he is now brindled with dirt and dust. Praise to the mule, his clothes is mostly strings and flaps. Yes, the looks of the general man is agreeable to Clancy.

'I asks him, delicate, if, by any chance, he brought away anybody's money with him from Guatemala. He sighs and humps his shoulders against the bench. Not a cent. All right. Maybe, he tells me, some of his friends in the tropic outfit will send him funds later. The general was as clear a case of no visible means as I ever saw.

'I told him not to move from the bench, and then I went up to the corner of Poydras and Carondelet. Along there is O'Hara's beat. In five minutes along comes O'Hara, a big, fine man, red-faced, with shinin' buttons, swingin' his club. 'Twould be a fine thing for Guatemala to move into O'Hara's precinct. 'Twould be a fine bit of recreation for Danny to suppress revolutions and uprisin's once or twice a week with his club.

'"Is 5046 workin' yet, Danny?" says I, walkin' up to him.

'"Overtime," says O'Hara, lookin' over me suspicious. "Want some of it?"

'Fifty-forty-six is the celebrated city ordinance authorizin' arrest, conviction and imprisonment of persons that succeed in concealin' their crimes from the police.

'"Don't ye know Jimmy Clancy?" says I. "Ye pink-gilled monster." So, when O'Hara recognized me beneath the scandalous exterior bestowed upon me by the tropics, I backed him into a doorway and told him what I wanted, and why I wanted it. "All right, Jimmy," says O'Hara. "Go back and hold the bench. I'll be along in ten minutes."

'In that time O'Hara strolled through Lafayette Square and spied two Weary Willies disgracin' one of the benches. In ten minutes more J. Clancy and General De Vega, late candidate for the presidency of Guatemala, was in the station house. The general is badly frightened, and calls upon me to proclaim his distinguishments and rank.

'"The man," says I to the police, "used to be a railroad man. He's on the bum now. 'Tis a little bughouse he is, on account of losin' his job."

'"*Carrambos!*" says the general, fizzin' like a little soda-water fountain, "you fought, señor, with my forces in my native country. Why do you say the lies? You shall say I am the General De Vega, one soldier, one *caballero* –"

'"Railroader," says I again. "On the hog. No good. Been livin' for three days on stolen bananas. Look at him. Ain't that enough?"

'Twenty-five dollars or sixty days, was what the recorder gave the general. He didn't have a cent, so he took the time. They let me go, as I knew they would, for I had money to show, and O'Hara spoke for me. Yes; sixty days he got. 'Twas just so long that I slung a pick for the great country of Kam – Guatemala.'

Clancy paused. The bright starlight showed a reminiscent look of happy content on his seasoned features. Keogh leaned in his chair and gave his partner a slap on his thinly-clad back that sounded like the crack of the surf on the sands.

'Tell 'em, ye divil,' he chuckled, 'how you got even with the tropical general in the way of agricultural manœuvrings.'

'Havin' no money,' concluded Clancy, with unction, 'they set him to work his fine out with a gang from the parish prison clearing Ursulines Street. Around the corner was a saloon decorated genially with electric fans and cool merchandise. I made that me headquarters, and every fifteen minutes I'd walk around and take a look at the little man filibusterin' with a rake and shovel. 'Twas just such a hot broth of a day as this has been. And I'd call at him "Hey, monseer!" and he'd look at me black, with the damp showin' through his shirt in places.

'"Fat, strong mans," says I to General De Vega, "is needed in New Orleans. Yes. To carry on the good work. *Carrambos!* Erin go bragh!"'

There had to be a king and queen, of course. The king was a terrible old man who wore six-shooters and spurs, and shouted in such a tremendous voice that the rattlers on the prairie would run into their holes under the prickly pear. Before there was a royal family they called the man 'Whispering Ben.' When he came to own 50,000 acres of land and more cattle than he could count, they called him O'Donnell 'the Cattle King.'

The queen had been a Mexican girl from Laredo. She made a good, mild, Colorado-claro wife, and even succeeded in teaching Ben to modify his voice sufficiently while in the house to keep the dishes from being broken. When Ben got to be king she would sit on the gallery of Espinosa Ranch and weave rush mats. When wealth became so irresistible and oppressive that upholstered chairs and a centre table were brought down from San Antone in the wagons, she bowed her smooth, dark head, and shared the fate of the Danaë.

To avoid *lèse-majesté* you have been presented first to the king and queen. They do not enter the story, which might be called 'The Chronicle of the Princess, the Happy Thought, and the Lion that Bungled his Job.'

Josefa O'Donnell was the surviving daughter, the princess. From her mother she inherited warmth of nature and a dusky, semi-tropic beauty. From Ben O'Donnell the royal she acquired a store of intrepidity, common sense, and the faculty of ruling. The combination was one worth going miles to see. Josefa while riding her pony at a gallop could put five out of six bullets through a tomato-can swinging at the end of a string. She could play for hours with a white kitten she owned, dressing it in all manner of absurd clothes. Scorning a pencil, she could tell you out of her head what 1,545 two-year-olds would bring on the hoof, at $8.50 per head. Roughly speaking, the Espinosa Ranch is forty miles long and thirty broad – but mostly leased land. Josefa, on her pony, had prospected over every mile of it. Every cow-puncher

on the range knew her by sight and was a loyal vassal. Ripley
Givens, foreman of one of the Espinosa outfits, saw her one day,
and made up his mind to form a royal matrimonial alliance.
Presumptuous? No. In those days in the Nueces country a man
was a man. And, after all, the title of cattle king does not
presuppose blood royal. Often it only signifies that its owner
wears the crown in token of his magnificent qualities in the art of
cattle stealing.

One day Ripley Givens rode over to the Double Elm Ranch to
inquire about a bunch of strayed yearlings. He was late in setting
out on his return trip, and it was sundown when he struck the
White Horse Crossing of the Nueces. From there to his own camp
it was sixteen miles. To the Espinosa ranch house it was twelve.
Givens was tired. He decided to pass the night at the Crossing.

There was a fine water hole in the river-bed. The banks were
thickly covered with great trees, undergrown with brush. Back
from the water hole fifty yards was a stretch of curly mesquite
grass – supper for his horse and bed for himself. Givens staked his
horse, and spread out his saddle blankets to dry. He sat down
with his back against a tree and rolled a cigarette. From somewhere in the dense timber along the river came a sudden, rageful,
shivering wail. The pony danced at the end of his rope and blew
a whistling snort of comprehending fear. Givens puffed at his
cigarette, but he reached leisurely for his pistol-belt, which lay on
the grass, and twirled the cylinder of his weapon tentatively. A
great gar plunged with a loud splash into the water hole. A little
brown rabbit skipped around a bunch of catclaw and sat twitch-
ing his whiskers and looking humorously at Givens. The pony
went on eating grass.

It is well to be reasonably watchful when a Mexican lion sings
soprano along the arroyos at sundown. The burden of his song
may be that young calves and fat lambs are scarce, and that he
has a carnivorous desire for your acquaintance.

In the grass lay an empty fruit can, cast there by some former
sojourner. Givens caught sight of it with a grunt of satisfaction.
In his coat pocket tied behind his saddle was a handful or two of
ground coffee. Black coffee and cigarettes! What ranchero could
desire more?

In two minutes he had a little fire going clearly. He started,
with his can, for the water hole. When within fifteen yards of its
edge he saw, between the bushes, a side-saddled pony with

down-dropped reins cropping grass a little distance to his left. Just rising from her hands and knees on the brink of the water hole was Josefa O'Donnell. She had been drinking water, and she brushed the sand from the palms of her hands. Ten yards away, to her right, half concealed by a clump of sacuista, Givens saw the crouching form of the Mexican lion. His amber eyeballs glared hungrily; six feet from them was the tip of the tail stretched straight, like a pointer's. His hind-quarters rocked with the motion of the cat tribe preliminary to leaping.

Givens did what he could. His six-shooter was thirty-five yards away lying on the grass. He gave a loud yell, and dashed between the lion and the princess.

The 'rucus,' as Givens called it afterward, was brief and somewhat confused. When he arrived on the line of attack he saw a dim streak in the air, and heard a couple of faint cracks. Then a hundred pounds of Mexican lion plumped down upon his head and flattened him, with a heavy jar, to the ground. He remembered calling out: 'Let up, now – no fair gouging!' and then he crawled from under the lion like a worm, with his mouth full of grass and dirt, and a big lump on the back of his head where it had struck the root of a water-elm. The lion lay motionless. Givens, feeling aggrieved, and suspicious of fouls, shook his fist at the lion, and shouted: 'I'll rastle you again for twenty – ' and then he got back to himself.

Josefa was standing in her tracks, quietly reloading her silver-mounted .38. It had not been a difficult shot. The lion's head made an easier mark than a tomato-can swinging at the end of a string. There was a provoking, teasing, maddening smile upon her mouth and in her dark eyes. The would-be-rescuing knight felt the fire of his fiasco burn down to his soul. Here had been his chance, the chance that he had dreamed of; and Momus, and not Cupid, had presided over it. The satyrs in the wood were, no doubt, holding their sides in hilarious, silent laughter. There had been something like vaudeville – say Signor Givens and his funny knockabout act with the stuffed lion.

'Is that you, Mr Givens?' said Josefa, in her deliberate, saccharine contralto. 'You nearly spoiled my shot when you yelled. Did you hurt your head when you fell?'

'Oh, no,' said Givens, quietly; 'that didn't hurt.' He stooped ignominiously and dragged his best Stetson hat from under the beast. It was crushed and wrinkled to a fine comedy effect. Then he knelt down and softly stroked the fierce, open-jawed head of the dead lion.

'Poor old Bill!' he exclaimed mournfully.

'What's that?' asked Josefa sharply.

'Of course you didn't know, Miss Josefa,' said Givens, with an air of one allowing magnanimity to triumph over grief. 'Nobody can blame you. I tried to save him, but I couldn't let you know in time.'

'Save who?'

'Why, Bill. I've been looking for him all day. You see, he's been our camp pet for two years. Poor old fellow, he wouldn't have hurt a cottontail rabbit. It'll break the boys all up when they hear about it. But you couldn't tell, of course, that Bill was just trying to play with you.'

Josefa's black eyes burned steadily upon him. Ripley Givens met the test successfully. He stood rumpling the yellow-brown curls on his head pensively. In his eyes was regret, not unmingled with a gentle reproach. His smooth features were set to a pattern of indisputable sorrow. Josefa wavered.

'What was your pet doing here?' she asked, making a last stand. 'There's no camp near the White Horse Crossing.'

'The old rascal ran away from camp yesterday,' answered Givens readily. 'It's a wonder the coyotes didn't scare him to death. You see, Jim Webster, our horse wrangler, brought a little terrier pup into camp last week. The pup made life miserable for Bill – he used to chase him around and chew his hind legs for hours at a time. Every night when bedtime came Bill would sneak under one of the boy's blankets and sleep to keep the pup from finding him. I reckon he must have been worried pretty desperate or he wouldn't have run away. He was always afraid to get out of sight of camp.'

Josefa looked at the body of the fierce animal. Givens patted one of the formidable paws that could have killed a yearling calf with one blow. Slowly a red flush widened upon the dark olive face of the girl. Was it the signal of shame of the true sportsman who has brought down ignoble quarry? Her eyes grew softer, and the lowered lids drove away all their bright mockery.

'I'm very sorry,' she said humbly; 'but he looked so big, and jumped so high that –'

'Poor old Bill was hungry,' interrupted Givens, in quick defence of the deceased. 'We always made him jump for his supper in camp. He would lie down and roll over for a piece of meat. When he saw you he thought he was going to get something to eat from you.'

Suddenly Josefa's eyes opened wide.

'I might have shot you!' she exclaimed. 'You ran right in between. You risked your life to save your pet! That was fine, Mr Givens. I like a man who is kind to animals.'

Yes; there was even admiration in her gaze now. After all, there was a hero rising out of the ruins of the anti-climax. The look on Givens's face would have secured him a high position in the S.P.C.A.

'I always loved 'em,' said he; 'horses, dogs, Mexican lions, cows, alligators –'

'I hate alligators,' instantly demurred Josefa; 'crawly, muddy things!'

'Did I say alligators?' said Givens. 'I meant antelopes, of course.'

Josefa's conscience drove her to make further amends. She held out her hand penitently. There was a bright, unshed drop in each of her eyes.

'Please forgive me, Mr Givens, won't you? I'm only a girl, you know, and I was frightened at first. I'm very, very sorry I shot Bill. You don't know how ashamed I feel. I wouldn't have done it for anything.'

Givens took the proffered hand. He held it for a time while he allowed the generosity of his nature to overcome his grief at the loss of Bill. At last it was clear that he had forgiven her.

'Please don't speak of it any more, Miss Josefa. 'Twas enough to frighten any young lady the way Bill looked. I'll explain it all right to the boys.'

'Are you really sure you don't hate me?' Josefa came closer to him impulsively. Her eyes were sweet – oh, sweet and pleading with gracious penitence. 'I would hate anyone who would kill my kitten. And how daring and kind of you to risk being shot when you tried to save him! How very few men would have done that!' Victory wrested from defeat! Vaudeville turned into drama! Bravo, Ripley Givens!

It was now twilight. Of course Miss Josefa could not be allowed to ride on to the ranch house alone. Givens resaddled his pony in spite of that animal's reproachful glances, and rode with her. Side by side they galloped across the smooth grass, the princess and the man who was kind to animals. The prairie odours of fruitful earth and delicate bloom were thick and sweet around them. Coyotes yelping over there on the hill! No fear. And yet –

Josefa rode closer. A little hand seemed to grope. Givens found it with his own. The ponies kept an even gait. The hands lingered together, and the owner of one explained:

'I never was frightened before, but just think! How terrible it would be to meet a really wild lion! Poor Bill! I'm so glad you came with me!'

O'Donnell was sitting on the ranch gallery.

'Hallo, Rip!' he shouted – 'that you?'

'He rode in with me,' said Josefa. 'I lost my way and was late.'

'Much obliged,' called the cattle king. 'Stop over, Rip, and ride to camp in the morning.'

But Givens would not. He would push on to camp. There was a bunch of steers to start off on the trail at daybreak. He said good night, and trotted away.

An hour later, when the lights were out, Josefa, in her night-robe, came to her door and called to the king in his own room across the brick-paved hallway:

'Say, pop, you know that old Mexican lion they call the "Gotch-eared Devil" – the one that killed Gonzales, Mr Martin's sheep herder, and about fifty calves on the Salado range? Well, I settled his hash this afternoon over at the White Horse Crossing. Put two balls in his head with my .38 while he was on the jump. I knew him by the slice gone from his left ear that old Gonzales cut off with his machete. You couldn't have made a better shot yourself, daddy.'

'Bully for you!' thundered Whispering Ben from the darkness of the royal chamber.

THE ATAVISM OF JOHN TOM
LITTLE BEAR

I saw a light in Jeff Peters's room over the Red Front Drug Store. I hastened toward it, for I had not known that Jeff was in town. He is a man of the Hadji breed, of a hundred occupations, with a story to tell (when he will) of each one.

I found Jeff re-packing his grip for a run down to Florida to look at an orange grove for which he had traded, a month before, his mining claim on the Yukon. He kicked me a chair, with the same old humorous, profound smile on his seasoned countenance. It had been eight months since we had met, but his greeting was such as men pass from day to day. Time is Jeff's servant, and the continent is a big lot across which he cuts to his many roads.

For a while we skirmished along the edges of unprofitable talk which culminated in that unquiet problem of the Philippines.

'All them tropical races,' said Jeff, 'could be run out better with their own jockeys up. The tropical man knows what he wants. All he wants is a season ticket to the cock-fights and a pair of Western Union climbers to go up the bread-fruit tree. The Anglo-Saxon man wants him to learn to conjugate and wear suspenders. He'll be happiest in his own way.'

I was shocked.

'Education, man,' I said, 'is the watchword. In time they will rise to our standard of civilization. Look at what education has done for the Indian.'

'O-ho!' sang Jeff, lighting his pipe (which was a good sign). 'Yes, the Indian! I'm looking. I hasten to contemplate the redman as a standard-bearer of progress. He's the same as the other brown boys. You can't make an Anglo-Saxon of him. Did I ever tell you about the time my friend John Tom Little Bear bit off the right ear of the arts of culture and education and spun the teetotum back round to where it was when Columbus was a little boy? I did not?

'John Tom Little Bear was an educated Cherokee Indian and an old friend of mine when I was in the Territories. He was a graduate of one of them Eastern football colleges that have been so successful in teaching the Indian to use the gridiron instead of burning his victims at the stake. As an Anglo-Saxon, John Tom was copper-coloured in spots. As an Indian, he was one of the whitest men I ever knew. As a Cherokee, he was a gentleman, on the first ballot. As a ward of the nation he was mighty hard to carry at the primaries.

'John Tom and me got together and began to make medicine – how to get up some lawful, genteel swindle which we might work in a quiet way so as not to excite the stupidity of the police or the cupidity of the larger corporations. We had close upon $500 between us, and we pined to make it grow, as all respectable capitalists do.

'So we figured out a proposition which seems to be as honourable as a gold mine prospectus and as profitable as a church raffle. And inside of thirty days you find us swarming into Kansas with a pair of fluent horses and a red camping-wagon on the European plan. John Tom is Chief Wish-Heap-Dough, the famous Indian medicine man and Samaritan Sachem of the Seven Tribes. Mr Peters is business manager and half owner. We needed a third man, so we looked around and found J. Conyngham Binkly leaning against the want column of a newspaper. This Binkly has a disease for Shakespearean rôles, and an hallucination about a 200 nights' run on the New York stage. But he confesses that he never could earn the butter to spread on his William S. rôles, so he is willing to drop to the ordinary baker's kind, and be satisfied with a 200-mile run behind the medicine ponies. Besides Richard III, he could do twenty-seven coon songs and banjo specialties, and was willing to cook, and curry the horses. We carried a fine line of excuses for taking money. One was a magic soap for removing grease spots and quarters from clothes. One was a Sum-wah-tah, the great Indian Remedy made from a prairie herb revealed by the Great Spirit in a dream to his favourite medicine men, the great chiefs MacGarrity and Silberstein, bottlers, Chicago. And the other was a frivolous system of pick-pocketing the Kansasters that had the department stores reduced to a decimal fraction. Look ye! A pair of silk garters, a dream book, one dozen clothes-pins, a gold tooth, and 'When Knighthood Was in Flower' all wrapped up in a genuine Japanese silkarina handkerchief and handed to the handsome lady by Mr Peters for the trivial sum of fifty cents, while Professor Binkly entertains us in a three-minute round with the banjo.

"'Twas an eminent graft we had. We ravaged peacefully through the State, determined to remove all doubt as to why 'twas called bleeding Kansas. John Tom Little Bear, in full Indian chief's costume, drew crowds away from the parchesi sociables and government ownership conversaziones. While at the football college in the East he had acquired quantities of rhetoric and the art of calisthenics and sophistry in his classes, and when he stood up in the red wagon and explained to the farmers, eloquent, about chilblains and hyperæsthesia of the cranium, Jeff couldn't hand out the Indian Remedy fast enough for 'em.

'One night we was camped on the edge of a little town out west of Salina. We always camped near a stream, and put up a little tent. Sometimes we sold out of the Remedy unexpected, and then Chief Wish-Heap-Dough would have a dream in which the Manitou commanded him to fill up a few bottles of Sum-wah-tah at the most convenient place. 'Twas about ten o'clock, and we'd just got in from a street performance. I was in the tent with the lantern, figuring up the day's profits. John Tom hadn't taken off his Indian make-up, and was sitting by the camp-fire minding a fine sirloin steak in the pan for the Professor till he finished his hair-raising scene with the trained horses.

'All at once out of dark bushes comes a pop like a fire-cracker, and John Tom gives a grunt and digs out of his bosom a little bullet that has dented itself against his collar-bone. John Tom makes a dive in the direction of the fireworks, and comes back dragging by the collar a kid about nine or ten years young, in a velveteen suit, with a little nickel-mounted rifle in his hand about as big as a fountain-pen.

'"Here, you pappoose," says John Tom, "what are you gunning for with that howitzer? You might hit somebody in the eye. Come out, Jeff, and mind the steak. Don't let it burn, while I investigate this demon with the pea-shooter."

'"Cowardly redskin," says the kid like he was quoting from a favourite author. "Dare to burn me at the stake and the paleface will sweep you from the prairies like – like everything. Now, you lemme go, or I'll tell mamma."

'John Tom plants the kid on a camp-stool, and sits down by him. "Now, tell the big chief," he says, "why you try to shoot pellets into your Uncle John's system. Didn't you know it was loaded?"

'"Are you a Indian?" asks the kid, looking up, cute as you

please, at John Tom's buckskin and eagle feathers. "I am," says John Tom.

"'Well, then, that's why," answers the boy, swinging his feet. I nearly let the steak burn watching the nerve of that youngster.

"'O-ho!' says John Tom, "I see. You're the Boy Avenger. And you've sworn to rid the continent of the savage redman. Is that about the way of it, son?"

'The kid half-way nodded his head. And then he looked glum. 'Twas indecent to wring his secret from his bosom before a single brave had fallen before his parlour-rifle.

"'Now, tell us where your wigwam is, pappoose," says John Tom – "where you live ? Your mamma will be worrying about you being out so late. Tell me, and I'll take you home."

'The kid grins. "I guess not," he says. "I live thousands and thousands of miles over there." He gyrated his hand toward the horizon. "I come on the train," he says, "by myself. I got off here because the conductor said my ticket had ex-pirated." He looks at John Tom with sudden suspicion. "I bet you ain't a Indian," he says. "You don't talk like a Indian. You look like one, but all a Indian can say is 'heap good' and 'paleface die.' Say, I bet you are one of them make-believe Indians that sell medicine on the streets. I saw one once in Quincy."

"'You never mind," says John Tom, "whether I'm a cigar-sign or a Tammany cartoon. The question before the council is what's to be done with you. You've run away from home. You've been reading Howells. You've disgraced the profession of boy avengers by trying to shoot a tame Indian, and never saying: ' Die, dog of a redskin! You have crossed the path of the Boy Avenger nineteen times too often.' What do you mean by it?"

'The kid thought for a minute. "I guess I made a mistake," he says. "I ought to have gone farther west. They find 'em wild out there in the cañons." He holds out his hand to John Tom, the little rascal. "Please excuse me, sir," says he, "for shooting at you. I hope it didn't hurt you. But you ought to be more careful. When a scout sees a Indian in his war-dress, his rifle must speak." Little Bear give a big laugh with a whoop at the end of it, and swings the kid ten feet high and sets him on his shoulder, and the runaway fingers the fringe and the eagle feathers and is full of the joy the white man knows when he dangles his heels against an inferior race. It is plain that Little Bear and that kid are chums from that on. The little renegade has already smoked the pipe of peace with the savage; and you can see in his eye that he is figuring on a tomahawk and a pair of moccasins, children's size.

'We have supper in the tent. The youngster looks upon me and the Professor as ordinary braves, only intended as a background to the camp scene. When he is seated on a box of Sum-wah-tah, with the edge of the table sawing his neck, and his mouth full of beefsteak, Little Bear calls for his name. "Roy," says the kid, with a sirloiny sound to it. But when the rest of it and his post-office address is referred to, he shakes his head. "I guess not," he says. "You'll send me back. I want to stay with you. I like this camping out. At home, we fellows had a camp in our back yard. They called me Roy, the Red Wolf. I guess that'll do for a name. Gimme another piece of beefsteak, please."

'We had to keep that kid. We knew there was a hullabaloo about him somewheres, and that Mamma, and Uncle Harry, and Aunt Jane, and the Chief of Police were hot after finding his trail, but not another word would he tell us. In two days he was the mascot of Big Medicine outfit, and all of us had a sneaking hope that his owners wouldn't turn up. When the red wagon was doing business he was in it, and passed up the bottles to Mr Peters as proud and satisfied as a prince that's abjured a two-hundred-dollar crown for a million-dollar parvenuess. Once John Tom asked him something about his papa. "I ain't got any papa," he says. "He runned away and left us. He made my mamma cry. Aunt Lucy says he's a shape." "A what?" somebody asks him. "A shape," says the kid: "some kind of a shape – lemme see – oh, yes, a feendenuman shape. I don't know what it means." John Tom was for putting our brand on him, and dressing him up like a little chief, with wampum and beads, but I vetoes it. "Somebody's lost that kid, is my view of it, and they may want him. You let me try him with a few stratagems, and see if I can't get a look at his visiting-card."

'So that night I goes up to Mr Roy Blank by the camp-fire, and looks at him contemptuous and scornful. "Snickenwitzel!" says I, like the word made me sick; "Snickenwitzel! Bah! Before I'd be named Snickenwitzel!"

'"What's the matter with you, Jeff?" says the kid, opening his eyes wide.

'"Snickenwitzel!" I repeats, and I spat the word out. "I saw a man to-day from your town, and he told me your name. I'm not surprised you was ashamed to tell it. Snickenwitzel! Whew!"

'"Ah, here, now," says the boy, indignant and wriggling all over, "what's the matter with you? That ain't my name. It's Conyers. What's the matter with you?"

'"And that's not the worst of it," I went on quick, keeping him hot and not giving him time to think. "We thought you was from a nice, well-to-do family. Here's Mr Little Bear, a chief of the Cherokees, entitled to wear nine otter tails on his Sunday blanket, and Professor Binkly, who plays Shakespeare and the banjo, and me, that's got hundreds of dollars in that black tin box in the wagon, and we've got to be careful about the company we keep. That man tells me your folks live 'way down in little Hencoop Alley, wheer there are no sidewalks, and the goats eat off the table with you."

'That kid was almost crying now. "'Tain't so," he splutters. "He – he don't know what he's talking about. We live on Poplar Av'noo. I don't 'sociate with goats. What's the matter with you?"

'"Poplar Avenue," says I, sarcastic. "Poplar Avenue! That's a street to live on! It only runs two blocks and then falls off a bluff. You can throw a keg of nails the whole length of it. Don't talk to me about Poplar Avenue."

'"It's – it's miles long," says the kid. "Our number's 862 and there's lots of houses after that. What's the matter with – aw, you make me tired, Jeff."

'"Well, well, now," says I. "I guess that man made a mistake. Maybe it was some other boy he was talking about. If I catch him I'll teach him to go around slandering people." And after supper I goes up-town and telegraphs to Mrs Conyers, 862 Poplar Avenue, Quincy, Ill., that the kid is safe and sassy with us, and will be held for further orders. In two hours an answer comes to hold him tight, and she'll start for him by next train.

'The next train was due at 6 p.m. the next day, and me and John Tom was at the depot with the kid. You might scour the plains in vain for the big Chief Wish-Heap-Dough. In his place is Mr Little Bear in the human habiliments of the Anglo-Saxon sect; and the leather of his shoes is patented and the loop of his necktie is copyrighted. For these things John Tom had grafted on him at college along with metaphysics and the knock-out guard for the low tackle. But for his complexion, which is some yellowish, and the black mop of his straight hair, you might have thought here was an ordinary man out of the city directory that subscribes for magazines and pushes the lawn-mower in his shirt-sleeves of evenings.

'Then the train rolled in, and a little woman in a grey dress, with a sort of illuminating hair, slides off and looks around quick. And the Boy Avenger sees her, and yells "Mamma," and she cries "Oh!" and they meet in a clinch, and now the pesky redskins can come forth from their caves on the plains without fear any more of the rifle of Roy, the Red Wolf. Mrs Conyers comes up and thanks me an' John Tom without the usual extremities you always look for in a woman. She says just enough, in a way to convince, and there is no incidental music by the orchestra. I made a few illiterate requisitions upon the art of conversation, at which the lady smiles friendly, as if she had known me a week. And then Mr Little Bear adorns the atmosphere with the various idioms into which education can fracture the wind of speech. I could see the kid's mother didn't quite place John Tom; but it seemed she was apprised in his dialects, and she played up to his lead in the science of making three words do the work of one.

'That kid introduced us, with some footnotes and explanations that made things plainer than a week of rhetoric. He danced around, and punched us in the back, and tried to climb John Tom's leg. "This is John Tom, mamma," says he. "He's a Indian. He sells medicine in a red wagon. I shot him, but he wasn't wild. The other one's Jeff. He's a fakir, too. Come on and see the camp where we live, won't you, mamma?"

'It is plain to see that the life of the woman is in that boy. She has got him again where her arms can gather him, and that's enough. She's ready to do anything to please him. She hesitates the eighth of a second and takes another look at these men. I imagine she says to herself about John Tom, "Seems to be a gentleman, if his hair don't curl." And Mr Peters she disposes of as follows: "No ladies' man, but a man who knows a lady."

'So we all rambled down to the camp as neighbourly as coming from a wake. And there she inspects the wagon, and pats the place with her hand where the kid used to sleep, and dabs around her eyewinkers with her handkerchief. And Professor Binkly gives us "Trovatore" on one string of the banjo, and is about to slide off into Hamlet's monologue when one of the horses gets tangled in his rope and he must go look after him, and says something about "foiled again."

'When it got dark me and John Tom walked back up to the Corn Exchange Hotel, and the four of us had supper there. I think the trouble started at that supper, for then was when Mr Little

Bear made an intellectual balloon ascension. I held on to the tablecloth, and listened to him soar. That redman, if I could judge, had the gift of information. He took language, and did with it all a Roman can do with macaroni. His vocal remarks was all embroidered over with the most scholarly verbs and prefixes. And his syllables was smooth, and fitted nicely to the joints of his idea. I thought I'd heard him talk before, but I hadn't. And it wasn't the size of his words, but the way they come; and 'twasn't his subjects, for he spoke of common things like cathedrals and footballs and poems and catarrh and souls and freight rates and sculpture. Mrs Conyers understood his accents, and the elegant sounds went back and forth between 'em. And now and then Jefferson D. Peters would intervene a few shop-worn, senseless words to have the butter passed or another leg of the chicken.

'Yes, John Tom Little Bear appeared to be inveigled some in his bosom about that Mrs Conyers. She was of the kind that pleases. She had the good looks and more, I'll tell you. You take one of these cloak models in a big store. They strike you as being on the impersonal system. They are adapted for the eye. What they run to is inches around and complexion, and the art of fanning the delusion that the sealskin would look just as well on the lady with the warts and the pocket-book. Now, if one of them models was off duty, and you took it, and it would say "Charlie" when you pressed it, and sit up at the table, why, then you would have something similar to Mrs Conyers. I could see how John Tom could resist any inclination to hate that white squaw.

'The lady and the kid stayed at the hotel. In the morning, they say, they will start for home. Me and Little Bear left at eight o'clock, and sold Indian Remedy on the courthouse square till nine. He leaves me and the Professor to drive down to camp, while he stays up town. I am not enamoured with that plan, for it shows John Tom is uneasy in his composures, and that leads to fire-water, and sometimes to the green corn dance and costs. Not often does Chief Wish-Heap-Dough get busy with the fire-water, but whenever he does there is heap much doing in the lodges of the palefaces who wear blue and carry the club.

'At half-past nine Professor Binkly is rolled in his quilt snoring in blank verse, and I am sitting by the fire listening to the frogs. Mr Little Bear slides into camp, and sits down against a tree. There is no symptoms of fire-water.

'"Jeff," says he, after a long time, "a little boy came West to hunt Indians."

'"Well, then?" says I, for I wasn't thinking as he was.

'"And he bagged one," says John Tom, "and 'twas not with a gun, and he never had on a velveteen suit of clothes in his life." And then, I began to catch his smoke.

'"I know it," says I. "And I'll bet you his pictures are on valentines, and fool men are his game, red and white."

'"You win on the red," says John Tom, calm. "Jeff, for how many ponies do you think I could buy Mrs Conyers?"

'"Scandalous talk!" I replies. "'Tis not a paleface custom." John Tom laughs loud and bites into a cigar. "No," he answers; "'tis the savage equivalent for the dollars of the white man's marriage settlement. Oh, I know. There's an eternal wall between the races. If I could do it, Jeff, I'd put a torch to every white college that a redman has ever set foot inside. Why don't you leave us alone," says he, "to our own ghost-dances and dog-feasts, and our dingy squaws to cook our grasshopper soup and darn our moccasins?"

'"Now, you sure don't mean disrespect to the perennial blossom entitled education?" says I, scandalized, "because I wear it in the bosom of my own intellectual shirt-waist. I've had education," says I, "and never took any harm from it."

'"You lasso us," goes on Little Bear, not noticing my prose insertions, "and teach us what is beautiful in literature and in life, and how to appreciate what is fine in men and women. What have you done to me?" says he. "You've made me a Cherokee Moses. You've taught me to hate the wigwams and love the white man's ways. I can look over into the promised land and see Mrs Conyers, but my place is – on the reservation."

'Little Bear stands up in his chief's dress, and laughs again. "But, white man Jeff," he goes on, "the paleface provides a recourse. 'Tis a temporary one, but it gives a respite and the name of it is whisky."

'And straight off he walks up the path to town again. "Now," says I in my mind, "may the Manitou move him to do only bailable things this night!" For I perceive that John Tom is about to avail himself of the white man's solace.

'Maybe it was 10.30, as I sat smoking, when I hear pit-a-pats on the path, and here comes Mrs Conyers running, her hair twisted up any way, and a look on her face that says burglars and mice and the flour's all-out rolled in one. "Oh, Mr Peters," she calls out, as they will, "oh, oh!" I made a quick think, and I spoke the gist of it out loud. "Now," says I, "we've been brothers, me and that Indian, but I'll make a good one of him in two minutes if –"

'"No, no," she says, wild and cracking her knuckles. "I haven't seen Mr Little Bear. 'Tis my – husband. He's stolen my boy. Oh," she says, "just when I had him back in my arms again! That heartless villain! Every bitterness life knows," she says, "he's made me drink. My poor little lamb, that ought to be warm in his bed, carried off by that fiend!"

'"How did all this happen?" I ask. "Let's have the facts."

'"I was fixing his bed," she explains, "and Roy was playing on the hotel porch and he drives up to the steps. I heard Roy scream and ran out. My husband had him in the buggy then. I begged him for my child. This is what he gave me." She turns her face to the light. There is a crimson streak running across her cheek and mouth. "He did that with his whip," she says.

'"Come back to the hotel," says I, "and we'll see what can be done."

'On the way she tells me some of the wherefores. When he slashed her with the whip he told her he found out she was coming for the kid, and he was on the same train. Mrs Conyers had been living with her brother, and they'd watched the boy always, as her husband had tried to steal him before. I judge that man was worse than a street railway promoter. It seems he had spent her money and slugged her and killed her canary bird, and told it around that she had cold feet.

'At the hotel we found a mass meeting of five infuriated citizens chewing tobacco and denouncing the outrage. Most of the town was asleep by ten o'clock. I talks the lady some quiet, and tells her I will take the one o'clock train for the next town, forty miles east, for it is likely that the esteemed Mr Conyers will drive there to take the cars. "I don't know," I tells her, "but what he has legal rights; but if I find him I can give him an illegal left in the eye, and tie him up for a day or two, anyhow, on a disturbal of the peace proposition."

'Mrs Conyers goes inside and cries with the landlord's wife, who is fixing some catnip tea that will make everything all right for the poor dear. The landlord comes out on the porch, thumbing his one suspender, and says to me:

'"Ain't had so much excitements in town since Bedford

Steegall's wife swallered a spring lizard. I seen him through the winder hit her with the buggy whip, and everything. What's that suit of clothes cost you you got on? 'Pears like we'd have some rain, don't it? Say, doc, that Indian of yorn's on a kind of whizz tonight, ain't he? He comes along just before you did, and I told him about this here occurrence. He gives a cur'us kind of a hoot, and trotted off. I guess our constable 'll have him in the lock-up 'fore morning."

'I thought I'd sit on the porch and wait for the one o'clock train. I wasn't feeling saturated with mirth. Here was John Tom on one of his sprees, and this kidnapping business losing sleep for me. But then, I'm always having trouble with other people's troubles. Every few minutes Mrs Conyers would come out on the porch and look down the road the way the buggy went, like she expected to see that kid coming back on a white pony with a red apple in his hand. Now, wasn't that like a woman? And that brings up cats. "I saw a mouse go in this hole," says Mrs Cat; "you can go prize up a plank over there if you like; I'll watch this hole."

'About a quarter to one o'clock the lady comes out again, restless, crying easy, as females do for their own amusement, and she looks down that road again and listens. "Now, ma'am," says I, "there's no use watching cold wheel-tracks. By this time they're half-way to –" "Hush," she says, holding up her hand. And I do hear something coming "flip-flap" in the dark; and then there is the awfullest war-whoop ever heard outside of Madison Square Garden at a Buffalo Bill matinée. And up the steps and on to the porch jumps the disrespectable Indian. The lamp in the hall shines on him, and I fail to recognize Mr J. T. Little Bear, alumnus of the class of '91. What I see is a Cherokee brave, and the warpath is what he has been travelling. Fire-water and other things have got him going. His buckskin is hanging in strings, and his feathers are mixed up like a frizzly hen's. The dust of miles is on his moccasins, and the light in his eye is the kind the aborigines wear. But in his arms he brings that kid, his eyes half closed, with his little shoes dangling and one hand fast around the Indian's collar.

'"Pappoose!" says John Tom, and I notice that the flowers of the white man's syntax have left his tongue. He is the original proposition in bear's claws and copper colour. "Me bring," says he, and he lays the kid in his mother's arms. "Run fifteen mile," says John Tom –"Ugh! Catch white man. Bring pappoose."

'The little woman is in extremities of gladness. She must wake up that stir-up trouble youngster and hug him and make proclamation that he is his mamma's own precious treasure. I was about to ask questions, but I looked at Mr Little Bear, and my eye caught the sight of something in his belt. "Now go to bed, ma'am," says I, "and this gadabout youngster likewise, for there's no more danger, and the kidnapping business is not what it was earlier in the night."

'I inveigled John Tom down to camp quick, and when he tumbled over asleep I got that thing out of his belt and disposed of it where the eye of education can't see it. For even the football colleges disapprove of the art of scalp-taking in their curriculums.

'It is ten o'clock next day when John Tom wakes up and looks around. I am glad to see the nineteenth century in his eye again.

'"What was it, Jeff?" he asks.

'"Heap fire-water," says I.

'John Tom frowns, and thinks a little. "Combined," says he directly, "with the interesting little physiological shake-up known as reversion to type. I remember now. Have they gone yet?"

'"On the 7.30 train," I answers.

'"Ugh!" says John Tom; "better so. Paleface, bring big Chief Wish-Heap-Dough a little bromoseltzer, and then he'll take up the redman's burden again."'

THE BRIEF DEBUT OF TILDY

If you do not know Bogle's Chop House and Family Restaurant it is your loss. For if you are one of the fortunate ones who dine expensively you should be interested to know how the other half consumes provisions. And if you belong to the half to whom waiters' checks are things of moment, you should know Bogle's, for there you get your money's worth – in quantity, at least.

Bogle's is situated in that highway of *bourgeoisie*, that boulevard of Brown-Jones-and-Robinson, Eighth Avenue. There are two rows of tables in the room, six in each row. On each table is a castor-stand, containing cruets of condiments and seasons. From the pepper cruet you may shake a cloud of something tasteless and melancholy, like volcanic dust. From the salt cruet you may expect nothing. Though a man should extract a sanguinary stream from the pallid turnip, yet will his prowess be baulked when he comes to wrest salt from Bogle's cruets. Also upon each table stands the counterfeit of that benign sauce made 'from the recipe of a nobleman in India.'

At the cashier's desk sits Bogle, cold, sordid, slow, smouldering, and takes your money. Behind a mountain of toothpicks he makes your change, files your check, and ejects at you, like a toad, a word about the weather. Beyond a corroboration of his meteorological statement you would better not venture. You are not Bogle's friend; you are a fed, transient customer, and you and he may not meet again until the blowing of Gabriel's dinner horn. So take your change and go – to the devil if you like. There you have Bogle's sentiments.

The needs of Bogle's customers were supplied by two waitresses and a Voice. One of the waitresses was named Aileen. She was tall, beautiful, lively, gracious and learned in persiflage. Her other name? There was no more necessity for another name at Bogle's than there was for finger-bowls.

The name of the other waitress was Tildy. Why do you suggest Matilda? Please listen this time – Tildy – Tildy. Tildy was dumpy, plain-faced, and too anxious to please to please. Repeat the last clause to yourself once or twice, and make the acquaintance of the duplicate infinite.

The Voice at Bogle's was invisible. It came from the kitchen, and did not shine in the way of originality. It was a heathen Voice, and contented itself with vain repetitions of exclamations emitted by the waitresses concerning food.

Will it tire you to be told again that Aileen was beautiful? Had she donned a few hundred dollars' worth of clothes and joined the Easter parade, and had you seen her, you would have hastened to say so yourself.

The customers at Bogle's were her slaves. Six tables full she could wait upon at once. They who were in a hurry restrained their impatience for the joy of merely gazing upon her swiftly moving, graceful figure. They who had finished eating ate more that they might continue in the light of her smiles. Every man there – and they were mostly men – tried to make his impression upon her.

Aileen could successfully exchange repartee against a dozen at once. And every smile that she sent forth lodged, like pellets from a scatter-gun, in as many hearts. And all this while she would be performing astounding feats with orders of pork and beans, pot roasts, ham-and, sausage-and-the-wheats, and any quantity of things on the iron and in the pan and straight up and on the side. With all this feasting and flirting and merry exchange of wit Bogle's came mighty near being a salon, with Aileen for its Madame Récamier.

If the transients were entranced by the fascinating Aileen, the regulars were her adorers. There was much rivalry among many of the steady customers. Aileen could have had an engagement every evening. At least twice a week someone took her to a theatre or to a dance. One stout gentleman whom she and Tildy had privately christened 'The Hog' presented her with a turquoise ring. Another one known as 'Freshy,' who rode on the Traction Company's repair wagon, was going to give her a poodle as soon as his brother got the hauling contract in the Ninth. And the man who always ate spareribs and spinach and said he was a stock-broker asked her to go to 'Parsifal' with him.

'I don't know where this place is,' said Aileen while talking it over with Tildy, 'but the wedding-ring's got to be on before I put a stitch into a travelling dress – ain't that right? Well, I guess!'

But, Tildy!

In steaming, chattering, cabbage-scented Bogle's there was almost a heart tragedy. Tildy with the blunt nose, the hay-coloured hair, the freckled skin, the bag-o'-meal figure, had never had an admirer. Not a man followed her with his eyes when she went to and fro in the restaurant save now and then when they glared with the beast-hunger for food. None of them bantered her gaily to coquettish interchanges of wit. None of them loudly 'jollied' her of mornings as they did Aileen, accusing her, when the eggs were slow in coming, of late hours in the company of envied swains. No one had ever given her a turquoise ring or invited her upon a voyage to mysterious distant 'Parsifal.'

Tildy was a good waitress, and the men tolerated her. They who sat at her tables spoke to her briefly with quotations from the bill of fare; and then raised their voices in honeyed and otherwise-flavoured accents, eloquently addressed to the fair Aileen. They writhed in their chairs to gaze around and over the impending form of Tildy, that Aileen's pulchritude might season and make ambrosia of their bacon and eggs.

And Tildy was content to be the unwooed drudge if Aileen could receive the flattery and the homage. The blunt nose was loyal to the short Grecian. She was Aileen's friend; and she was glad to see her rule hearts and wean the attention of men from smoking pot-pie and lemon meringue. But deep below our freckles and hay-coloured hair the unhandsomest of us dream of a prince or a princess, not vicarious, but coming to us alone.

There was a morning when Aileen tripped in to work with a slightly bruised eye; and Tildy's solicitude was almost enough to heal any optic.

'Fresh guy,' explained Aileen, 'last night as I was going home at Twenty-third and Sixth. Sashayed up, so he did, and made a break. I turned him down, cold, and he made a sneak; but followed me down to Eighteenth, and tried his hot air again. Gee! but I slapped him a good one, side of the face. Then he give me that eye. Does it look real awful, Til? I should hate that Mr Nicholson should see it when he comes in for his tea and toast at ten.'

Tildy listened to the adventure with breathless admiration. No man had ever tried to follow her. She was safe abroad at any hour of the twenty-four. What bliss it must have been to have had a man follow one and black one's eye for love!

Among the customers at Bogle's was a young man named

Seeders, who worked in a laundry office. Mr Seeders was thin and had light hair, and appeared to have been recently rough-dried and starched. He was too diffident to aspire to Aileen's notice; so he usually sat at one of Tildy's tables, where he devoted himself to silence and boiled weakfish.

One day when Mr Seeders came in to dinner he had been drinking beer. There were only two or three customers in the restaurant. When Mr Seeders had finished his weakfish he got up, put his arm around Tildy's waist, kissed her loudly and impudently, walked out upon the street, snapped his fingers in the direction of the laundry, and hied himself to play pennies in the slot machines at the Amusement Arcade.

For a few moments Tildy stood petrified. Then she was aware of Aileen shaking at her an arch forefinger, and saying:

'Why, Til, you naughty girl! Ain't you getting to be awful, Miss Slyboots! First thing I know you'll be stealing some of my fellows. I must keep an eye on you, my lady.'

Another thing dawned upon Tildy's recovering wits. In a moment she had advanced from a hopeless, lowly admirer to be an Eve-sister of the potent Aileen. She herself was now a man-charmer, a mark for Cupid, a Sabine who must be coy when the Romans were at their banquet boards. Man had found her waist achievable and her lips desirable. The sudden and amatory Seeders had, as it were, performed for her a miraculous piece of one-day laundry-work. He had taken the sackcloth of her uncomeliness, had washed, dried, starched and ironed it, and returned it to her sheer embroidered lawn – robe of Venus herself.

The freckles on Tildy's cheeks merged into a rosy flush. Now both Circe and Psyche peeped from her brightened eyes. Not even Aileen herself had been publicly embraced and kissed in the restaurant.

Tildy could not keep the delightful secret. When trade was slack she went and stood at Bogle's desk. Her eyes were shining; she tried not to let her words sound proud and boastful.

'A gentleman insulted me to-day,' she said. 'He hugged me around the waist and kissed me.'

'That so?' said Bogle, cracking open his business armour. 'After this week you get a dollar a week more.'

At the next regular meal when Tildy set food before customers with whom she had acquaintance she said to each of them modestly, as one whose merit needed no bolstering:

'A gentleman insulted me to-day in the restaurant. He put his arm around my waist and kissed me.'

The diners accepted the revelation in various ways – some incredulously, some with congratulations; others turned upon her the stream of badinage that had hitherto been directed at Aileen alone. And Tildy's heart swelled in her bosom, for she saw at last the towers of Romance rise above the horizon of the grey plain in which she had for so long travelled.

For two days Mr Seeders came not again. During that time Tildy established herself firmly as a woman to be wooed. She bought ribbons, and arranged her hair like Aileen's, and tightened her waist two inches. She had a thrilling but delightful fear that Mr Seeders would rush in suddenly and shoot her with a pistol. He must have loved her desperately; and impulsive lovers are always blindly jealous.

Even Aileen had not been shot at with a pistol. And then Tildy rather hoped that he would not shoot at her, for she was always loyal to Aileen; and she did not want to overshadow her friend.

At four o'clock on the afternoon of the third day Mr Seeders came in. There were no customers at the tables. At the back end of the restaurant Tildy was refilling the mustard pots and Aileen was quartering pies. Mr Seeders walked back to where they stood.

Tildy looked up and saw him, gasped, and pressed the mustard spoon upon her heart. A red hair-bow was in her hair; she wore Venus's Eighth Avenue badge, the blue bead necklace with the swinging silver symbolic heart.

Mr Seeders was flushed and embarrassed. He plunged one hand into his hip pocket and the other into a fresh pumpkin pie.

'Miss Tildy,' said he, 'I want to apologize for what I done the other evenin'. Tell you the truth, I was pretty well tanked up or I wouldn't of done it. I wouldn't do no lady that a-way when I was sober. So I hope, Miss Tildy, you'll accept my 'pology, and believe that I wouldn't of done it if I'd known what I was doin' and hadn't of been drunk.'

With this handsome plea Mr Seeders backed away, and departed, feeling that reparation had been made.

But behind the convenient screen Tildy had thrown herself flat upon a table among the butter chips and the coffee cups, and was sobbing her heart out – out and back again to the grey plain wherein travel they with blunt noses and hay-coloured hair. From her knot she had torn the red hair-bow and cast it upon the floor.

Seeders she despised utterly; she had but taken his kiss as that of a pioneer and prophetic prince who might have set the clocks going and the pages to running in fairyland. But the kiss had been maudlin and unmeant; the court had not stirred at the false alarm; she must for evermore remain the Sleeping Beauty.

Yet not all was lost. Aileen's arm was around her; and Tildy's red hand groped among the butter chips till it found the warm grasp of her friend's.

'Don't you fret, Til,' said Aileen, who did not understand entirely. 'That turnip-faced little clothes-pin of a Seeders ain't worth it. He ain't anything of a gentleman or he wouldn't ever of apologized.'

THE COP AND THE ANTHEM

On his bench in Madison Square Soapy moved uneasily. When wild goose honk high of nights, and when women without sealskin coats grow kind to their husbands, and when Soapy moves uneasily on his bench in the park, you may know that winter is near at hand.

A dead leaf fell in Soapy's lap. That was Jack Frost's card. Jack is kind to the regular denizens of Madison Square, and gives fair warning of his annual call. At the corners of four streets he hands his pasteboard to the North Wind, footman of the mansion of All Outdoors, so that the inhabitants thereof may make ready.

Soapy's mind became cognizant of the fact that the time had come for him to resolve himself into a singular Committee of Ways and Means to provide against the coming rigour. And therefore he moved uneasily on his bench.

The hibernatorial ambitions of Soapy were not of the highest. In them were no considerations of Mediterranean cruises, of soporific Southern skies or drifting in the Vesuvian Bay. Three months on the Island was what his soul craved. Three months of assured board and bed and congenial company, safe from Boreas and bluecoats, seemed to Soapy the essence of things desirable.

For years the hospitable Blackwell's had been his winter quarters. Just as his more fortunate fellow New Yorkers had bought their tickets to Palm Beach and the Riviera each winter, so Soapy had made his humble arrangements for his annual hegira to the Island. And now the time was come. On the previous night three Sabbath newspapers, distributed beneath his coat, about his ankles and over his lap, had failed to repulse the cold as he slept on his bench near the spurting fountain in the ancient square. So the Island loomed large and timely in Soapy's mind. He scorned the provisions made in the name of charity for the city's dependents. In Soapy's opinion the Law was more benign than Philanthropy. There was an endless round of institutions, municipal and eleemosynary, on which he might set out and receive lodging and food accordant with the simple life. But to one of Soapy's proud spirit the gifts of charity are encumbered. If not in coin you must pay in humiliation of spirit for every benefit received at the hands of philanthropy. As Cæsar had his Brutus, every bed of charity must have its toll of a bath, every loaf of bread its compensation of a private and personal inquisition. Wherefore it is better to be a guest of the law, which, though conducted by rules, does not meddle unduly with a gentleman's private affairs.

Soapy, having decided to go to the Island, at once set about accomplishing his desire. There were many easy ways of doing this. The pleasantest was to dine luxuriously at some expensive restaurant; and then, after declaring insolvency, be handed over quietly and without uproar to a policeman. An accommodating magistrate would do the rest.

Soapy left his bench and strolled out of the square and across the level sea of asphalt, where Broadway and Fifth Avenue flow together. Up Broadway he turned, and halted at a glittering café, where are gathered together nightly the choicest products of the grape, the silkworm and the protoplasm.

Soapy had confidence in himself from the lowest button of his vest upward. He was shaven, and his coat was decent and his neat black, ready-tied four-in-hand had been presented to him by a lady missionary on Thanksgiving Day. If he could reach a table in the restaurant unsuspected success would be his. The portion of him that would show above the table would raise no doubt in the waiter's mind. A roasted mallard duck, thought Soapy, would be about the thing – with a bottle of Chablis, and then Camembert, a demitasse and a cigar. One dollar for the cigar would be enough. The total would not be so high as to call forth any supreme manifestation of revenge from the café management; and yet the meat would leave him filled and happy for the journey to his winter refuge.

But as Soapy set foot inside the restaurant door the head waiter's eye fell upon his frayed trousers and decadent shoes. Strong and ready hands turned him about and conveyed him in silence and haste to the sidewalk and averted the ignoble fate of the menaced mallard.

Soapy turned off Broadway. It seemed that his route to the coveted Island was not to be an epicurean one. Some other way of entering limbo must be thought of.

At a corner of Sixth Avenue electric lights and cunningly

displayed wares behind plate-glass made a shop window conspicuous. Soapy took a cobblestone and dashed it through the glass.
People came running round the corner, a policeman in the lead.
Soapy stood still, with his hands in his pockets, and smiled at the
sight of brass buttons.

'Where's the man that done that?' inquired the officer excitedly.

'Don't you figure out that I might have had something to do
with it?' said Soapy, not without sarcasm, but friendly, as one
greets good fortune.

The policeman's mind refused to accept Soapy even as a clue.
Men who smash windows do not remain to parley with the law's
minions. They take to their heels. The policeman saw a man
halfway down the block running to catch a car. With drawn club
he joined in the pursuit. Soapy, with disgust in his heart, loafed
along, twice unsuccessful.

On the opposite side of the street was a restaurant of no great
pretensions. It catered to large appetites and modest purses. Its
crockery and atmosphere were thick; its soup and napery thin.
Into this place Soapy took his accusive shoes and tell-tale trousers
without challenge. At a table he sat and consumed beefsteak,
flap-jacks, doughnuts and pie. And then to the waiter he betrayed
the fact that the minutest coin and himself were strangers.

'Now, get busy and call a cop,' said Soapy. 'And don't keep a
gentleman waiting.'

'No cop for youse,' said the waiter, with a voice like butter
cakes and an eye like the cherry in a Manhattan cocktail. 'Hey,
Con!'

Neatly upon his left ear on the callous pavement two waiters
pitched Soapy. He arose, joint by joint, as a carpenter's rule opens,
and beat the dust from his clothes. Arrest seemed but a rosy
dream. The Island seemed very far away. A policeman who stood
before a drug store two doors away laughed and walked down
the street.

Five blocks Soapy travelled before his courage permitted him
to woo capture again. This time the opportunity presented what
he fatuously termed to himself a 'cinch.' A young woman of a
modest and pleasing guise was standing before a show window
gazing with sprightly interest at its display of shaving mugs and
inkstands, and two yards from the window a large policeman of
severe demeanour leaned against a water-plug.

It was Soapy's design to assume the rôle of the despicable and execrated 'masher.' The refined and elegant appearance of his victim and the contiguity of the conscientious cop encouraged him to believe that he would soon feel the pleasant official clutch upon his arm that would ensure his winter quarters on the right little, tight little isle.

Soapy straightened the lady missionary's ready-made tie, dragged his shrinking cuffs into the open, set his hat at a killing cant and sidled toward the young woman. He made eyes at her, was taken with sudden coughs and 'hems,' smiled, smirked and went brazenly through the impudent and contemptible litany of the 'masher.' With half an eye Soapy saw that the policeman was watching him fixedly. The young woman moved away a few steps, and again bestowed her absorbed attention upon the shaving mugs. Soapy followed, boldly stepping to her side, raised his hat and said:

'Ah there, Bedelia! Don't you want to come and play in my yard?'

The policeman was still looking. The persecuted young woman had but to beckon a finger and Soapy would be practically *en route* for his insular haven. Already he imagined he could feel the cosy warmth of the station-house. The young woman faced him and, stretching out a hand, caught Soapy's coatsleeve.

'Sure, Mike,' she said joyfully, 'if you'll blow me to a pail of suds. I'd have spoke to you sooner, but the cop was watching.'

With the young woman playing the clinging ivy to his oak Soapy walked past the policeman, overcome with gloom. He seemed doomed to liberty.

At the next corner he shook off his companion and ran. He halted in the district where by night are found the lightest streets, hearts, vows and librettos. Women in furs and men in greatcoats moved gaily in the wintry air. A sudden fear seized Soapy that some dreadful enchantment had rendered him immune to arrest. The thought brought a little of panic upon it, and when he came upon another policeman lounging grandly in front of a transplendent theatre he caught at the immediate straw of 'disorderly conduct.'

On the sidewalk Soapy began to yell drunken gibberish at the top of his harsh voice. He danced, howled, raved and otherwise disturbed the welkin.

The policeman twirled his club, turned his back to Soapy and remarked to a citizen:

''Tis one of them Yale lads celebratin' the goose egg they give to the Hartford College. Noisy; but no harm. We've instructions to lave them be.'

Disconsolate, Soapy ceased his unavailing racket. Would never a policeman lay hands on him? In his fancy the Island seemed an unattainable Arcadia. He buttoned his thin coat against the chilling wind.

In a cigar store he saw a well-dressed man lighting a cigar at a swinging light. His silk umbrella he had set by the door on entering. Soapy stepped inside, secured the umbrella and sauntered off with it slowly. The man at the cigar light followed hastily.

'My umbrella,' he said sternly.

'Oh, is it?' sneered Soapy, adding insult to petit larceny. 'Well, why don't you call a policeman? I took it. Your umbrella! Why don't you call a cop? There stands one at the corner.'

The umbrella owner slowed his steps. Soapy did likewise, with a presentiment that luck would again run against him. The policeman looked at the two curiously.

'Of course,' said the umbrella man – 'that is – well, you know how these mistakes occur – I – if it's your umbrella I hope you'll excuse me – I picked it up this morning in a restaurant – If you recognize it as yours, why – I hope you'll –'

'Of course it's mine,' said Soapy viciously.

The ex-umbrella man retreated. The policeman hurried to assist a tall blonde in an opera cloak across the street in front of a street car that was approaching two blocks away.

Soapy walked eastward through a street damaged by improvements. He hurled the umbrella wrathfully into an excavation. He muttered against the men who wear helmets and carry clubs. Because he wanted to fall into their clutches, they seemed to regard him as a king who could do no wrong.

At length Soapy reached one of the avenues to the east where the glitter and turmoil was but faint. He set his face down this toward Madison Square, for the homing instinct survives even when the home is a park bench.

But on an unusually quiet corner Soapy came to a standstill. Here was an old church, quaint and rambling and gabled. Through one violet-stained window a soft light glowed, where, no doubt, the organist loitered over the keys, making sure of his mastery of the coming Sabbath anthem. For there drifted out to Soapy's ears sweet music that caught and held him transfixed against the convolutions of the iron fence.

The moon was above, lustrous and serene; vehicles and pedestrians were few; sparrows twittered sleepily in the eaves – for a little while the scene might have been a country churchyard. And the anthem that the organist played cemented Soapy to the iron fence, for he had known it well in the days when his life contained such things as mothers and roses and ambitions and friends and immaculate thoughts and collars.

The conjunction of Soapy's receptive state of mind and the influences about the old church wrought a sudden and wonderful change in his soul. He viewed with swift horror the pit into which he had tumbled, the degraded days, unworthy desires, dead hopes, wrecked faculties and base motives that made up his existence.

And also in a moment his heart responded thrillingly to this novel mood. An instantaneous and strong impulse moved him to battle with his desperate fate. He would pull himself out of the mire; he would make a man of himself again; he would conquer the evil that had taken possession of him. There was time; he was comparatively young yet; he would resurrect his old eager ambitions and pursue them without faltering. Those solemn but sweet organ notes had set up a revolution in him. To-morrow he would go into the roaring down-town district and find work. A fur importer had once offered him a place as driver. He would find him to-morrow and ask for the position. He would be somebody in the world. He would –

Soapy felt a hand laid on his arm. He looked quickly around into the broad face of a policeman.

'What are you doin' here?' asked the officer.

'Nothin',' said Soapy.

'Then come along,' said the policeman.

'Three months on the Island,' said the Magistrate in the Police Court the next morning.

I never got inside of the legitimate line of graft but once. But, one time, as I say, I reversed the decision of the revised statutes and undertook a thing that I'd have to apologize for even under the New Jersey trust laws.

Me and Caligula Polk, of Muskogee in the Creek Nation, was down in the Mexican State of Tamaulipas running a peripatetic lottery and monte game. Now, selling lottery tickets is a government graft in Mexico, just like selling forty-eight cents' worth of postage-stamps for forty-nine cents is over here. So Uncle Porfirio he instructs the *rurales* to attend to our case.

Rurales? They're a sort of country police; but don't draw any mental crayon portraits of the worthy constable with a tin star and a grey goatee. The *rurales* – well, if we'd mount our Supreme Court on broncos, arm 'em with Winchesters, and start 'em out after John Doe *et al.*, we'd have about the same thing.

When the *rurales* started for us we started for the States. They chased us as far as Matamoras. We hid in a brickyard; and that night we swum the Rio Grande, Caligula with a brick in each hand, absent-minded, which he drops upon the soil of Texas, forgetting he had 'em.

From there we emigrated to San Antone, and then over to New Orleans, where we took a rest. And in that town of cotton bales and other adjuncts to female beauty we made the acquaintance of drinks invented by the Creoles during the period of Louey Cans, in which they are still served at the side doors. The most I can remember of this town is that me and Caligula and a Frenchman named McCarty – wait a minute; Adolph McCarty – was trying to make the French Quarter pay up the back trading-stamps due on the Louisiana Purchase, when somebody hollers that the johndarms are coming. I have an insufficient recollection of buying two yellow tickets through a window; and I seemed to see a man swing a lantern and say 'All aboard!' I remembered no more, except that the train butcher was covering me and Caligula up with Augusta J. Evans' works and figs.

When we become revised, we find that we have collided up against the State of Georgia at a spot hitherto unaccounted for in time-tables except by an asterisk, which means that trains stop every other Thursday on signal by tearing up a rail. We was waked up in a yellow pine hotel by the noise of flowers and the smell of birds. Yes, sir, for the wind was banging sunflowers as big as buggy wheels against the weatherboarding and the chicken-coop was right under the window. Me and Caligula dressed and went downstairs. The landlord was shelling peas on the front porch, He was six feet of chills and fever, and Hong-Kong in complexion though in other respects he seemed amenable in the exercise of his sentiments and features.

Caligula, who is a spokesman by birth, and a small man, though red-haired and impatient of painfulness of any kind, speaks up.

'Pardner,' says he, 'good morning, and be darned to you. Would you mind telling us why we are at? We know the reason we are where, but can't exactly figure out on account of at what place.'

'Well, gentlemen,' says the landlord, 'I reckoned you-all would be inquiring this morning. You-all dropped off at the nine-thirty train here last night; and you was right tight. Yes, you was right smart in liquor. I can inform you that you are now in the town of Mountain Valley, in the State of Georgia.'

'On top of that,' says Caligula, 'don't say that we can't have anything to eat.'

'Sit down, gentlemen,' says the landlord, 'and in twenty minutes I'll call you to the best breakfast you can get anywhere in town.'

That breakfast turned out to be composed of fried bacon and a yellowish edifice that proved up something between pound cake and flexible sandstone. The landlord calls it corn pone; and then he sets out a dish of the exaggerated breakfast food known as hominy; and so me and Caligula makes the acquaintance of the celebrated food that enabled every Johnny Reb to lick one and two-thirds Yankees for nearly four years at a stretch.

'The wonder to me is,' says Caligula, 'that Uncle Robert Lee's boys didn't chase the Grant and Sherman outfit clear up into Hudson's Bay. It would have made me that mad to eat this truck they call mahogany!'

'Hog and hominy,' I explains, 'is the staple food of this section.'

'Then,' says Caligula, 'they ought to keep it where it belongs. I thought this was a hotel and not a stable. Now, if we was in Muskogee at the St Lucifer House, I'd show you some breakfast grub. Antelope steaks and fried liver to begin on, and venison cutlets with *chili con carne* and pineapple fritters, and then some sardines and mixed pickles; and top it off with a can of yellow clings and a bottle of beer. You won't find a layout like that on the bill of affairs of any of your Eastern restauraws.'

'Too lavish,' say I. 'I've travelled, and I'm unprejudiced. There'll never be a perfect breakfast eaten until some man grows arms long enough to stretch down to New Orleans for his coffee and over to Norfolk for his rolls, and reaches up to Vermont and digs a slice of butter out of a springhouse, and then turns over a beehive close to a white clover patch out in Indiana for the rest. Then he'd come pretty close to making a meal on the amber that the gods eat on Mount Olympia.'

'Too ephemeral,' says Caligula. 'I'd want ham and eggs, or rabbit stew, anyhow, for a chaser. What do you consider the most edifying and casual in the way of a dinner?'

'I've been infatuated from time to time,' I answers, 'with fancy ramifications of grub such as terrapins, lobsters, reed birds, jambolaya, and canvas-covered ducks; but, after all, there's nothing less displeasing to me than a beefsteak smothered in mushrooms on a balcony in sound of the Broadway street-cars, with a hand-organ playing down below, and the boys hollering extras about the latest suicide. For the wine, give me a reasonable Ponty Cany. And that's all, except a *demi-tasse*.'

'Well,' says Caligula, 'I reckon in New York you get to be a conniseer; and when you go around with the *demi-tasse* you are naturally bound to buy 'em stylish grub.'

'It's a great town for epicures,' says I. 'You'd soon fall into their ways if you was there.'

'I've heard it was,' says Caligula. 'But I reckon I wouldn't. I can polish my finger-nails all they need myself.'

II

After breakfast we went out on the front porch, lighted up two of the landlord's *flor de upas* perfectos, and took a look at Georgia.

The instalment of scenery visible to the eye looked mighty poor.

As far as we could see was red hills all washed down with gullies and scattered over with patches of piny woods. Blackberry bushes was all that kept the rail fences from falling down. About fifteen miles over to the north was a little range of well-timbered mountains.

That town of Mountain Valley wasn't going. About a dozen people permeated along the sidewalks; but what you saw mostly was rain-barrels and roosters, and boys poking around with sticks in piles of ashes made by burning the scenery of Uncle Tom shows.

And just then there passes down on the other side of the street a high man in a long black coat and a beaver hat. All the people in sight bowed, and some crossed the street to shake hands with him; folks came out of stores and houses to holler at him; women leaned out of windows and smiled; and all the kids stopped playing to look at him. Our landlord stepped out on the porch and bent himself double like a carpenter's rule, and sung out, 'Good morning, Colonel,' when he was a dozen yards gone by.

'And is that Alexander, pa?' says Caligula to the landlord; 'and why is he called great?'

'That, gentlemen,' says the landlord, 'is no less than Colonel Jackson T. Rockingham, the president of the Sunrise & Edenville Tap Railroad, mayor of Mountain Valley, and chairman of the Perry County board of immigration and public improvements.'

'Been away a good many years, hasn't he?' I asked.

'No, sir; Colonel Rockingham is going down to the post office for his mail. His fellow-citizens take pleasure in greeting him thus every morning. The colonel is our most prominent citizen. Besides the height of the stock of the Sunrise & Edenville Tap Railroad, he owns a thousand acres of that land across the creek. Mountain Valley delights, sir, to honour a citizen of such worth and public spirit.'

For an hour that afternoon Caligula sat on the back of his neck on the porch and studied a newspaper, which was unusual in a man who despised print. When he was through he took me to the end of the porch among the sunlight and drying dish-towels. I knew that Caligula had invented a new graft. For he chewed the ends of his moustache and ran the left catch of his suspenders up and down, which was his way.

'What is it now?' I asks. 'Just so it ain't floating mining stocks or raising Pennsylvania pinks, we'll talk it over.'

Pennsylvania pinks? Oh, that refers to a coin-raising scheme of the Keystoners. They burn the soles of old women's feet to make them tell where their money's hid.

Caligula's words in business was always few and bitter.

'You see them mountains,' said he, pointing. 'And you seen that colonel man that owns railroads and cuts more ice when he goes to the post office than Roosevelt does when he cleans 'em out. What we're going to do is to kidnap the latter into the former, and inflict a ransom of ten thousand dollars.'

'Illegality,' says I, shaking my head.

'I knew you'd say that,' says Caligula. 'At first sight it does seem to jar peace and dignity. But it don't. I got the idea out of that newspaper. Would you commit aspersions on a equitable graft that the United States itself has condoned and indorsed and ratified?'

'Kidnapping,' says I, 'is an immoral function in the derogatory list of the statutes. If the United States upholds it, it must be a recent enactment of ethics, along with race suicide and rural delivery.'

'Listen,' says Caligula, 'and I'll explain the case set down in the papers. Here was a Greek citizen named Burdick Harris,' says he, 'captured for a graft by Africans; and the United States sends two gunboats to the State of Tangiers and makes the King of Morocco give up seventy thousand dollars to Raisuli.'

'Go slow,' says I. 'That sounds too international to take in all at once. It's like "thimble, thimble, who's got the naturalization papers?"'

''Twas Press despatches from Constantinople,' says Caligula. 'You'll see, six months from now. They'll be confirmed by the monthly magazines; and then it won't be long till you'll notice 'em alongside of photos of the Mount Pelée eruption photos in the while-you-get-your-hair-cut weeklies. It's all right, Pick. This African man Raisuli hides Burdick Harris up in the mountains, and advertises his price to the governments of different nations. Now, you wouldn't think for a minute,' goes on Caligula, 'that John Hay would have chipped in and helped this graft along if it wasn't a square game, would you?'

'Why, no,' says I. 'I've always stood right in with Bryan's policies, and I couldn't consciously say a word against the Republican administration just now. But if Harris was a Greek, on what system of international protocols did Hay interfere?'

'It ain't exactly set forth in the papers,' says Caligula. 'I suppose it's a matter of sentiment. You know he wrote this poem, "Little Breeches"; and them Greeks wear little or none. But anyhow, John Hay sends the *Brooklyn* and the *Olympia* over, and they cover Africa with thirty-inch guns. And then Hay cables after the health of the *persona grata*. "And how are they this morning?" he wires. "Is Burdick Harris alive yet, or Mr Raisuli dead?" And the King of Morocco sends up the seventy thousand dollars, and they turn Burdick Harris loose. And there's not half the hard feelings among the nations about this little kidnapping matter as there was about the peace congress. And Burdick Harris says to the reporters, in the Greek language, that he's often heard about the United States, and he admires Roosevelt next to Raisuli, who is one of the whitest and most gentlemanly kidnappers that he ever worked alongside of. So you see, Pick,' winds up Caligula, 'we've got the law of nations on our side. We'll cut this colonel man out of the herd, and corral him in them little mountains, and stick up his heirs and assigns for ten thousand dollars.'

'Well, you seldom little red-headed territorial terror,' I answers, 'you can't bluff your uncle Tecumseh Pickens! I'll be your company in this graft. But I misdoubt if you've absorbed the inwardness of this Burdick Harris case, Calig; and if on any morning we get a telegram from the Secretary of State asking about the health of the scheme, I propose to acquire the most propinquitous and celeritous mule in this section and gallop diplomatically over into the neighbouring and peaceful nation of Alabama.'

III

Me and Caligula spent the next three days investigating the bunch of mountains into which we proposed to kidnap Colonel Jackson T. Rockingham. We finally selected an upright slice of topography covered with bushes and trees that you could only reach by a secret path that we cut out up the side of it. And the only way to reach the mountain was to follow up the bend of a branch that wound among the elevations.

Then I took in hand an important sub-division of the proceedings. I went up to Atlanta on the train and laid in a two-hundred-and-fifty-dollar supply of the most gratifying and efficient lines of grub that money could buy. I always was an admirer of viands in their more palliative and revised stages. Hog and hominy are not only inartistic to my stomach, but they give indigestion to my moral sentiments. And I thought of Colonel Jackson T. Rockingham, president of the Sunrise & Edenville Tap Railroad, and how he would miss the luxury of his home fare as is so famous among wealthy Southerners. So I sunk half of mine and Caligula's capital in as elegant a layout of fresh and canned provisions as Burdick Harris or any other professional kidnappee ever saw in a camp.

I put another hundred in a couple of cases of Bordeaux, two quarts of cognac, two hundred Havana regalias with gold bands, and a camp-stove and stools and folding cots. I wanted Colonel Rockingham to be comfortable; and I hoped after he gave up the ten thousand dollars he would give me and Caligula as good a name for gentlemen and entertainers as the Greek man did the friend of his that made the United States his bill collector against Africa.

When the goods came down from Atlanta, we hired a wagon, moved them up on the little mountain, and established camp. And then we laid for the colonel.

We caught him one morning about two miles out from Mountain Valley, on his way to look after some of his burnt umber farm land. He was an elegant old gentleman, as thin and tall as a trout rod, with frazzled shirt-cuffs and specs on a black string. We explained to him, brief and easy, what we wanted; and Caligula showed him, careless, the handle of his forty-five under his coat.

'What?' says Colonel Rockingham. 'Bandits in Perry County, Georgia! I shall see that the board of immigration and public improvements hears of this!'

'Be so unfoolhardy as to climb into that buggy,' says Caligula, 'by order of the board of perforation and public depravity. This is a business meeting, and we're anxious to adjourn *sine qua non.*'

We drove Colonel Rockingham over the mountain and up the side of it as far as the buggy could go. Then we tied the horse, and took our prisoner on foot up to the camp.

'Now, colonel,' I says to him, 'we're after the ransom, me and my partner; and no harm will come to you if the King of Mor – if your friends send up the dust. In the meantime we are gentlemen the same as you. And if you give us your word not to try to escape, the freedom of the camp is yours.'

'I give you my word,' says the colonel.

'All right,' says I; 'and now it's eleven o'clock, and me and Mr Polk will proceed to inoculate the occasion with a few well-timed trivialities in the line of grub.'

'Thank you,' says the colonel; 'I believe I could relish a slice of bacon and a plate of hominy.'

'But you won't,' says I emphatic. 'Not in this camp. We soar in higher regions than them occupied by your celebrated but repulsive dish.'

While the colonel read his paper, me and Caligula took off our coats and went in for a little luncheon *de luxe* just to show him. Caligula was a fine cook of the Western brand. He could toast a buffalo or fricassee a couple of steers as easy as a woman could make a cup of tea. He was gifted in the way of knocking together edibles when haste and muscle and quantity was to be considered. He held the record west of the Arkansas River for frying pancakes with his left hand, broiling venison cutlets with his right, and skinning a rabbit with his teeth at the same time. But I could do things *en casserole* and *à la creole*, and handle the oil and tabasco as gently as a French *chef*.

So at twelve o'clock we had a hot lunch ready that looked like a banquet on a Mississippi River steamboat. We spread it on the tops of two or three big boxes, opened two quarts of the red wine, set the olives and a canned oyster cocktail and a ready-made Martini by the colonel's plate, and called him to grub.

Colonel Rockingham drew up his camp-stool, wiped off his specs, and looked at the things on the table. Then I thought he was swearing; and I felt mean because I hadn't taken more pains with the victuals. But he wasn't; he was asking a blessing; and me and Caligula hung our heads, and I saw a tear drop from the colonel's eye into his cocktail.

I never saw a man eat with so much earnestness and application – not hastily, like a grammarian, or one of the canal, but slow and appreciative, like a anaconda, or a real *vive bonjour*.

In an hour and a half the colonel leaned back. I brought him a pony of brandy and his black coffee, and set the box of Havana regalias on the table.

'Gentlemen,' says he, blowing out the smoke and trying to breathe it back again, 'when we view the eternal hills and the smiling and beneficent landscape, and reflect upon the goodness of the Creator who –'

'Excuse me, colonel,' says I, 'but there's some business to

attend to now'; and I brought out paper and pen and ink and laid 'em before him. 'Who do you want to send to for the money?' I asks.

'I reckon,' says he, after thinking a bit, 'to the vice-president of our railroad, at the general offices of the Company in Edenville.'

'How far is it to Edenville from here?' I asked.

'About ten miles,' says he.

Then I dictated these lines, and Colonel Rockingham wrote them out:

'I am kidnapped and held a prisoner by two desperate outlaws in a place which is useless to attempt to find. They demand ten thousand dollars at once for my release. The amount must be raised immediately, and these directions followed. Come alone with the money to Stony Creek, which runs out of Blacktop Mountains. Follow the bed of the creek till you come to a big flat rock on the left bank, on which is marked a cross in red chalk. Stand on the rock and wave a white flag. A guide will come to you and conduct you to where I am held. Lose no time.'

After the colonel had finished this, he asked permission to tack on a postscript about how white he was being treated, so the railroad wouldn't feel uneasy in its bosom about him. We agreed to that. He wrote down that he had just had lunch with the two desperate ruffians; and then he set down the whole bill of fare, from cocktails to coffee. He wound up with the remark that dinner would be ready about six, and would probably be a more licentious and intemperate affair than lunch.

Me and Caligula read it, and decided to let it go; for we, being cooks, were amenable to praise, though it sounded out of place on a sight draft for ten thousand dollars.

I took the letter over to the Mountain Valley road and watched for a messenger. By and by a coloured equestrian came along on horseback, riding toward Edenville. I gave him a dollar to take the letter to the railroad offices; and then I went back to camp.

IV

About four o'clock in the afternoon, Caligula, who was acting as look-out, calls to me:

'I have to report a white shirt signalling on the starboard bow, sir.'

I went down the mountain and brought back a fat, red man in an alpaca coat and no collar.

'Gentlemen,' says Colonel Rockingham, 'allow me to introduce my brother, Captain Duval C. Rockingham, vice-president of the Sunrise & Edenville Tap Railroad.'

'Otherwise the King of Morocco,' says I. 'I reckon you don't mind my counting the ransom, just as a business formality.'

'Well, no, not exactly,' says the fat man, 'Not when it comes. I turned that matter over to our second vice-president. I was anxious after Brother Jackson's safetiness. I reckon he'll be along right soon. What does that lobster salad you mentioned taste like, Brother Jackson?'

'Mr Vice-President,' says I, 'you'll oblige us by remaining here till the second V.-P. arrives. This is a private rehearsal, and we don't want any roadside speculators selling tickets.'

In half an hour Caligula sings out again:

'Sail ho! Looks like an apron on a broomstick.'

I perambulated down the cliff again, and escorted up a man six foot three, with a sandy beard and no other dimensions that you could notice. Thinks I to myself, if he's got ten thousand dollars on his person it's in one bill and folded lengthwise.

'Mr Patterson G. Coble, our second vice-president,' announces the colonel.

'Glad to know you, gentlemen,' says this Coble. 'I came up to disseminate the tidings that Major Tallahassee Tucker, our general passenger agent, is now negotiating a peach-crate full of our railroad bonds with the Perry County Bank for a loan. My dear Colonel Rockingham, was that chicken gumbo or cracked goobers on the bill of fare in your note? Me and the conductor of fifty-six was having a dispute about it.'

'Another white wings on the rocks!' hollers Caligula. 'If I see any more I'll fire on 'em and swear they was torpedo-boats!'

The guide goes down again, and convoys into the lair a person in blue overalls carrying an amount of inebriety and a lantern. I am so sure that this is Major Tucker that I don't even ask him until we are up above; and then I discover that it is Uncle Timothy, the yard switchman at Edenville, who is sent ahead to flag our understandings with the gossip that Judge Pendergast, the railroad's attorney, is in the process of mortgaging Colonel Rockingham's farming lands to make up the ransom.

While he is talking, two men crawl from under the bushes into camp, and Caligula, with no white flag to disinter him from his plain duty, draws his gun. But again Colonel Rockingham intervenes and introduces Mr Jones and Mr Batts, engineer and fireman of train number forty-two.

'Excuse us,' says Batts, 'but me and Jim have hunted squirrels all over this mounting, and we don't need no white flag. Was that straight, colonel, about the plum pudding and pineapples and real store cigars?'

'Towel on a fishing-pole in the offing!' howls Caligula. 'Suppose it's the firing-line of the freight conductors and brakemen.'

'My last trip down,' says I, wiping off my face. 'If the S. & E.T. wants to run an excursion up here just because we kidnapped their president, let 'em. We'll put out our sign. "The Kidnapper's Café and Trainmen's Home."'

This time I caught Major Tallahassee Tucker by his own confession, and I felt easier. I asked him into the creek, so I could drown him if he happened to be a track-walker or caboose porter. All the way up the mountain he drivelled to me about asparagus on toast, a thing that his intelligence in life had skipped.

Up above I got his mind segregated from food and asked if he had raised the ransom.

'My dear sir,' says he, 'I succeeded in negotiating a loan on thirty thousand dollars' worth of the bonds of our railroad, and –'

'Never mind just now, major,' says I. 'It's all right, then. Wait till after dinner, and we'll settle the business. All of you gentlemen,' I continues to the crowd, 'are invited to stay to dinner. We have mutually trusted one another, and the white flag is supposed to wave over the proceedings.'

'The correct idea,' says Caligula, who was standing by me. 'Two baggage-masters and a ticket-agent dropped out of a tree while you was below the last time. Did the major man bring the money?'

'He says,' I answered, 'that he succeeded in negotiating the loan.'

If any cooks ever earned ten thousand dollars in twelve hours, me and Caligula did that day. At six o'clock we spread the top of the mountain with as fine a dinner as the personnel of any railroad ever engulfed. We opened all the wine, and we concocted entrées and *pièces de résistance*, and stirred up little savoury *chef de cuisines* and organized a mass of grub such as has been seldom instigated out of canned and bottled goods. The railroad gathered around it, and the wassail and diversions was intense.

After the feast, me and Caligula, in the line of business, takes Major Tucker to one side and talks ransom. The major pulls out an agglomeration of currency about the size of the price of a town lot in the suburbs of Rabbitville, Arizona, and makes this outcry:

'Gentlemen,' says he, 'the stock of the Sunrise & Edenville Railroad has depreciated some. The best I could do with thirty thousand dollars' worth of the bonds was to secure a loan of eighty-seven dollars and fifty cents. On the farming lands of Colonel Rockingham, Judge Pendergast was able to obtain, on a ninth mortgage, the sum of fifty dollars. You will find the amount, one hundred and thirty-seven fifty, correct.'

'A railroad president,' said I, looking this Tucker in the eye, 'and the owner of a thousand acres of land; and yet –'

'Gentlemen,' says Tucker, 'the railroad is ten miles long. There don't any train run on it except when the crew goes out in the pines and gathers enough light-wood knots to get up steam. A long time ago, when times was good, the net earnings used to run as high as eighteen dollars a week. Colonel Rockingham's land has been sold for taxes thirteen times. There hasn't been a peach crop in this part of Georgia for two years. The wet spring killed the watermelons. Nobody around here has money enough to buy fertilizer; and land is so poor the corn crop failed, and there wasn't enough grass to support the rabbits. All the people have had to eat in this section for over a year is hog and hominy, and –'

'Pick,' interrupts Caligula, mussing up his red hair, 'what are you going to do with that chicken-feed?'

I hands the money back to Major Tucker; and then I goes over to Colonel Rockingham and slaps him on the back.

'Colonel,' says I, 'I hope you've enjoyed our little joke. We don't want to carry it too far. Kidnappers! Well, wouldn't it tickle your uncle? My name's Rhinegelder, and I'm a nephew of Chaucey Depew. My friend's a second cousin of the editor of *Puck*. So you can see. We are down South enjoying ourselves in our humorous way. Now, there's two quarts of cognac to open yet, and then the joke's over.'

What's the use to go into details? One or two will be enough. I remember Major Tallahassee Tucker playing on a jews' harp, and Caligula waltzing with his head on the watch-pocket of a tall baggage-master. I hesitate to refer to the cake-walk done by me and Mr Patterson G. Coble with Colonel Jackson T. Rockingham between us.

And even on the next morning, when you wouldn't think it possible, there was a consolation for me and Caligula. We knew that Raisuli himself never made half the hit with Burdick Harris that we did with the Sunrise & Edenville Tap Railroad.

THE GIFT OF THE MAGI

One dollar and eighty-seven cents. That was all. And sixty cents of it was in pennies. Pennies saved one and two at a time by bulldozing the grocer and the vegetable man and the butcher until one's cheek burned with the silent imputation of parsimony that such close dealing implied. Three times Della counted it. One dollar and eighty-seven cents. And the next day would be Christmas.

There was clearly nothing left to do but flop down on the shabby little couch and howl. So Della did it. Which instigates the moral reflection that life is made up of sobs, sniffles, and smiles, with sniffles predominating.

While the mistress of the home is gradually subsiding from the first stage to the second, take a look at the home. A furnished flat at $8 per week. It did not exactly beggar description, but it certainly had that word on the look-out for the mendicancy squad.

In the vestibule below was a letter-box into which no letter would go, and an electric button from which no mortal finger could coax a ring. Also appertaining thereunto was a card bearing the name 'Mr James Dillingham Young.'

The 'Dillingham' had been flung to the breeze during a former period of prosperity when its possessor was being paid $30 per week. Now, when the income was shrunk to $20, the letters of 'Dillingham' looked blurred, as though they were thinking seriously of contracting to a modest and unassuming D. But whenever Mr James Dillingham Young came home and reached his flat above he was called 'Jim' and greatly hugged by Mrs James Dillingham Young, already introduced to you as Della. Which is all very good.

Della finished her cry and attended to her cheeks with the powder rag. She stood by the window and looked out dully at a grey cat walking a grey fence in a grey backyard. To-morrow would be Christmas Day, and she had only $1.87 with which to buy Jim a present. She had been saving every penny she could for months, with this result. Twenty dollars a week doesn't go far. Expenses had been greater than she had calculated. They always are. Only $1.87 to buy a present for Jim. Her Jim. Many a happy hour she had spent planning for something nice for him. Something fine and rare and sterling – something just a little bit near to being worthy of the honour of being owned by Jim.

There was a pier-glass between the windows of the room. Perhaps you have seen a pier-glass in an $8 flat. A very thin and very agile person may, by observing his reflection in a rapid sequence of longitudinal strips, obtain a fairly accurate conception of his looks. Della, being slender, had mastered the art.

Suddenly she whirled from the window and stood before the glass. Her eyes were shining brilliantly, but her face had lost its colour within twenty seconds. Rapidly she pulled down her hair and let it fall to its full length.

Now, there were two possessions of the James Dillingham Youngs in which they both took a mighty pride. One was Jim's gold watch that had been his father's and his grandfather's. The other was Della's hair. Had the Queen of Sheba lived in the flat across the airshaft, Della would have let her hair hang out the window some day to dry just to depreciate Her Majesty's jewels and gifts. Had King Solomon been the janitor, with all his treasures piled up in the basement, Jim would have pulled out his watch every time he passed, just to see him pluck at his beard from envy.

So now Della's beautiful hair fell about her, rippling and shining like a cascade of brown waters. It reached below her knee and made itself almost a garment for her. And then she did it up again nervously and quickly. Once she faltered for a minute and stood still while a tear or two splashed on the worn red carpet.

On went her old brown jacket; on went her old brown hat. With a whirl of skirts and with the brilliant sparkle still in her eyes, she fluttered out of the door and down the stairs to the street.

Where she stopped the sign read: 'Mme Sofronie. Hair Goods of All Kinds.' One flight up Della ran, and collected herself, panting. Madame, large, too white, chilly, hardly looked the 'Sofronie.'

'Will you buy my hair?' asked Della.

'I buy hair,' said Madame. 'Take yer hat off and let's have a sight at the looks of it.'

Down rippled the brown cascade.

'Twenty dollars,' said Madame, lifting the mass with a practised hand.

'Give it to me quick,' said Della.

Oh, and the next two hours tripped by on rosy wings. Forget the hashed metaphor. She was ransacking the stores for Jim's present.

She found it at last. It surely had been made for Jim and no one else. There was no other like it in any of the stores, and she had turned all of them inside out. It was a platinum fob chain simple and chaste in design, properly proclaiming its value by substance alone and not by meretricious ornamentation – as all good things should do. It was even worthy of The Watch. As soon as she saw it she knew that it must be Jim's. It was like him. Quietness and value – the description applied to both. Twenty-one dollars they took from her for it, and she hurried home with the 87 cents. With that chain on his watch Jim might be properly anxious about the time in any company. Grand as the watch was, he sometimes looked at it on the sly on account of the old leather strap that he used in place of a chain.

When Della reached home her intoxication gave way a little to prudence and reason. She got out her curling irons and lighted the gas and went to work repairing the ravages made by generosity added to love. Which is always a tremendous task, dear friends – a mammoth task.

Within forty minutes her head was covered with tiny, close-lying curls that made her look wonderfully like a truant schoolboy. She looked at her reflection in the mirror long, carefully, and critically.

'If Jim doesn't kill me,' she said to herself, 'before he takes a second look at me, he'll say I look like a Coney Island chorus girl. But what could I do – oh! what could I do with a dollar and eighty-seven cents?'

At seven o'clock the coffee was made and the frying-pan was on the back of the stove, hot and ready to cook the chops.

Jim was never late. Della doubled the fob chain in her hand and sat on the corner of the table near the door that he always entered. Then she heard his step on the stair away down on the first flight, and she turned white for just a moment. She had a habit of saying little silent prayers about the simplest everyday things, and now she whispered: 'Please God, make him think I am still pretty.'

The door opened and Jim stepped in and closed it. He looked thin and very serious. Poor fellow, he was only twenty-two – and to be burdened with a family! He needed a new overcoat and he was without gloves.

Jim stepped inside the door, as immovable as a setter at the scent of quail. His eyes were fixed upon Della, and there was an expression in them that she could not read, and it terrified her. It was not anger, nor surprise, nor disapproval, nor horror, nor any of the sentiments that she had been prepared for. He simply stared at her fixedly with that peculiar expression on his face.

Della wriggled off the table and went for him.

'Jim, darling,' she cried, 'don't look at me that way. I had my hair cut off and sold it because I couldn't have lived through Christmas without giving you a present. It'll grow out again – you won't mind, will you? I just had to do it. My hair grows awfully fast. Say "Merry Christmas!" Jim, and let's be happy. You don't know what a nice – what a beautiful, nice gift I've got for you.'

'You've cut off your hair?' asked Jim, laboriously, as if he had not arrived at that patent fact yet even after the hardest mental labour.

'Cut it off and sold it,' said Della. 'Don't you like me just as well, anyhow? I'm me without my hair, ain't I?'

Jim looked about the room curiously.

'You say your hair is gone?' he said with an air almost of idiocy.

'You needn't look for it,' said Della. 'It's sold, I tell you – sold and gone, too. It's Christmas Eve, boy. Be good to me, for it went for you. Maybe the hairs of my head were numbered,' she went on with a sudden serious sweetness, 'but nobody could ever count my love for you. Shall I put the chops on, Jim?'

Out of his trance Jim seemed quickly to wake. He enfolded his Della. For ten seconds let us regard with discreet scrutiny some inconsequential object in the other direction. Eight dollars a week or a million a year – what is the difference? A mathematician or a wit would give you the wrong answer. The magi brought valuable gifts, but that was not among them. This dark assertion will be illuminated later on.

Jim drew a package from his overcoat pocket and threw it upon the table.

'Don't make any mistake, Dell,' he said, 'about me. I don't

think there's anything in the way of a haircut or a shave or a shampoo that could make me like my girl any less. But if you'll unwrap that package you may see why you had me going awhile at first.'

White fingers and nimble tore at the string and paper. And then an ecstatic scream of joy; and then, alas! a quick feminine change to hysterical tears and wails, necessitating the immediate employment of all the comforting powers of the lord of the flat.

For there lay The Combs – the set of combs, side and back, that Della had worshipped for long in a Broadway window. Beautiful combs, pure tortoiseshell, with jewelled rims – just the shade to wear in the beautiful vanished hair. They were expensive combs, she knew, and her heart had simply craved and yearned over them without the least hope of possession. And now they were hers, but the tresses that should have adorned the coveted adornments were gone.

But she hugged them to her bosom, and at length she was able to look up with dim eyes and a smile and say: 'My hair grows so fast, Jim!'

And then Della leaped up like a little singed cat and cried, 'Oh, oh!'

Jim had not yet seen his beautiful present. She held it out to him eagerly upon her open palm. The dull precious metal seemed to flash with a reflection of her bright and ardent spirit.

'Isn't it a dandy, Jim? I hunted all over town to find it. You'll have to look at the time a hundred times a day now. Give me your watch. I want to see how it looks on it.'

Instead of obeying, Jim tumbled down on the couch and put his hands under the back of his head and smiled.

'Dell,' said he, 'let's put our Christmas presents away and keep 'em awhile. They're too nice to use just at present. I sold the watch to get the money to buy your combs. And now suppose you put the chops on.'

The magi, as you know, were wise men – wonderfully wise men – who brought gifts to the Babe in the manger. They invented the art of giving Christmas presents. Being wise, their gifts were no doubt wise ones, possibly bearing the privilege of exchange in case of duplication. And here I have lamely related to you the uneventful chronicle of two foolish children in a flat who most unwisely sacrificed for each other the greatest treasures of their house. But in a last word to the wise of these days, let it be said that of all who give gifts these two were the wisest. Of all who give and receive gifts, such as they are wisest. Everywhere they are wisest. They are the magi.

TELEMACHUS, FRIEND

Returning from a hunting trip, I waited at the little town of Los Piños, in New Mexico, for the south-bound train, which was one hour late. I sat on the porch of the Summit House and discussed the functions of life with Telemachus Hicks, the hotel proprietor.

Perceiving that personalities were not out of order, I asked him what species of beast had long ago twisted and mutilated his left ear. Being a hunter, I was concerned in the evils that may befall one in the pursuit of game.

'That ear,' said Hicks, 'is the relic of true friendship.'

'An accident?' I persisted.

'No friendship is an accident,' said Telemachus; and I was silent.

'The only perfect case of true friendship I ever knew,' went on my host, 'was a cordial intent between a Connecticut man and a monkey. The monkey climbed palms in Barranquilla and threw down coco-nuts to the man. The man sawed them in two and made dippers, which he sold for two *reales* each and bought rum. The monkey drank the milk of the nuts. Through each being satisfied with his own share of the graft, they lived like brothers.

'But in the case of human beings, friendship is a transitory art subject to discontinuance without further notice.

'I had a friend once, of the entitlement of Paisley Fish, that I imagined was sealed to me for an endless space of time. Side by side for seven years we had mined, ranched, sold patent churns, herded sheep, took photographs and other things, built wire fences, and picked prunes. Thinks I, neither homicide nor flattery nor riches nor sophistry nor drink can make trouble between me and Paisley Fish. We was friends an amount you could hardly guess at. We was friends in business, and we let our amicable qualities lap over and season our hours of recreation and folly. We certainly had days of Damon and nights of Pythias.

'One summer me and Paisley gallops down into these San

Andrés mountains for the purpose of a month's surcease and levity, dressed in the natural store habiliments of man. We hit this town of Los Piños, which certainly was a roof-garden spot of the world, and flowing with condensed milk and honey. It had a street or two, and air, and hens, and a eating-house; and that was enough for us.

'We strikes the town after supper-time, and we concludes to sample whatever efficacy there is in this eating-house down by the railroad tracks. By the time we had set down and pried up our plates with a knife from the red oil-cloth, along intrudes Widow Jessup with the hot biscuit and the fried liver.

'Now, there was a woman that would have tempted an anchovy to forget his vows. She was not so small as she was large; and a kind of welcome air seemed to mitigate her vicinity. The pink of her face was the *in hoc signo* of a culinary temper and a warm disposition, and her smile would have brought out the dogwood blossoms in December.

'Widow Jessup talks to us a lot of garrulousness about the climate and history and Tennyson and prunes and the scarcity of mutton, and finally wants to know where we came from.

'"Spring Valley,"' says I.

'"Big Spring Valley," chips in Paisley, out of a lot of potatoes and knuckle-bone of ham in his mouth.

'That was the first sign I noticed that the old *fidus Diogenes* business between me and Paisley Fish was ended for ever. He knew how I hated a talkative person, and yet he stampedes into the conversation with his amendments and addendums of syntax. On the map it was Big Spring Valley; but I had heard Paisley himself call it Spring Valley a thousand times.

'Without saying any more, we went out after supper and set on the railroad track. We had been pardners too long not to know what was going on in each other's mind.

'"I reckon you understand," says Paisley, "that I've made up my mind to accrue that widow woman as part and parcel in and to my hereditaments for ever, both domestic, sociable, legal, and otherwise, until death us do part."

'"Why, yes," says I. "I read it between the lines, though you only spoke one. And I suppose you are aware," says I, "that I have a movement on foot that leads up to the widow's changing her name to Hicks, and leaves you writing to the society column to inquire whether the best man wears a japonica or seamless socks at the wedding!"

'"There'll be some hiatuses in your programme," says Paisley, chewing up a piece of a railroad tie. "I'd give in to you," says he, "in 'most any respect if it was secular affairs, but this is not so. The smiles of woman," goes on Paisley, "is the whirlpool of Squills and Chalybeates, into which vortex the good ship Friendship is often drawn and dismembered. I'd assault a bear that was annoying you," says Paisley, "or I'd endorse your note, or rub the place between your shoulder-blades with opodeldoc the same as ever; but there my sense of etiquette ceases. In this fracas with Mrs Jessup we play it alone. I've notified you fair."

'And then I collaborates with myself, and offers the following resolutions and bye-laws –

'"Friendship between man and man," says I, "is an ancient historical virtue enacted in the days when men had to protect each other against lizards with eighty-foot tails and flying turtles. And they've kept up the habit to this day, and stand by each other till the bellboy comes up and tells them the animals are not really there. I've often heard," I says, "about ladies stepping in and breaking up a friendship between men. Why should that be? I'll tell you, Paisley, the first sight and hot biscuit of Mrs Jessup appears to have inserted a oscillation into each of our bosoms. Let the best man of us have her. I'll play you a square game, and won't do any underhanded work. I'll do all of my courting of her in your presence, so you will have an equal opportunity. With that arrangement I don't see why our steamboat of friendship should fall overboard in the medicinal whirlpools you speak of, whichever of us wins out."

'"Good old hoss!" says Paisley, shaking my hand. "And I'll do the same," says he. "We'll court the lady synonymously, and without any of the prudery and bloodshed usual to such occasions. And we'll be friends still, win or lose."

'At one side of Mrs Jessup's eating-house was a bench under some trees where she used to sit in the breeze after the southbound had been fed and gone. And there me and Paisley used to congregate after supper and make partial payments on our respects to the lady of our choice. And we was so honourable and circuitous in our calls that if one of us got there first we waited for the other before beginning any gallivantery.

'The first evening that Mrs Jessup knew about our arrangement I got to the bench before Paisley did. Supper was just over, and

Mrs Jessup was out there with a fresh pink dress on, and almost cool enough to handle.

'I sat down by her and made a few specifications about the moral surface of nature as set forth by the landscape and the contiguous perspective. That evening was surely a case in point. The moon was attending to business in the section of sky where it belonged, and the trees was making shadows on the ground according to science and nature, and there was a kind of conspicuous hullabaloo going on in the bushes between the bullbats and the orioles and the jack-rabbits and other feathered insects of the forest. And the wind out of the mountains was singing like a jew's harp in the pile of old tomato cans by the railroad track.

'I felt a kind of sensation in my left side – something like dough rising in a crock by the fire. Mrs Jessup had moved up closer.

'"Oh, Mr Hicks," says she, "when one is alone in the world, don't they feel it more aggravated on a beautiful night like this?"

'I rose up off the bench at once.

'"Excuse me, ma'am," says I, "but I'll have to wait till Paisley comes before I can give a audible hearing to leading questions like that."

'And then I explained to her how we was friends cinctured by years of embarrassment and travel and complicity, and how we had agreed to take no advantage of each other in any of the more mushy walks of life, such as might be fomented by sentiment and proximity. Mrs Jessup appears to think serious about the matter for a minute, and then she breaks into a species of laughter that makes the wild-wood resound.

'In a few minutes Paisley drops around, with oil of bergamot on his hair, and sits on the other side of Mrs Jessup, and inaugurates a sad tale of adventure in which him and Pieface Lumley has a skinning match of dead cows in '95 for a silver-mounted saddle in the Santa Rita valley during the nine months' drought.

'Now, from the start of that courtship I had Paisley Fish hobbled and tied to a post. Each one of us had a different system of reaching out for the easy places in the female heart. Paisley's scheme was to petrify 'em with wonderful relations of events that he had either come across personally or in large print. I think he must have got his idea of subjugation from one of Shakespeare's shows I see once called *Othello*. There is a coloured man in it who acquires a duke's daughter by disbursing to her a mixture of the talk turned out by Rider Haggard, Lew Dockstader, and Dr

Parkhurst. But that style of courting don't work well off the stage.

'Now, I give you my own recipe for inveigling a woman into that state of affairs when she can be referred to as "*née* Jones." Learn how to pick up her hand and hold it, and she's yours. It ain't so easy. Some men grab at it so much like they was going to set a dislocation of the shoulder that you can smell the arnica and hear 'em tearing off bandages. Some take it up like a hot horse-shoe, and hold it off at arm's length like a druggist pouring tincture of asafœtida in a bottle. And most of 'em catch hold of it and drag it right out before the lady's eyes like a boy finding a baseball in the grass, without giving her a chance to forget that the hand is growing on the end of her arm. Them ways are all wrong.

'I'll tell you the right way. Did you ever see a man sneak out in the back yard and pick up a rock to throw at a tom-cat that was sitting on a fence looking at him? He pretends he hasn't got a thing in his hand, and that the cat don't see him, and that he don't see the cat. That's the idea. Never drag her hand out where she'll have to take notice of it. Don't let her know that you think she knows you have the least idea she is aware you are holding her hand. That was my rule of tactics; and as far as Paisley's serenade about hostilities and misadventure went, he might as well have been reading to her a time-table of the Sunday trains that stop at Ocean Grove, New Jersey.

'One night when I beat Paisley to the bench by one pipeful, my friendship gets subsidized for a minute, and I asks Mrs Jessup if she didn't think a "H" was easier to write than a "J". In a second her head was mashing the oleander flower in my buttonhole, and I leaned over and – but I didn't.

'"If you don't mind," says I, standing up, "we'll wait for Paisley to come before finishing this. I've never done anything dishonour-able yet to our friendship, and this won't be quite fair."

'"Mr Hicks," says Mrs Jessup, looking at me peculiar in the dark, "if it wasn't for but one thing, I'd ask you to hike yourself down the gulch and never disresume your visits to my house."

'"And what is that, ma'am?" I asks.

'"You are too good a friend not to make a good husband," says she.

'In five minutes Paisley was on his side of Mrs Jessup.

'"In Silver City, in the summer of '98," he begins, "I see Jim Bartholomew chew off a Chinaman's ear in the *Blue Light Saloon* on account of a cross-barred muslin shirt that – what was that noise?"

'I had resumed matters again with Mrs Jessup right where we had left off.

'"Mrs Jessup," says I, "has promised to make it Hicks. And this is another of the same sort."

'Paisley winds his feet around a leg of the bench and kind of groans.'

'"Lem," says he, "we been friends for seven years. Would you mind not kissing Mrs Jessup quite so loud? I'd do the same for you."

'"All right," says I. "The other kind will do as well."

'"This Chinaman," goes on Paisley, "was the one that shot a man named Mullins in the spring of '97, and that was –"

'Paisley interrupted himself again.

'"Lem," says he, "if you was a true friend you wouldn't hug Mrs Jessup quite so hard. I felt the bench shake all over just then. You know you told me you would give me an even chance as long as there was any."

'"Mr Man," says Mrs Jessup, turning around to Paisley, "if you was to drop in to the celebration of mine and Mr Hicks's silver wedding, twenty-five years from now, do you think you could get it into that Hubbard squash you call your head that you are *nix cum rous* in this business? I've put up with you a long time because you was Mr Hicks's friend; but it seems to me it's time for you to wear the willow and trot off down the hill."

'"Mrs Jessup," says I, without losing my grasp on the situation as fiancé, "Mr Paisley is my friend, and I offered him a square deal and a equal opportunity as long as there was a chance."

'"A chance!" says she. "Well, he may think he has a chance; but I hope he won't think he's got a cinch, after what he's been next to all the evening."

'Well, a month afterward me and Mrs Jessup was married in the Los Piños Methodist Church; and the whole town closed up to see the performance.

'When we lined up in front, and the preacher was beginning to sing out his rituals and observances, I looks around and misses Paisley. I calls time on the preacher. "Paisley ain't here," says I. "We've got to wait for Paisley. A friend once, a friend always – that's Telemachus Hicks," says I. Mrs Jessup's eyes snapped some; but the preacher holds up the incantations according to instructions.

'In a few minutes Paisley gallops up the aisle, putting on a cuff as he comes. He explains that the only dry-goods store in town was closed for the wedding, and he couldn't get the kind of a boiled shirt that his taste called for until he had broke open the back window of the store and helped himself. Then he ranges up on the other side of the bride, and the wedding goes on. I always imagined that Paisley calculated as a last chance that the preacher might marry him to the widow by mistake.

'After the proceedings was over we had tea and jerked antelope and canned apricots, and then the populace hiked itself away. Last of all Paisley shook me by the hand and told me I'd acted square and on the level with him, and he was proud to call me a friend.

'The preacher had a small house on the side of the street that he'd fixed up to rent; and he allowed me and Mrs Hicks to occupy it till the ten-forty train the next morning, when we was going on a bridal tour of El Paso. His wife had decorated it all up with hollyhocks and poison ivy, and it looked real festal and bowery.

'About ten o'clock that night I sets down in the front door and pulls off my boots a while in the cool breeze, while Mrs Hicks was fixing around in the room. Right soon the light went out inside; and I sat there a while reverberating over old times and scenes. And then I heard Mrs Hicks call out, "Ain't you coming in soon, Lem?"

'"Well, well!" says I, kind of rousing up. "Durn me if I wasn't waiting for old Paisley to –"

'But when I got that far,' concluded Telemachus Hicks, 'I thought somebody had shot this left ear of mine off with a forty-five. But it turned out to be only a lick from a broom-handle in the hands of Mrs Hicks.'

A RAMBLE IN APHASIA

My wife and I parted on that morning in precisely our usual manner. She left her second cup of tea to follow me to the front door. There she plucked from my lapel the invisible strand of lint (the universal act of woman to proclaim ownership) and bade me take care of my cold. I had no cold. Next came her kiss of parting – the level kiss of domesticity flavoured with Young Hyson. There was no fear of the extemporaneous, of variety spicing her infinite custom. With the deft touch of long malpractice, she dabbed awry my well-set scarf-pin; and then, as I closed the door, I heard her morning slippers pattering back to her cooling tea.

When I set out I had no thought or premonition of what was to occur. The attack came suddenly.

For many weeks I had been toiling, almost night and day, at a famous railroad law case that I won triumphantly but a few days previously. In fact, I had been digging away at the law almost without cessation for many years. Once or twice good Doctor Volney, my friend and physician, had warned me.

'If you don't slacken up, Bellford,' he said, 'you'll go suddenly to pieces. Either your nerves or your brain will give way. Tell me, does a week pass in which you do not read in the papers of a case of aphasia – of some man lost, wandering nameless, with his past and his identity blotted out – and all from that little brain-clot made by overwork or worry?'

'I always thought,' said I, 'that the clot in those instances was really to be found on the brains of the newspaper reporters.'

Dr Volney shook his head.

'The disease exists,' he said. 'You need a change or a rest. Court-room, office and home – there is the only route you travel. For recreation you – read law books. Better take warning in time.'

'On Thursday nights,' I said defensively, 'my wife and I play cribbage. On Sundays she reads to me the weekly letter from her mother. That law books are not a recreation remains yet to be established.'

That morning as I walked I was thinking of Doctor Volney's words. I was feeling as well as I usually did – possibly in better spirits than usual.

I awoke with stiff and cramped muscles from having slept long on the incommodious seat of a day coach. I leaned my head against the seat and tried to think. After a long time I said to myself: 'I must have a name of some sort.' I searched my pockets. Not a card; not a letter; not a paper or monogram could I find. But I found in my coat pocket nearly $3,000 in bills of large denomination. 'I must be someone, of course,' I repeated to myself, and began again to consider.

The car was well crowded with men, among whom I told myself, there must have been some common interest, for they intermingled freely, and seemed in the best good-humour and spirits. One of them – a stout, spectacled gentleman enveloped in a decided odour of cinnamon and aloes – took the vacant half of my seat with a friendly nod, and unfolded a newspaper. In the intervals between his periods of reading, we conversed, as travellers will, on current affairs. I found myself able to sustain the conversation on such subjects with credit, at least to my memory. By and by my companion said:

'You are one of us, of course. Fine lot of men the West sends in this time. I'm glad they held the convention in New York; I've never been East before. My name's R. P. Bolder – Bolder & Son, of Hickory Grove, Missouri.'

Though unprepared, I rose to the emergency, as men will when put to it. Now must I hold a christening, and be at once babe, parson, and parent. My senses came to the rescue of my slower brain. The insistent odour of drugs from my companion supplied one idea; a glance at his newspaper, where my eye met a conspicuous advertisement, assisted me further.

'My name,' said I glibly, 'is Edward Pinkhammer. I am a druggist, and my home is in Cornopolis, Kansas.'

'I knew you were a druggist,' said my fellow-traveller affably. 'I saw the callous spot on your right forefinger where the handle of the pestle rubs. Of course, you are a delegate to our National Convention.'

'Are all these men druggists?' I asked wonderingly.

'They are. This car came through from the West. And they're your old-time druggists, too – none of your patent tablet-and-granule pharmashootists that use slot machines instead of a prescription desk. We percolate our own paregoric and roll our own pills, and we ain't above handling a few garden seeds in the spring, and carrying a sideline of confectionery and shoes. I tell you, Hampinker, I've got an idea to spring on this convention – new ideas is what they want. Now, you know the shelf bottles of tartar emetic and Rochelle salt Ant. et Pot. Tart. and Sod. et Pot. Tart. – one's poison, you know, and the other's harmless. It's easy to mistake one label for the other. Where do druggists mostly keep 'em? Why, as far apart as possible, on different shelves. That's wrong. I say keep 'em side by side so when you want one you can always compare it with the other and avoid mistakes. Do you catch the idea?'

'It seems to me a very good one,' I said.

'All right! When I spring it on the convention you back it up. We'll make some of these Eastern orange-phosphate-and-massage-cream professors that think they're the only lozenges in the market look like hypodermic tablets.'

'If I can be of any aid,' I said, warming, 'the two bottles of – er –'

'Tartrate of antimony and potash, and tartrate of soda and potash.'

'Shall henceforth sit side by side,' I concluded firmly.

'Now, there's another thing,' said Mr Bolder. 'For an excipient in manipulating a pill mass which do you prefer – the magnesia carbonate or the pulverized glycerrhiza radix?'

'The – er – magnesia,' I said. It was easier to say than the other word.

Mr Bolder glanced at me distrustfully through his spectacles.

'Give me the glycerrhiza,' said he. 'Magnesia cakes.'

'Here's another one of these fake aphasia cases,' he said, presently, handing me his newspaper, and laying his finger upon an article. 'I don't believe in 'em. I put nine out of ten of 'em down as frauds. A man gets sick of his business and his folks and wants to have a good time. He skips out somewhere, and when they find him he pretends to have lost his memory – don't know his own name, and won't even recognize the strawberry mark on his wife's left shoulder. Aphasia! Tut! Why can't they stay at home and forget?'

I took the paper and read, after the pungent headlines, the following:

'Denver, June 12 – Elwyn C. Bellford, a prominent lawyer, is myste-riously missing from his home since three days ago, and all efforts to locate him have been in vain. Mr Bellford is a well-known citizen of the highest standing, and has enjoyed a large and lucrative law practice. He is married and owns a fine home and the most extensive private library in the State. On the day of his disappearance, he drew quite a large sum of money from his bank. No one can be found who saw him after he left the bank. Mr Bellford was a man of singularly quiet and domestic tastes, and seemed to find his happiness in his home and profession. If any clue at all exists to his strange disappearance, it may be found in the fact that for some months he had been deeply absorbed in an important law case in connection with the Q. Y. and Z. Railroad Company. It is feared that overwork may have affected his mind. Every effort is being made to discover the whereabouts of the missing man.'

'It seems to me you are not altogether uncynical, Mr Bolder,' I said, after I had read the despatch. 'This has the sound, to me, of a genuine case. Why should this man, prosperous, happily married and respected, choose suddenly to abandon every-thing? I know that these lapses of memory do occur, and that men do find themselves adrift without a name, a history or a home.'

'Oh, gammon and jalap!' said Mr Bolder. 'It's larks they're after. There's too much education nowadays. Men know about aphasia, and they use it for an excuse. The women are wise, too. When it's all over they look you in the eye, as scientific as you please, and say: "He hypnotized me."'

Thus Mr Bolder diverted, but did not aid me with his comments and philosophy.

We arrived in New York about ten at night. I rode in a cab to an hotel, and I wrote my name 'Edward Pinkhammer' in the register. As I did so I felt pervade me a splendid, wild, intoxicating buoyancy – a sense of unlimited freedom, of newly attained possibilities. I was just born into the world. The old fetters – whatever they had been – were stricken from my hands and feet. The future lay before me a clear road such as an infant enters, and I could set out upon it equipped with a man's learning and experience.

I thought the hotel clerk looked at me five seconds too long. I had no baggage.

'The Druggists' Convention,' I said. 'My trunk has somehow failed to arrive.' I drew out a roll of money.

'Ah!' said he, showing an auriferous tooth, 'we have quite a number of the Western delegates stopping here.' He struck a bell for the boy.

I endeavoured to give colour to my rôle.

'There is an important movement on foot among us West-erners,' I said, 'in regard to a recommendation to the convention that the bottles containing the tartrate of antimony and potash, and the tartrate of sodium and potash, be kept in a contiguous position on the shelf.'

'Gentleman to three-fourteen,' said the clerk hastily. I was whisked away to my room.

The next day I bought a trunk and clothing, and began to live the life of Edward Pinkhammer. I did not tax my brain with endeavours to solve problems of the past.

It was a piquant and sparkling cup that the great island city held up to my lips. I drank of it gratefully. The keys of Manhattan belong to him who is able to bear them. You must be either the city's guest or its victim.

The following few days were as gold and silver. Edward Pinkhammer, yet counting back to his birth by hours only, knew the rare joy of having come upon so diverting a world full-fledged and unrestrained. I sat entranced on the magic carpets provided in theatres and roof-gardens, that transported one into strange and delightful lands full of frolicsome music, pretty girls and grotesque, drolly extravagant parodies upon humankind. I went here and there at my own dear will, bound by no limits of space, time or comportment. I dined in weird cabarets, at weirder tables d'hôte to the sound of Hungarian music and the wild shouts of mercurial artists and sculptors. Or, again, where the night life quivers in the electric glare like a kinetoscopic picture, and the millinery of the world, and its jewels, and the ones whom they adorn, and the men who make all three possible are met for good cheer and the spectacular effect. And among all these scenes that I have mentioned I learned one thing that I never knew before. And that is that the key to liberty is not in the hands of Licence, but Convention holds it. Comity has a toll-gate at which you must pay, or you may not enter the land of Freedom. In all the glitter, the seeming disorder, the parade, the abandon, I saw this law, unobtrusive, yet like iron, prevail. Therefore, in Manhattan you must obey these unwritten laws, and then you will be freest of the free. If you decline to be bound by them, you put on shackles.

Sometimes, as my mood urged me, I would seek the stately, softly murmuring palm-rooms, redolent with high-born life and delicate restraint, in which to dine. Again I would go down to the waterways in steamers packed with vociferous, bedecked, unchecked, love-making clerks and shop-girls to their crude pleasures on the island shores. And there was always Broadway – glistening, opulent, wily, varying, desirable Broadway – growing upon one like an opium habit.

One afternoon as I entered my hotel a stout man with a big nose and a black moustache blocked my way in the corridor. When I would have passed around him, he greeted me with offensive familiarity.

'Hallo, Bellford!' he cried loudly. 'What the deuce are you doing in New York? Didn't know anything could drag you away from that old book den of yours. Is Mrs B. alone or is this a little business run alone, eh?'

'You have made a mistake, sir,' I said coldly, releasing my hand from his grasp. 'My name is Pinkhammer. You will excuse me.'

The man dropped to one side, apparently astonished. As I walked to the clerk's desk I heard him call to a bell-boy and say something about telegraph blanks.

'You will give me my bill,' I said to the clerk, 'and have my baggage brought down in half an hour. I do not care to remain where I am annoyed by confidence men.'

I moved that afternoon to another hotel, a sedate, old-fashioned one on lower Fifth Avenue.

There was a restaurant a little way off Broadway where one could be served almost *al fresco* in a tropic array of screening flora. Quiet and luxury and a perfect service made it an ideal place in which to take luncheon or refreshment. One afternoon I was there picking my way to a table among the ferns when I felt my sleeve caught.

'Mr Bellford!' exclaimed an amazingly sweet voice.

I turned quickly to see a lady seated alone – a lady of about thirty, with exceedingly handsome eyes, who looked at me as though I had been her very dear friend.

'You were about to pass me,' she said accusingly. 'Don't tell me you did not know me. Why should we not shake hands – at least once in fifteen years?'

I shook hands with her at once. I took a chair opposite her at the table. I summoned with my eyebrows a hovering waiter. The lady was philandering with an orange ice. I ordered a *crème de menthe*. Her hair was reddish bronze. You could not look at it, because you could not look away from her eyes. But you were conscious of it as you are conscious of sunset while you look into the profundities of a wood at twilight.

'Are you sure you know me?' I asked.

'No,' she said, smiling, 'I was never sure of that.'

'What would you think,' I said, a little anxiously, 'if I were to tell you that my name is Edward Pinkhammer, from Cornopolis, Kansas.'

'What would I think?' she repeated, with a merry glance. 'Why, that you had not brought Mrs Bellford to New York with you, of course. I do wish you had. I would have liked to see Marian.' Her voice lowered slightly – 'You haven't changed much, Elwyn.'

I felt her wonderful eyes searching mine and my face more closely.

'Yes, you have,' she amended, and there was a soft, exultant note in her latest tones; ' I see it now. You haven't forgotten. You haven't forgotten for a year or a day or an hour. I told you you never could.'

I poked my straw anxiously in the *crème de menthe*.

'I'm sure I beg your pardon,' I said, a little uneasy at her gaze. 'But that is just the trouble. I have forgotten. I've forgotten everything.'

She flouted my denial. She laughed deliciously at something she seemed to see in my face.

'I've heard of you at times,' she went on. 'You're quite a big lawyer out West – Denver, isn't it, or Los Angeles? Marian must be very proud of you. You knew, I suppose, that I married six months after you did. You may have seen it in the papers. The flowers alone cost two thousand dollars.'

She had mentioned fifteen years. Fifteen years is a long time.

'Would it be too late,' I asked somewhat timorously, 'to offer you congratulations?'

'Not if you dare do it,' she answered, with such fine intrepidity that I was silent, and began to crease patterns on the cloth with my thumb-nail.

'Tell me one thing,' she said, leaning toward me rather eagerly – 'a thing I have wanted to know for many years – just from a woman's curiosity, of course – have you ever dared since that night to touch, smell or look at white roses – at white roses wet with rain and dew?'

I took a sip of *crème de menthe*.

'It would be useless, I suppose,' I said, with a sigh, 'for me to repeat that I have no recollection at all about these things. My memory is completely at fault. I need not say how much I regret it.'

The lady rested her arms upon the table, and again her eyes disdained my words and went travelling by their own route direct to my soul. She laughed softly, with a strange quality in the sound – it was a laugh of happiness – yes, and of content – and of misery. I tried to look away from her.

'You lie, Elwyn Bellford,' she breathed blissfully. 'Oh, I know you lie!'

I gazed dully into the ferns.

'My name is Edward Pinkhammer,' I said. 'I came with the delegates to the Druggists' National Convention. There is a movement on foot for arranging a new position for the bottles of tartrate of antimony and tartrate of potash, in which, very likely, you would take little interest.'

A shining landau stopped before the entrance. The lady rose. I took her hand, and bowed.

'I am deeply sorry,' I said to her, 'that I cannot remember. I could explain, but fear you would not understand. You will not concede Pinkhammer; and I really cannot at all conceive of the – the roses and other things.'

'Good-bye, Mr Bellford,' she said, with her happy, sorrowful smile, as she stepped into her carriage.

I attended the theatre that night. When I returned to my hotel, a quiet man in dark clothes, who seemed interested in rubbing his finger-nails with a silk handkerchief, appeared, magically, at my side.

'Mr Pinkhammer,' he said casually, giving the bulk of his attention to his forefinger, 'may I request you to step aside with me for a little conversation? There is a room here.'

'Certainly,' I answered.

He conducted me into a small, private parlour. A lady and a gentleman were there. The lady, I surmised, would have been unusually good-looking had her features not been clouded by an expression of keen worry and fatigue. She was of a style of figure and possessed colouring and features that were agreeable to my fancy. She was in a travelling-dress; she fixed upon me an earnest look of extreme anxiety, and pressed an unsteady hand to her bosom. I think she would have started forward, but the gentleman arrested her movement with an authoritative motion of his hand. He then came, himself, to meet me. He was a man of forty, a little grey about the temples, and with a strong, thoughtful face.

'Bellford, old man,' he said cordially, 'I'm glad to see you again. Of course we know everything is all right. I warned you, you know, that you were overdoing it. Now, you'll go back with us, and be yourself again in no time.'

I smiled ironically.

'I have been "Bellforded" so often,' I said, 'that it has lost its edge. Still, in the end, it may grow wearisome. Would you be willing at all to entertain the hypothesis that my name is Edward Pinkhammer, and that I never saw you before in my life?'

Before the man could reply a wailing cry came from the woman. She sprang past his detaining arm. 'Elwyn !' she sobbed, and cast herself upon me, and clung tight. 'Elwyn,' she cried again, 'don't break my heart. I am your wife – call my name once – just once! I could see you dead rather than this way.'

I unwound her arms respectfully, but firmly.

'Madam,' I said severely, 'pardon me if I suggest that you accept a resemblance too precipitately. It is a pity,' I went on, with an amused laugh, as the thought occurred to me, 'that this Bellford and I could not be kept side by side upon the same shelf like tartrates of sodium and antimony for purposes of identification. In order to understand the allusion,' I concluded airily, 'it may be necessary for you to keep an eye on the proceedings of the Druggists' National Convention.'

The lady turned to her companion, and grasped his arm.

'What is it, Doctor Volney? Oh, what is it?' she moaned.

He led her to the door.

'Go to your room for a while,' I heard him say. 'I will remain and talk with him. His mind? No, I think not – only a portion of the brain. Yes, I am sure he will recover. Go to your room and leave me with him.'

The lady disappeared. The man in dark clothes also went outside, still manicuring himself in a thoughtful way. I think he waited in the hall.

'I would like to talk with you a while, Mr Pinkhammer, if I may,' said the gentleman who remained.

'Very well, if you care to,' I replied, 'and will excuse me if I take it comfortably; I am rather tired.' I stretched myself upon a couch by a window and lit a cigar. He drew a chair near by.

'Let us speak to the point,' he said soothingly. 'Your name is not Pinkhammer.'

'I know that as well as you do,' I said coolly. 'But a man must have a name of some sort. I can assure you that I do not extravagantly admire the name of Pinkhammer. But when one christens one's self, suddenly the fine names do not seem to suggest themselves. But suppose it had been Scheringhausen or Scroggins! I think I did very well with Pinkhammer.'

'Your name,' said the other man seriously, 'is Elwyn C. Bellford. You are one of the first lawyers in Denver. You are suffering from an attack of aphasia, which has caused you to forget your identity. The cause of it was over-application to your profession, and, perhaps, a life too bare of natural recreation and pleasures. The lady who has just left the room is your wife.'

'She is what I would call a fine-looking woman,' I said, after a judicial pause. 'I particularly admire the shade of brown in her hair.'

'She is a wife to be proud of. Since your disappearance, nearly two weeks ago, she has scarcely closed her eyes. We learned that you were in New York through a telegram sent by Isidore Newman, a travelling man from Denver. He said that he had met you in an hotel here, and that you did not recognize him.'

'I think I remember the occasion,' I said. 'The fellow called me "Bellford," if I am not mistaken. But don't you think it about time, now, for you to introduce yourself?'

'I am Robert Volney – Doctor Volney. I have been your close friend for twenty years, and your physician for fifteen. I came with Mrs Bellford to trace you as soon as we got the telegram. Try, Elwyn, old man – try to remember!'

'What's the use to try!' I asked, with a little frown. 'You say you are a physician. Is aphasia curable? When a man loses his memory, does it return slowly, or suddenly?'

'Sometimes gradually and imperfectly; sometimes as suddenly as it went.'

'Will you undertake the treatment of my case, Doctor Volney?' I asked.

'Old friend,' said he, 'I'll do everything in my power, and will have done everything that science can do to cure you.'

'Very well,' said I. 'Then you will consider that I am your patient. Everything is in confidence now – professional confidence.'

'Of course,' said Doctor Volney.

I got up from the couch. Someone had set a vase of white roses on the centre table – a cluster of white roses freshly sprinkled and fragrant. I threw them far out of the window, and then I laid myself upon the couch again.

'It will be best, Bobby,' I said, 'to have this cure happen suddenly. I'm rather tired of it all, anyway. You may go now and bring Marian in. But, oh, Doc,' I said, with a sigh, as I kicked him on the shin – 'good old Doc – it was glorious!'

A RULER OF MEN

I walked the streets of the City of Insolence, thirsting for the sight of a stranger face. For the City is a desert of familiar types as thick and alike as the grains in a sandstorm; and you grow to hate them as you do a friend who is always by you, or one of your own kin.

And my desire was granted, for I saw, near a corner of Broadway and Twenty-ninth Street, a little flaxen-haired man with a face like a scaly-bark hickory-nut, selling to a fast-gathering crowd a tool that omnigeneously proclaimed itself a can-opener, a screwdriver, a button-hook, a nail-file, a shoe-horn, a watch-guard, a potato-peeler, and an ornament to any gentleman's key-ring.

And then a stall-fed cop shoved himself through the congregation of customers. The vendor, plainly used to having his seasons of trade thus abruptly curtailed, closed his satchel and slipped like a weasel through the opposite segment of the circle. The crowd scurried aimlessly away like ants from a disturbed crumb. The cop, suddenly becoming oblivious of the earth and its inhabitants, stood still, swelling his bulk and putting his club through an intricate drill of twirls. I hurried after Kansas Bill Bowers, and caught him by an arm.

Without his looking at me or slowing his pace, I found a five-dollar bill crumpled neatly into my hand.

'I wouldn't have thought, Kansas Bill,' I said, 'that you'd hold an old friend that cheap.'

Then he turned his head, and the hickory-nut cracked into a wide smile.

'Give back the money,' said he, 'or I'll have the cop after you for false pretences. I thought you was the cop.'

'I want to talk to you, Bill,' I said. 'When did you leave Oklahoma? Where is Reddy McGill now? Why are you selling those impossible contraptions on the street? How did your Big Horn gold-mine pan out? How did you get so badly sun-burned? What will you drink?'

'A year ago,' answered Kansas Bill systematically. 'Putting up windmills in Arizona. For pin money to buy etceteras with. Salted. Been down in the tropics. Beer.'

We forgathered in a propitious place and became Elijahs, while a waiter of dark plumage played the raven to perfection. Reminiscence needs must be had before I could steer Bill into his epic mood.

'Yes,' said he, 'I mind the time Timoteo's rope broke on that cow's horns while the calf was chasing you. You and that cow! I'd never forget it.'

'The tropics,' said I, 'are a broad territory. What part of Cancer or Capricorn have you been honouring with a visit?'

'Down along China or Peru – or may be the Argentine Confederacy,' said Kansas Bill. 'Anyway 'twas a great race of peoples, off-coloured but progressive. I was there three months.'

'No doubt you are glad to be back among the truly great race,' I surmised. 'Especially among New Yorkers, the most progressive and independent citizens of any country in the world,' I continued, with the fatuity of the provincial who has eaten the Broadway lotus.

'Do you want to start an argument?' asked Bill.

'Can there be one?' I answered.

'Has an Irishman humour, do you think?' asked he.

'I have an hour or two to spare,' said I, looking at the café clock.

'Not that the Americans aren't a great commercial nation,' conceded Bill. 'But the fault lay with the people who wrote lies for fiction.'

'What was this Irishman's name?' I asked.

'Was that last beer cold enough?' said he.

'I see there is talk of further outbreaks among the Russian peasants,' I remarked.

'His name was Barney O'Connor,' said Bill.

Thus, because of our ancient prescience of each other's trail of thought, we travelled ambiguously to the point where Kansas Bill's story began:

'I met O'Connor in a boarding-house on the West Side. He invited me to his hall-room to have a drink, and we became like a dog and a cat that had been raised together. There he sat, a tall, fine, handsome man, with his feet against one wall and his back against the other, looking over a map. On the bed and sticking three feet out of it was a beautiful gold sword with tassels on it and rhinestones in the handle.

"'What's this?' says I (for by that time we were well acquainted). "The annual parade in vilification of the ex-snakes of Ireland? And what's the line of march? Up Broadway to Forty-second; thence east to McCarthy's café; thence –"

"'Sit down on the wash-stand,' says O'Connor, "and listen. And cast no perversions on the sword. 'Twas me father's in old Munster. And this map, Bowers, is no diagram of a holiday procession. If ye look again ye'll see that it's the continent known as South America, comprising fourteen green, blue, red, and yellow countries, all crying out from time to time to be liberated from the yoke of the oppressor."

"'I know,' says I to O'Connor. "The idea is a literary one. The ten-cent magazine stole it from Ridpath's *History of the World from the Sandstone Period to the Equator*. You'll find it in every one of 'em. It's a continued story of a soldier of fortune, generally named O'Keefe, who gets to be dictator while the Spanish-American populace cries 'Cospetto!' and other Italian maledictions. I misdoubt if it's ever been done. You're not thinking of trying that, are you, Barney?" I asks.

"'Bowers,' says he, "you're a man of education and courage."

"'How can I deny it?' says I. "Education runs in my family; and I have acquired courage by a hard struggle with life."

"'The O'Connors,' says he, "are a warlike race. There is me father's sword; and here is the map. A life of inaction is not for me. The O'Connors were born to rule. 'Tis a ruler of men I must be."

"'Barney,' I says to him, "why don't you get on the force and settle down to a quiet life of carnage and corruption instead of roaming off to foreign parts? In what better way can you indulge your desire to subdue and maltreat the oppressed?"

"'Look again at the map,' says he, "at the country I have the point of me knife on. 'Tis that one I have selected to aid and overthrow with me father's sword."

"'I see,' says I. "It's the green one, and that does credit to your patriotism; and it's the smallest one, and that does credit to your judgment."

"'Do ye accuse me of cowardice?' says Barney, turning pink.

"'No man,' says I, "who attacks and confiscates a country

single-handed could be called a coward. The worst you can be charged with is plagiarism or imitation. If Anthony Hope and Roosevelt let you get away with it, nobody else will have any right to kick."

'"I'm not joking," says O'Connor. "And I've got $1,500 cash to work the scheme with. I've taken a liking to you. Do you want it, or not?"

'"I'm not working," I told him; "but how is it to be? Do I eat during the fomentation of the insurrection, or am I only to be Secretary of War after the country is conquered? Is it to be a pay envelope or only a portfolio?"

'"I'll pay all expenses," says O'Connor. "I want a man I can trust. If we succeed you may pick out any appointment you want in the gift of the government."

'"All right, then," says I. "You can get me a bunch of draying contracts and then a quick-action consignment to a seat on the Supreme Court bench so I won't be in line for the presidency. The kind of cannon they chasten their presidents with in that country hurt too much. You can consider me on the payroll."

'Two weeks afterward O'Connor and me took a steamer for the small, green, doomed country. We were three weeks on the trip. O'Connor said he had his plans all figured out in advance; but being the commanding general, it consorted with his dignity to keep the details concealed from his army and cabinet, commonly known as William T. Bowers. Three dollars a day was the price for which I joined the cause of liberating an undiscovered country from the ills that threatened or sustained it. Every Saturday night on the steamer I stood in line at parade rest, and O'Connor handed over the twenty-one dollars.

'The town we landed at was named Guayaquerita, so they told me. "Not for me," says I. "It'll be little old Hilldale or Tompkinsville or Cherry Tree Corners when I speak of it. It's a clear case where spelling reform ought to butt in and disenvowel it."

'But the town looked fine from the bay when we sailed in. It was white, with green ruching and lace ruffles on the skirt when the surf slashed up on the sand. It looked as tropical and *dolce far ultra* as the pictures of Lake Ronkonkoma in the brochure of the passenger department of the Long Island Railroad.

'We went through the quarantine and custom-house indignities; and then O'Connor leads me to a 'dobe house on a street called "The Avenue of the Dolorous Butterflies of the Individual and Collective Saints." Ten feet wide it was, and knee-deep in alfalfa and cigar stumps.

'"Hooligan Alley," says I, re-christening it.

'"'Twill be our headquarters," says O'Connor. "My agent here, Don Fernando Pacheco, secured it for us."

'So in that house O'Connor and me established the revolutionary centre. In the front room we had ostensible things such as fruit, a guitar, and a table with a conch shell on it. In the back room O'Connor had his desk and a large looking-glass and his sword hid in a roll of straw matting. We slept on hammocks that we hung to hooks in the wall; and took our meals at the Hotel Ingles, a beanery run on the American plan by a German proprietor with Chinese cooking served à la Kansas City lunch counter.

'It seems that O'Connor really did have some sort of system planned out beforehand. He wrote plenty of letters; and every day or two some native gent would stroll round to headquarters and be shut up in the back room for half an hour with O'Connor and the interpreter. I noticed that when they went in they were always smoking eight-inch cigars and at peace with the world; but when they came out they would be folding up a ten- or twenty-dollar bill and cursing the government horribly.

'One evening after we had been in Guaya – in this town of Smellville-by-the-Sea – about a month, and me and O'Connor were sitting outside the door helping old *tempus fugit* with rum and ice and limes, I says to him:

'"If you'll excuse a patriot that don't exactly know what he's patronizing, for the question – what is your scheme for subjugating this country? Do you intend to plunge it into bloodshed, or do you mean to buy its votes peacefully and honourably at the polls?"

'"Bowers," says he, "ye're a fine little man and I intend to make great use of ye after the conflict. But ye do not understand statecraft. Already by now we have a network of strategy clutching with invisible fingers at the throat of the tyrant Calderas. We have agents at work in every town in the republic. The Liberal Party is bound to win. On our secret lists we have the names of enough sympathizers to crush the administration forces at a single blow."

'"A straw vote," says I, "only shows which way the hot air blows."

'"Who has accomplished this?" goes on O'Connor. "I have. I

have directed everything. The time was ripe when we came, so my agents inform me. The people are groaning under burdens of taxes and levies. Who will be their natural leader when they rise? Could it be anyone but meself? 'Twas only yesterday that Zaldas, our representative in the province of Durasnas, tells me that the people, in secret, already call me 'El Library Door,' which is the Spanish manner of saying 'The Liberator.'"

'"Was Zaldas that maroon-coloured old Aztec with a paper collar on and unbleached domestic shoes?" I asked.

'"He was," says O'Connor.

'"I saw him tucking a yellow-back into his vest pocket as he came out," says I. "It may be," says I, "that they call you a library door, but they treat you more like the side-door of a bank. But let us hope for the worst."

'"It has cost money, of course," says O'Connor; "but we'll have the country in our hands inside of a month."

'In the evenings we walked about in the plaza and listened to the band playing and mingled with the populace at its distressing and obnoxious pleasures. There were thirteen vehicles belonging to the upper classes, mostly rockaways and old-style barouches, such as the mayor rides in at the unveiling of the new poor-house at Milledgeville, Alabama. Round and round the desiccated fountain in the middle of the plaza they drove, and lifted their high silk hats to their friends. The common people walked around in barefooted bunches, puffing stogies that a Pittsburg millionaire wouldn't have chewed for a dry smoke on Ladies' Day at his club. And the grandest figure in the whole turnout was Barney O'Connor. Six foot two he stood in his Fifth Avenue clothes, with his eagle eye and his black moustache that tickled his ears. He was a born dictator and tsar and hero and harrier of the human race. It looked to me that all eyes were turned upon O'Connor, and that every woman there loved him, and every man feared him. Once or twice I looked at him and thought of funnier things that had happened than his winning out in his game; and I began to feel like a Hidalgo de Officio de Grafto de South America myself. And then I would come down again to solid bottom and let my imagination gloat, as usual, upon the twenty-one American dollars due me on Saturday night.

'"Take note," says O'Connor to me as thus we walked, "of the mass of the people. Observe their oppressed and melancholy air. Can ye not see that they are ripe for revolt? Do ye not perceive that they are disaffected?"

'"I do not," says I. "Nor disinfected either. I'm beginning to understand these people. When they look unhappy they're enjoying themselves. When they feel unhappy they go to sleep. They're not the kind of people to take an interest in revolutions."

'"They'll flock to our standard," says O'Connor. "Three thousand men in this town alone will spring to arms when the signal is given. I am assured of that. But everything is in secret. There is no chance for us to fail."

'On Hooligan Alley, as I prefer to call the street our headquarters was on, there was a row of flat 'dobe houses with red tile roofs, some straw shacks full of Indians and dogs, and one two-story wooden house with balconies a little farther down. That was where General Tumbalo, the commandant and commander of the military forces, lived. Right across the street was a private residence built like a combination bake-oven and folding-bed. One day, O'Connor and me were passing it, single file, on the flange they called a sidewalk, when out of the window flies a big red rose. O'Connor, who is ahead, picks it up, presses it to his fifth rib, and bows to the ground. By Carrambos! that man certainly had the Irish drama chaunceyized. I looked around expecting to see the little boy and girl in white sateen ready to jump on his shoulder while he jolted their spinal columns and ribs together through a breakdown, and sang: "Sleep, Little One, Sleep."

'As I passed the window I glanced inside and caught a glimpse of a white dress and a pair of big flashing eyes and gleaming teeth under a dark lace mantilla.

'When we got back to our house O'Connor began to walk up and down the floor and twist his moustache.

'"Did ye see her eyes, Bowers?" he asks me.

'"I did," says I, "and I can see more than that. It's all coming out according to the story-books. I knew there was something missing. 'Twas the love interest. What is it that comes in Chapter VII to cheer the gallant Irish adventurer? Why, Love, of course – Love that makes the hat go around. At last we have the eyes of midnight hue and the rose flung from the barred window. Now, what comes next? The underground passage – the intercepted letter – the traitor in camp – the hero thrown into a dungeon – the mysterious message from the señorita – then the outburst – the fighting on the plaza – the –"

'"Don't be a fool," says O'Connor, interrupting. "But that's the only woman in the world for me, Bowers. The O'Connors are as quick to love as they are to fight. I shall wear that rose over me heart when I lead me men into action. For a good battle to be fought there must be some woman to give it power."

'"Every time," I agreed, "if you want to have a good lively scrap. There's only one thing bothering me. In the novels the light-haired friend of the hero always gets killed. Think 'em all over that you've read, and you'll see that I'm right. I think I'll step down to the Botica Española and lay in a bottle of walnut stain before war is declared."

'"How will I find out her name?" says O'Connor, laying his chin in his hand.

'"Why don't you go across the street and ask her?" says I.

'"Will ye never regard anything in life seriously?" says O'Connor, looking down at me like a schoolmaster.

'"Maybe she meant the rose for me," I said, whistling the Spanish fandango.

'For the first time since I'd known O'Connor, he laughed. He got up and roared and clapped his knees, and leaned against the wall till the tiles on the roof clattered to the noise of his lungs. He went into the back room and looked at himself in the glass and began and laughed all over from the beginning again. Then he looked at me and repeated himself. That's why I asked you if you thought an Irishman had any humour. He'd been doing farce comedy from the day I saw him without knowing it; and the first time he had an idea advanced to him with any intelligence he acted in it like two-twelfths of the sextet in a "Floradora" road company.

'The next afternoon he comes in with a triumphant smile and begins to pull something like ticker tape out of his pocket.

'"Great!" says I. "This is something like home. How is Amalgamated Copper to-day?"

'"I've got her name," says O'Connor, and he reads off something like this: "Dona Isabel Antonia Inez Lolita Carreras y Buencaminos y Monteleon. She lives with her mother," explains O'Connor. "Her father was killed in the last revolution. She is sure to be in sympathy with our cause."

'And sure enough the next day she flung a little bunch of roses clear across the street into our door. O'Connor dived for it and found a piece of paper curled around a stem with a line in Spanish on it. He dragged the interpreter out of his corner and got him busy. The interpreter scratched his head, and gave us as a translation three best bets: "Fortune has got a face like the man fighting"; "Fortune looks like a brave man"; and "Fortune favours the brave." We put our money on the last one.

'"Do ye see?" says O'Connor. "She intends to encourage me sword to save her country."

'"It looks to me like an invitation to supper," says I.

'So every day this señorita sits behind the barred windows and exhausts a conservatory or two, one posy at a time. And O'Connor walks like a Dominecker rooster and swells his chest and swears to me he will win her by feats of arms and big deeds on the gory field of battle.

'By and by the revolution began to get ripe. One day O'Connor takes me into the back room and tells me all.

'"Bowers," he says, "at twelve o'clock one week from to-day the struggle will take place. It has pleased ye to find amusement and diversion in this project because ye have not sense enough to perceive that it is easily accomplished by a man of courage, intelligence, and historical superiority, such as meself. The whole world over," says he, "the O'Connors have ruled men, women, and nations. To subdue a small and indifferent country like this is a trifle. Ye see what little barefooted manikins the men of it are. I could lick four of 'em single-handed."

'"No doubt," says I. "But could you lick six? And suppose they hurl an army of seventeen against you?"

'"Listen," says O'Connor, "to what will occur. At noon next Tuesday 25,000 patriots will rise up in the towns of the republic. The government will be absolutely unprepared. The public buildings will be taken, the regular army made prisoners, and the new administration set up. In the capital it will not be so easy on account of most of the army being stationed there. They will occupy the president's palace and the strongly fortified government buildings, and stand a siege. But on the very day of the outbreak a body of our troops will begin a march to the capital from every town as soon as the local victory has been won. The thing is so well planned that it is an impossibility for us to fail. I meself will lead the troops from here. The new president will be Señor Espadas, now Minister of Finance in the present cabinet."

'"What do you get?" I asked.

'"'Twill be strange," said O'Connor smiling, "if I don't have all the jobs handed to me on a silver salver to pick what I choose. I've been the brains of the scheme, and when the fighting opens I guess I won't be in the rear rank. Who managed it so our troops could get arms smuggled into this country? Didn't I arrange it with a New York firm before I left there? Our financial agents inform me that 20,000 stands of Winchester rifles have been delivered a month ago at a secret place up coast and distributed among the towns. I tell you, Bowers, the game is already won."

'Well, that kind of talk kind of shook my disbelief in the infallibility of the serious Irish gentleman soldier of fortune. It certainly seemed that the patriotic grafters had gone about the thing in a business way. I looked upon O'Connor with more respect, and began to figure on what kind of uniform I might wear as Secretary of War.

'Tuesday, the day set for the revolution, came around according to schedule. O'Connor said that a signal had been agreed upon for the uprising. There was an old cannon on the beach near the national warehouse. That had been secretly loaded, and promptly at twelve o'clock was to be fired off. Immediately the revolutionists would seize their concealed arms, attack the comandante's troops in the cuartel, and capture the custom-house and all government property and supplies.

'I was nervous all the morning. And about eleven o'clock O'Connor became infused with the excitement and martial spirit of murder. He geared his father's sword around him, and walked up and down in the back room like a lion in the Zoo suffering from corns. I smoked a couple of dozen cigars, and decided on yellow stripes down the trouser legs of my uniform.

'At half-past eleven O'Connor asks me to take a short stroll through the streets to see if I could notice any signs of the uprising. I was back in fifteen minutes.

'"Did you hear anything?" he asks.

'"I did," says I. "At first I thought it was drums. But it wasn't; it was snoring. Everybody in town's asleep."

'O'Connor tears out his watch.

'"Fools!" says he. "They've set the time right at the siesta hour when everybody takes a nap. But the cannon will wake 'em up. Everything will be all right, depend upon it."

'Just at twelve o'clock we heard the sound of a cannon – BOOM! – shaking the whole town.

'O'Connor loosens his sword in its scabbard and jumps for the door. I went as far as the door and stood in it.

'People were sticking their heads out of doors and windows. But there was one grand sight that made the landscape look tame.

'General Tumbalo, the comandante, was rolling down the steps of his residential dug-out, waving a five-foot sabre in his hand. He wore his cocked and plumed hat and his dress-parade coat covered with gold braid and buttons. Sky-blue pyjamas, one rubber boot, and one red-plush slipper completed his make-up.

'The general had heard the cannon, and he puffed down the sidewalk towards the soldiers' barracks as fast as his rudely awakened two hundred pounds could travel.

'O'Connor sees him and lets out a battle-cry and draws his father's sword and rushes across the street and tackles the enemy.

'Right there in the street he and the general gave an exhibition of blacksmithing and butchery. Sparks flew from their blades, the general roared, and O'Connor gave the slogan of his race and proclivities.

'Then the general's sabre broke in two; and he took to his ginger-coloured heels crying out, "Policios," at every jump. O'Connor chased him a block, imbued with the sentiment of manslaughter, and slicing buttons off the general's coat-tails with the paternal weapon. At the corner five bare-footed policemen in cotton undershirts and straw hats climbed over O'Connor and subjugated him according to the municipal statutes.

'They brought him past the late revolutionary headquarters on the way to jail. I stood in the door. A policeman had him by each hand and foot, and they dragged him on his back through the grass like a turtle. Twice they stopped, and the odd policeman took another's place while he rolled a cigarette. The great soldier of fortune turned his head and looked at me as they passed. I blushed, and lit another cigar. The procession passed on, and at ten minutes past twelve everybody had gone back to sleep again.

'In the afternoon the interpreter came around and smiled as he laid his hand on the big red jar we usually kept ice-water in.

'"The ice-man didn't call to-day," says I. "What's the matter with everything, Sancho?"

'"Ah, yes," says the liver-coloured linguist. "They just tell me in the town. Verree bad act that Señor O'Connor make fight with General Tumbalo. Yes. General Tumbalo great soldier and big mans."

'"What'll they do to Mr O'Connor?" I asks.

'"I talk little while presently with the Juez de la Paz – what you call Justice-with-the-peace," says Sancho. "He tell me it verree bad crime that one Señor Americano try kill General Tumbalo. He says they keep Señor O'Connor in jail six months; then have trial and shoot him with guns. Verree sorree."

'"How about this revolution that was to be pulled off?" I asks.

'"Oh," says this Sancho, "I think too hot weather for revolution. Revolution better in winter-time. Maybe so next winter. Quien sabe?"

'"But the cannon went off," says I. "The signal was given."

'"That big sound?" says Sancho, grinning. "The boiler in ice factory he blow up – BOOM! Wake everybody up from siesta. Verree sorree. No ice. Mucho hot day."

'About sunset I went over to the jail, and they let me talk to O'Connor through the bars.

'"What's the news, Bowers?" says he. "Have we taken the town? I've been expecting a rescue party all the afternoon. I haven't heard any firing. Has any word been received from the capital?"

'"Take it easy, Barney," says I. "I think there's been a change of plans. There's something more important to talk about. Have you any money?"

'"I have not," says O'Connor. "The last dollar went to pay our hotel bill yesterday. Did our troops capture the custom-house? There ought to be plenty of government money there."

'"Segregate your mind from battles," says I. "I've been making inquiries. You're to be shot six months from date for assault and battery. I'm expecting to receive fifty years at hard labour for vagrancy. All they furnish you while you're a prisoner is water. You depend on your friends for food. I'll see what I can do."

'I went away and found a silver Chile dollar in an old vest of O'Connor's. I took him some fried fish and rice for his supper. In the morning I went down to a lagoon and had a drink of water, and then went back to the jail. O'Connor had a porterhouse steak look in his eye.

'"Barney," says I. "I've found a pond full of the finest kind of water. It's the grandest, sweetest, purest water in the world. Say the word and I'll go fetch you a bucket of it and you can throw this vile government stuff out of the window. I'll do anything I can for a friend."

'"Has it come to this?" says O'Connor, raging up and down

his cell. "Am I to be starved to death and then shot? I'll make those traitors feel the weight of an O'Connor's hand when I get out of this." And then he comes to the bars and speaks softer. "Has nothing been heard from Dona Isabel?" he asks. "Though every one else in the world fail," says he, "I trust those eyes of hers. She will find a way to effect my release. Do ye think ye could communicate with her? One word from her – even a rose would make me sorrow light. But don't let her know except with the utmost delicacy, Bowers. These high-bred Castilians are sensitive and proud."

'"Well said, Barney," says I. "You've given me an idea. I'll report later. Something's got to be pulled off quick, or we'll both starve."

'I walked out and down to Hooligan Alley, and then on the other side of the street. As I went past the window of Dona Isabel Antonia Concha Regalia, out flies the rose as usual and hits me on the ear.

'The door was open, and I took off my hat and walked in. It wasn't very light inside, but there she sat in a rocking-chair by the window smoking a black cheroot. And when I got closer I saw that she was about thirty-nine, and had never seen a straight front in her life. I sat down on the arm of her chair, and took the cheroot out of her mouth and stole a kiss.

'"Hullo, Izzy," I says. "Excuse my unconventionality, but I feel like I have known you for a month. Whose Izzy is oo?"

'The lady ducked her head under her mantilla, and drew in a long breath. I thought she was going to scream, but with all that intake of air she only came out with: "Me likee Americanos."

'As soon as she said that, I knew that O'Connor and me would be doing things with a knife and fork before the day was over. I drew a chair beside her, and inside of half an hour we were engaged. Then I took my hat and said I must go out for a while.

'"You come back?" says Izzy, in alarm.

'"Me go bring preacher," says I. "Come back twenty minutes. We marry now. How you likee?"

'"Marry to-day?" says Izzy. "Good!"

'I went down on the beach to the United States consul's shack. He was a grizzly man, eighty-two pounds, smoked glasses, five foot eleven, pickled. He was playing chess with an india-rubber man in white clothes.

'"Excuse me for interrupting," says I, "but can you tell me how a man could get married quick?"

'The consul gets up and fingers in a pigeon-hole.

'"I believe I had a licence to perform the ceremony myself, a year or two ago," he said. "I'll look, and –"

'I caught hold of his arm.

'"Don't look it up," says I. "Marriage is a lottery, anyway. I'm willing to take the risk about the licence if you are."

'The consul went back to Hooligan Alley with me. Izzy called her ma to come in, but the old lady was picking a chicken in the patio and begged to be excused. So we stood up and the consul performed the ceremony.

'That evening Mrs Bowers cooked a great supper of stewed goat, tamales, baked bananas, fricasséed red peppers and coffee. Afterward I sat in the rocking-chair by the front window, and she sat on the floor plucking at a guitar and happy, as she should be, as Mrs William T. B.

'All at once I sprang up in a hurry. I'd forgotten all about O'Connor. I asked Izzy to fix up a lot of truck for him to eat.

'"That big, oogly man," said Izzy. "But all right – he your friend."

'I pulled a rose out of a bunch in a jar, and took the grub-basket around to the jail. O'Connor ate like a wolf. Then he wiped his face with a banana peel and said: "Have you heard nothing from Dona Isabel yet?"

'"Hist!" says I, slipping the rose between the bars. "She sends you this. She bids you take courage. At nightfall two masked men brought it to the ruined chateau in the orange grove. How did you like that goat hash, Barney?"

'O'Connor pressed the rose to his lips.

'"This is more to me than all the food in the world," says he. "But the supper was fine. Where did you raise it?"

'"I've negotiated a stand-off at a delicatessen hut down-town," I tells him. "Rest easy. If there's anything to be done I'll do it."

'So things went along that way for some weeks. Izzy was a great cook; and if she had had a little more poise of character and smoked a little better brand of tobacco we might have drifted into some sense of responsibility for the honour I had conferred on her. But as time went on I began to hunger for the sight of a real lady standing before me in a street-car. All I was staying in that land of bilk and money for was because I couldn't get away, and I thought it no more than decent to stay and see O'Connor shot.

'One day our old interpreter drops around and after smoking an hour says that the judge of the peace sent him to request me to call on him. I went to his office in a lemon grove on a hill at the edge of the town; and there I had a surprise. I expected to see one of the usual cinnamon-coloured natives in congress gaiters and one of Pizzaro's cast-off hats. What I saw was an elegant gentleman of a slightly claybank complexion sitting in an upholstered leather chair, sipping a high-ball and reading Mrs Humphry Ward. I had smuggled into my brain a few words of Spanish by the help of Izzy, and I began to remark in a rich Andalusian brogue:

'"Buenas dias, señor. Yo tengo – yo tengo –"

'"Oh, sit down, Mr Bowers," says he. "I spent eight years in your country in colleges and law schools. Let me mix you a high-ball. Lemon peel, or not?"

'Thus we got along. In about half an hour I was beginning to tell him about the scandal in our family when Aunt Elvira ran away with a Cumberland Presbyterian preacher. Then he says to me:

'"I have sent for you, Mr Bowers, to let you know that you can have your friend Mr O'Connor now. Of course we had to make a show of punishing him on account of his attack on General Tumbalo. It is arranged that he shall be released to-morrow night. You and he will be conveyed on board the fruit steamer *Voyager*, bound for New York, which lies in the harbour. Your passage will be arranged for."

'"One moment, judge," says I; "that revolution –"

'The judge lays back in his chair and howls.

'"Why," says he presently, "that was all a little joke fixed up by the boys around the court-room, and one or two of our cup-ups, and a few clerks in the stores. The town is bursting its sides with laughing. The boys made themselves up to be conspirators, and they – what you call it? – stick Señor O'Connor for his money. It is very funny."

'"It was," says I. "I saw the joke all along. I'll take another high-ball, if your honour don't mind."

'The next evening just at dark a couple of soldiers brought O'Connor down to the beach, where I was waiting under a coco-nut tree.

'"Hist!" says I in his ear: "Dona Isabel has arranged our escape. Not a word!"

'They rowed us in a boat out to a little steamer that smelled of table d'hôte salad oil and bone phosphate.

'The great, mellow, tropical moon was rising as we steamed away. O'Connor leaned on the taffrail or rear balcony of the ship and gazed silently at Guaya – at Buncoville-on-the-Beach.

'He had the red rose in his hand.

'"She will wait," I heard him say. "Eyes like hers never deceive. But I shall see her again. Traitors cannot keep an O'Connor down for ever."

'"You talk like a sequel," says I. "But in Volume II please omit the light-haired friend who totes the grub to the hero in his dungeon cell."

'And thus reminiscing, we came back to New York.'

There was a little silence broken only by the familiar roar of the streets after Kansas Bill Bowers ceased talking.

'Did O'Connor ever go back?' I asked.

'He attained his heart's desire,' said Bill. 'Can you walk two blocks? I'll show you.'

He led me eastward and down a flight of stairs that was covered by a curious-shaped, glowing, pagoda-like structure. Signs and figures on the tiled walls and supporting columns attested that we were in the Grand Central station of the subway. Hundreds of people were on the midway platform.

An up-town express dashed up and halted. It was crowded. There was a rush for it by a still larger crowd.

Towering above every one there a magnificent, broad-shouldered, athletic man leaped into the centre of the struggle. Men and women he seized in either hand and hurled them like manikins toward the open gates of the train.

Now and then some passenger with a shred of soul and self-respect left to him turned to offer remonstrances; but the blue uniform on the towering figure, the fierce and conquering glare of his eye and the ready impact of his ham-like hands glued together the lips that would have spoken complaint.

When the train was full, then he exhibited to all who might observe and admire his irresistible genius as a ruler of men. With his knees, with his elbows, with his shoulders, with his resistless feet he shoved, crushed, slammed, heaved, kicked, flung, pounded the overplus of passengers aboard. Then with the sounds of its wheels drowned by the moans, shrieks, prayers, and curses of its unfortunate crew, the express dashed away.

'That's him. Ain't he a wonder?' said Kansas Bill admiringly. 'That tropical country wasn't the place for him. I wish the distinguished traveller, writer, war correspondent, and playwright, Richmond Hobson Davis, could see him now. O'Connor ought to be dramatized.'

JEFF PETERS AS A PERSONAL MAGNET

Jeff Peters has been engaged in as many schemes for making money as there are recipes for cooking rice in Charleston, S.C.

Best of all I like to hear him tell of his earlier days when he sold liniments and cough cures on street corners, living hand to mouth, heart to heart, with the people, throwing heads or tails with fortune for his last coin.

'I struck Fisher Hill, Arkansaw,' said he, 'in a buckskin suit, moccasins, long hair and a thirty-carat diamond ring that I got from an actor in Texarkana. I don't know what he ever did with the pocket-knife I swapped him for it.

'I was Dr Waugh-hoo, the celebrated Indian medicine man. I carried only one best bet just then, and that was Resurrection Bitters. It was made of life-giving plants and herbs accidentally discovered by Ta-qua-la, the beautiful wife of the chief of the Choctaw Nation, while gathering truck to garnish a platter of boiled dog for the annual corn dance.

'Business hadn't been good at the last town, so I only had five dollars. I went to the Fisher Hill druggist and he credited me for half a gross of eight-ounce bottles and corks. I had the labels and ingredients in my valise, left over from the last town. Life began to look rosy again after I got in my hotel room with the water running from the tap, and the Resurrection Bitters lining up on the table by the dozen.

'Fake? No, sir. There was two dollars' worth of fluid extract of cinchona and a dime's worth of aniline in that half-gross of bitters. I've gone through towns years afterwards and had folks ask for 'em again.

'I hired a wagon that night and commenced selling the bitters on Main Street. Fisher Hill was a low, malarial town; and a compound hypothetical pneumocardiac anti-scorbutic tonic was just what I diagnosed the crowd was needing. The bitters started off like sweetbreads-on-toast at a vegetarian dinner. I had sold two dozen at fifty cents apiece when I felt somebody pull my coat tail. I knew what that meant; so I climbed down and sneaked a five-dollar bill into the hand of a man with a German silver star on his lapel.

'"Constable," says I, "it's a fine night."

'"Have you got a city licence," he asks, "to sell this illegitimate essence of spooju that you flatter by the name of medicine?"

'"I have not," says I. "I didn't know you had a city. If I can find it to-morrow I'll take one out if it's necessary."

'"I'll have to close you up till you do," says the constable.

'I quit selling and went back to the hotel. I was talking to the landlord about it.

'"Oh, you won't stand no show in Fisher Hill," says he. "Dr Hoskins, the only doctor here, is a brother-in-law of the Mayor, and they won't allow no fake doctor to practise in town."

'"I don't practise medicine," says I, "I've got a State pedlar's licence, and I take out a city one wherever they demand it."

'I went to the Mayor's office the next morning and they told me he hadn't showed up yet. They didn't know when he'd be down. So Doc Waugh-hoo hunches down again in a hotel chair and lights a jimpson-weed regalia, and waits.

'By and by a young man in a blue neck-tie slips into the chair next to me and asks the time.

'"Half-past ten," says I, "and you are Andy Tucker. I've seen you work. Wasn't it you that put up the Great Cupid Combination package on the Southern States? Let's see, it was a Chilian diamond engagement ring, a wedding-ring, a potato masher, a bottle of soothing syrup and Dorothy Vernon – all for fifty cents."

'Andy was pleased to hear that I remembered him. He was a good street man; and he was more than that – he respected his profession, and he was satisfied with 300 per cent. profit. He had plenty of offers to go into the illegitimate drug and garden seed business; but he was never to be tempted off of the straight path.

'I wanted a partner; so Andy and me agreed to go out together. I told him about the situation in Fisher Hill and how finances was low on account of the local mixture of politics and jalap. Andy had just got in on the train that morning. He was pretty low himself, and was going to canvass the town for a few dollars to build a new battleship by popular subscription at Eureka Springs. So we went out and sat on the porch and talked it over.

'The next morning at eleven o'clock, when I was sitting there alone, an Uncle Tom shuffles into the hotel and asked for the doctor to come and see Judge Banks, who, it seems, was the Mayor and a mighty sick man.

'"I'm no doctor," says I. "Why don't you go and get the doctor?"

'"Boss," says he, "Doc Hoskins am done gone twenty miles in de country to see some sick persons. He's de only doctor in de town, and Massa Banks am powerful bad off. He sent me to ax you to please, suh, come."

'"As man to man," says I, "I'll go and look him over." So I put a bottle of Resurrection Bitters in my pocket and goes up on the hill to the Mayor's mansion, the finest house in town, with a mansard roof and two cast-iron dogs on the lawn.

'This Mayor Banks was in bed all but his whiskers and feet. He was making internal noises that would have had everybody in San Francisco hiking for the parks. A young man was standing by the bed holding a cup of water.

'"Doc," says the Mayor, "I'm awful sick. I'm about to die. Can't you do nothing for me?"

'"Mr Mayor," says I, "I'm not a regular pre-ordained disciple of S. Q. Lapius. I never took a course in a medical college," says I, "I've just come as a fellow-man to see if I could be of assistance."

'"I'm deeply obliged," says he. "Doc Waugh-hoo, this is my nephew, Mr Biddle. He has tried to alleviate my distress, but without success. Oh, Lordy! Ow-ow-ow!!" he sings out.

'I nods at Mr Biddle and sets down by the bed and feels the Mayor's pulse. "Let me see your liver – your tongue, I mean," says I. Then I turns up the lids of his eyes and looks close at the pupils of 'em.

'"How long have you been sick?" I asked.

'"I was taken down – ow-ouch – last night," says the Mayor. "Gimme something for it, doc, won't you?"

'"Mr Fiddle," says I, "raise the window shade a bit, will you?"

'"Biddle," says the young man. "Do you feel like you could eat some ham and eggs, Uncle James?"

'"Mr Mayor," says I, after laying my ear to his right shoulder-blade and listening, "you've got a bad attack of super-inflammation of the right clavicle of the harpsichord!"

'"Good Lord!" says he, with a groan. "Can't you rub something on it, or set it or anything?"

'I picks up my hat and starts for the door.

'"You ain't going, doc?" says the Mayor with a howl. "You

ain't going away and leave me to die with this – superfluity of the clapboards, are you?"

"'Common humanity, Dr Whoa-ha,' says Mr Biddle, "ought to prevent your deserting a fellow-human in distress."

"'Dr Waugh-hoo, when you get through ploughing," says I. And then I walks back to the bed and throws back my long hair.

"'Mr Mayor,' says I, "there is only one hope for you. Drugs will do you no good. But there is another power higher yet, although drugs are high enough," says I.

"'And what is that?" says he.

"'Scientific demonstrations,' says I. "The triumph of mind over sarsaparilla. The belief that there is no pain and sickness except what is produced when we ain't feeling well. Declare yourself in arrears. Demonstrate."

"'What is this paraphernalia you speak of, doc ?" says the Mayor. "You ain't a Socialist, are you?"

"'I am speaking," says I, "of the great doctrine of psychic financiering – of the enlightened school of long-distance, sub-con-scientious treatment of fallacies and meningitis – of that wonderful indoor sport known as personal magnetism."

"'Can you work it, doc?" asks the Mayor.

"'I'm one of the Sole Sanhedrims and Ostensible Hooplas of the Inner Pulpit," says I. "The lame talk and the blind rubber whenever I make a pass at 'em. I am a medium, a coloratura hypnotist and a spirituous control. It was only through me at the recent séances at Ann Arbour that the late president of the Vinegar Bitters Company could revisit the earth to communicate with his sister Jane. You see me peddling medicine on the streets," says I, "to the poor. I don't practise personal magnetism on them. I do not drag it in the dust," says I, "because they haven't got the dust."

"'Will you treat my case?" asks the Mayor.

"'Listen," says I. "I've had a good deal of trouble with medical societies everywhere I've been. I don't practise medicine. But, to save your life, I'll give you the psychic treatment if you'll agree as Mayor not to push the licence question."

"'Of course I will," says he. "And now get to work, doc, for them pains are coming on again."

"'My fee will be $250.00, cure guaranteed in two treatments," says I.

"'All right," says the Mayor. "I'll pay it. I guess my life's worth that much."

'I sat down by the bed and looked him straight in the eye.

'"Now," says I, "get your mind off the disease. You ain't sick. You haven't got a heart or a clavicle or a funny-bone or brains or anything. You haven't got any pain. Declare error. Now you feel the pain that you didn't have leaving, don't you?"

'"I do feel some little better, doc," says the Mayor, "darned if I don't. Now state a few lies about my not having this swelling in my left side, and I think I could be propped up and have some sausage and buckwheat cakes."

'I made a few passes with my hands.

'"Now," says I, "the inflammation's gone. The right lobe of the perihelion has subsided. You're getting sleepy. You can't hold your eyes open any longer. For the present the disease is checked. Now, you are asleep."

'The Mayor shut his eyes slowly and began to snore.

'"You observe, Mr Tiddle," says I, "the wonders of modern science."

'"Biddle," says he. "When will you give uncle the rest of the treatment, Dr Pooh-pooh?"

'"Waugh-hoo," says I. "I'll come back at eleven to-morrow. When he wakes up give him eight drops of turpentine and three pounds of steak. Good morning."

'The next morning I went back on time. "Well, Mr Riddle," says I, when he opened the bedroom door, "and how is uncle this morning?"

'"He seems much better," says the young man.

'The Mayor's colour and pulse was fine. I gave him another treatment, and he said the last of the pain left him.

'"Now," says I, "you'd better stay in bed for a day or two, and you'll be all right. It's a good thing I happened to be in Fisher Hill, Mr Mayor," says I, "for all the remedies in the cornucopia that the regular schools of medicine use couldn't have saved you. And now that error has flew and pain proved a perjurer, let's allude to a cheerfuller subject – say the fee of $250. No cheques, please; I hate to write my name on the back of a cheque almost as bad as I do on the front."

'"I've got the cash here," says the Mayor, pulling a pocket-book from under his pillow.

'He counts out five fifty-dollar notes and holds 'em in his hand.

'"Bring the receipt," he says to Biddle.

'I signed the receipt and the Mayor handed me the money. I put it in my inside pocket careful.

'"Now do your duty, officer," says the Mayor, grinning much unlike a sick man.

'Mr Biddle lays his hand on my arm.

'"You're under arrest, Dr Waugh-hoo, alias Peters," says he, "for practising medicine without authority under the State law."

'"Who are you?" I asks.

'"I'll tell you who he is," says Mr Mayor, sitting up in bed. "He's a detective employed by the State Medical Society. He's been following you over five counties. He came to me yesterday and we fixed up this scheme to catch you. I guess you won't do any more doctoring around these parts, Mr Faker. What was it you said I had, doc?" the Mayor laughs, "compound – well, it wasn't softening of the brain, I guess, anyway."

'"A detective," says I.

'"Correct," says Biddle. "I'll have to turn you over to the sheriff."

'"Let's see you do it," says I, and I grabs Biddle by the throat and half throws him out of the window, but he pulls a gun and sticks it under my chin, and I stand still. Then he puts handcuffs on me, and takes the money out of my pocket.

'"I witness," says he, "that they're the same bills that you and I marked, Judge Banks. I'll turn them over to the sheriff when we get to his office, and he'll send you a receipt. They'll have to be used as evidence in the case."

'"All right, Mr Biddle," says the Mayor. "And now, Doc Waugh-hoo," he goes on, "why don't you demonstrate? Can't you pull the cork out of your magnetism with your teeth and hocus-pocus them handcuffs off?"

'"Come on, officer," says I, dignified. "I may as well make the best of it." And then I turns to old Banks and rattles my chains.

'"Mr Mayor," says I, "the time will come soon when you'll believe that personal magnetism is a success. And you'll be sure that it succeeded in this case, too."

'And I guess it did.

'When we got nearly to the gate, I says: "We might meet somebody now, Andy. I reckon you better take 'em off, and –" Hey? Why, of course it was Andy Tucker. That was his scheme; and that's how we got the capital to go into business together.'

PAST ONE AT ROONEY'S

Only on the lower East Side of New York do the Houses of Capulet and Montague survive. There they do not fight by the book of arithmetic. If you but bite your thumb at an upholder of your opposing house you have work cut out for your steel. On Broadway you may drag your man along a dozen blocks by his nose, and he will only bawl for the watch; but in the domain of the East Side Tybalts and Mercutios you must observe the niceties of deportment to the wink of an eyelash and to an inch of elbow-room at the bar when its patrons include foes of your house and kin.

So, when Eddie McManus, known to the Capulets as Cork McManus, drifted into Dutch Mike's for a stein of beer, and came upon a bunch of Montagues making merry with the suds, he began to observe the strictest parliamentary rules. Courtesy forbade his leaving the saloon with his thirst unslaked; caution steered him to a place at the bar where the mirror supplied the cognizance of the enemy's movements that his indifferent gaze seemed to disdain; experience whispered to him that the finger of trouble would be busy among the chattering steins at Dutch Mike's that night. Close by his side drew Brick Cleary, his Mercutio, companion of his perambulations. Thus they stood, four of the Mulberry Hill Gang and two of the Dry Dock Gang, minding their P's and Q's so solicitously that Dutch Mike kept one eye on his customers and the other on an open space beneath his bar in which it was his custom to seek safety whenever the ominous politeness of the rival associations congealed into the shapes of bullets and cold steel.

But we have not to do with the wars of the Mulberry Hills and the Dry Docks. We must to Rooney's, where, on the most blighted dead branch of the tree of life, a little pale orchid shall bloom.

Overstrained etiquette at last gave way. It is not known who first overstepped the bounds of punctilio; but the consequences were immediate. Buck Malone, of the Mulberry Hills, with a

Dewey-like swiftness, got an eight-inch gun swung round from his hurricane deck. But McManus's simile must be the torpedo. He glided in under the guns and slipped a scant three inches of knife-blade between the ribs of the Mulberry Hill cruiser. Meanwhile Brick Cleary, a devotee to strategy, had skimmed across the lunch-counter and thrown the switch of the electrics, leaving the combat to be waged by the light of gunfire alone. Dutch Mike crawled from his haven and ran into the street crying for the watch instead of for a Shakespeare to immortalize the Cimmerian shindy.

The cop came, and found a prostrate, bleeding Montague supported by three distrait and reticent followers of the House. Faithful to the ethics of the gangs, no one knew whence the hurt came. There was no Capulet to be seen.

'Raus mit der interrogatories,' said Buck Malone to the officer. 'Sure I know who done it. I always manages to get a bird's-eye view of any guy that comes up an' makes a show-case for a hardware store out of me. No. I'm not telling you his name. I'll settle with um meself. Wow – ouch! Easy, boys! Yes, I'll attend to his case meself. I'm not making any complaint.'

At midnight McManus strolled around a pile of lumber near an East Side dock, and lingered in the vicinity of a certain water-plug. Brick Cleary drifted casually to the trysting-place ten minutes later. 'He'll maybe not croak,' said Brick; 'and he won't tell, of course. But Dutch Mike did. He told the police he was tired of having his place shot up. It's unhandy just now, because Tim Corrigan's in Europe for a week's end with Kings. He'll be back on the *Kaiser Williams* next Friday. You'll have to duck out of sight till then. Tim'll fix it up all right for us when he comes back.'

This goes to explain why Cork McManus went into Rooney's one night and there looked upon the bright, stranger face of Romance for the first time in his precarious career.

Until Tim Corrigan should return from his jaunt among Kings and Princes and hold up his big white finger in private offices, it was unsafe for Cork in any of the old haunts of his gang. So he lay, perdu, in the high rear room of a Capulet, reading pink sporting sheets and cursing the slow paddle-wheels of the *Kaiser Wilhelm*.

It was on Thursday evening that Cork's seclusion became intolerable to him. Never a hart panted for water fountain as he did for the cool touch of a drifting stein, for the firm security of a foot-rail in the hollow of his shoe and the quiet, hearty challenges of friendship and repartee along and across the shining bars. But he must avoid the district where he was known. The cops were looking for him everywhere, for news was scarce, and the newspapers were harping again on the failure of the police to suppress the gangs. If they got him before Corrigan came back, the big white finger could not be uplifted; it would be too late then. But Corrigan would be home the next day, so he felt sure there would be small danger in a little excursion that night among the crass pleasures that represented life to him.

At half-past twelve McManus stood in a darkish cross-town street looking up at the name 'Rooney's,' picked out by incandescent lights against a signboard over a second-story window. He had heard of the place as a tough 'hang-out'; with its frequenters and its locality he was unfamiliar. Guided by certain unerring indications common to all such resorts, he ascended the stairs and entered the large room over the café.

Here were some twenty or thirty tables, at this time about half filled with Rooney's guests. Waiters served drinks. At one end a human pianola with drugged eyes hammered the keys with automatic and furious unprecision. At merciful intervals a waiter would roar or squeak a song – songs full of 'Mr Johnsons' and 'babes' and 'coons' – historical word guarantees of the genuineness of African melodies composed by red-waistcoated young gentlemen, natives of the cotton fields and rice swamps of West Twenty-eighth Street.

For one brief moment you must admire Rooney with me as he receives, seats, manipulates, and chaffs his guests. He is twenty-nine. He has Wellington's nose, Dante's chin, the cheek-bones of an Iroquois, the smile of Talleyrand, Corbett's footwork, and the poise of an eleven-year-old East Side Central Park Queen of the May. He is assisted by a lieutenant known as Frank, a pudgy, easy chap, swell-dressed, who goes among the tables seeing that dull care does not intrude. Now, what is there about Rooney's to inspire all this pother? It is more than respectable by daylight; stout ladies with children and mittens and bundles and unpedigreed dogs drop up of afternoons for a stein and a chat. Even by gaslight the diversions are melancholy i' the mouth – drink and ragtime, and an occasional surprise when the waiter swabs the suds from under your sticky glass. There is an answer. Transmigration! The soul of Sir Walter Raleigh has travelled from beneath his slashed doublet to a kindred home under Rooney's visible plaid waistcoat. Rooney's is twenty years ahead of the times. Rooney has removed the embargo. Rooney has spread his cloak upon the soggy crossing of public opinion, and any Elizabeth who treads upon it is as much a queen as another. Attend to the revelation of the secret. In Rooney's ladies may smoke!

McManus sat down at a vacant table. He paid for the glass of beer that he ordered, tilted his narrow-brimmed derby to the back of his brick-dust head, twined his feet among the rungs of his chair, and heaved a sigh of contentment from the breathing spaces of his innermost soul; for this mud honey was clarified sweetness to his taste. The sham gaiety, the hectic glow of counterfeit hospitality, the self-conscious, joyless laughter, the wine-born warmth, the loud music retrieving the hour from frequent whiles of awful and corroding silence, the presence of well-clothed and frank-eyed beneficiaries of Rooney's removal of the restrictions laid upon the weed, the familiar blended odours of soaked lemon-peel, flat beer, and *peau d'Espagne* – all these were manna to Cork McManus, hungry from his week in the desert of the Capulet's high rear room.

A girl, alone, entered Rooney's, glanced around with leisurely swiftness, and sat opposite McManus at his table. Her eyes rested upon him for two seconds in the look with which woman reconnoitres all men whom she for the first time confronts. In that space of time she will decide upon one of two things – either to scream for the police, or that she may marry him later on.

Her brief inspection concluded, the girl laid on the table a worn red morocco shopping-bag with the inevitable topgallant sail of frayed lace handkerchief flying from a corner of it. After she had ordered a small beer from the immediate waiter she took from her bag a box of cigarettes and lighted one with slightly exaggerated ease of manner. Then she looked again in the eyes of Cork McManus and smiled.

Instantly the doom of each was sealed.

The unqualified desire of a man to buy clothes and build fires for a woman for a whole lifetime at first sight of her is not uncommon among that humble portion of humanity that does not care for Bradstreet or coats-of-arms or Shaw's plays. Love at first sight has occurred a time or two in high life; but, as a rule, the extempore mania is to be found among unsophisticated creatures such as the dove, the bluetailed dingbat, and the ten-dollar-a-week clerk. Poets, subscribers to all fiction magazines, and schatchens, take notice.

With the exchange of the mysterious magnetic current came to each of them the instant desire to lie, pretend, dazzle, and deceive, which is the worst thing about the hypocritical disorder known as love.

'Have another beer?' suggested Cork. In his circle the phrase was considered to be a card, accompanied by a letter of introduction and references.

'No, thanks,' said the girl, raising her eyebrows and choosing her conventional words carefully. 'I – merely dropped in for – a slight refreshment.' The cigarette between her fingers seemed to require explanation. 'My aunt is a Russian lady,' she concluded, 'and we often have a post perannual cigarette after dinner at home.'

'Cheese it!' said Cork, whom society airs oppressed. 'Your fingers are as yellow as mine.'

'Say,' said the girl, blazing upon him with low-voiced indignation, 'what do you think I am? Say, who do you think you are talking to? What?'

She was pretty to look at. Her eyes were big, brown, intrepid and bright. Under her flat sailor hat, planted jauntily on one side, her crinkly, tawny hair parted and was drawn back, low and massy, in a thick, pendent knot behind. The roundness of girlhood still lingered in her chin and neck, but her cheeks and fingers were thinning slightly. She looked upon the world with defiance, suspicion, and sullen wonder. Her smart, short tan coat was soiled and expensive. Two inches below her black dress dropped the lowest flounce of a heliotrope silk underskirt.

'Beg your pardon,' said Cork, looking at her admiringly. 'I didn't mean anything. Sure, it's no harm to smoke, Maudy.'

'Rooney's,' said the girl, softened at once by his amends, 'is the only place I know where a lady can smoke. Maybe it ain't a nice habit, but aunty lets us at home. And my name ain't Maudy, if you please; it's Ruby Delamere.'

'That's a swell handle,' said Cork approvingly. 'Mine's McManus – Cor – er – Eddie McManus.'

'Oh, you can't help that,' laughed Ruby. 'Don't apologize.'

Cork looked seriously at the big clock on Rooney's wall. The girl's ubiquitous eyes took in the movement.

'I know it's late,' she said, reaching for her bag; 'but you know how you want a smoke when you want one. Ain't Rooney's all right? I never saw anything wrong here. This is twice I've been in. I work in a bookbindery on Third Avenue. A lot of us girls have been working overtime three nights a week. They won't let you smoke there, of course. I just dropped in here on my way home for a puff. Ain't it all right in here? If it ain't, I won't come any more.'

'It's a little bit late for you to be out alone anywhere,' said Cork. 'I'm not wise to this particular joint; but anyhow you don't want to have your picture taken in it for a present to your Sunday-school teacher. Have one more beer, and then say I take you home.'

'But I don't know you,' said the girl, with fine scrupulosity. 'I don't accept the company of gentlemen I ain't acquainted with. My aunt never would allow that.'

'Why,' said Cork McManus, pulling his ear, 'I'm the latest thing in suitings with side vents and bell skirt when it comes to escortin' a lady. You bet you'll find me all right, Ruby. And I'll give you a tip as to who I am. My governor is one of the hottest cross-buns of the Wall Street push. Morgan's cab-horse casts a shoe every time the old man sticks his head out of the window. Me! Well, I'm in trainin' down the Street. The old man's goin' to put a seat on the Stock Exchange in my stockin' my next birthday. But it all sounds like a lemon to me. What I like is golf and yachtin' and – er – well, say a corkin' fast ten-round bout between welter-weights with walkin' gloves.'

'I guess you can walk to the door with me,' said the girl hesitatingly, but with a certain pleased flutter. 'Still I never heard anything extra good about Wall Street brokers, or sports who go to prizefights, either. Ain't you got any other recommendations?'

'I think you're the swellest looker I've had my lamps on in little old New York,' said Cork impressively.

'That'll be about enough of that, now. Ain't you the kidder!' She modified her chiding words by a deep, long, beaming, smile-embellished look at her cavalier. 'We'll drink our beer before we go, ha?'

A waiter sang. The tobacco smoke grew denser, drifting and rising in spirals, waves, tilted layers, cumulus clouds, cataracts and suspended fogs like some fifth element created from the ribs of the ancient four. Laughter and chat grew louder, stimulated by Rooney's liquids and Rooney's gallant hospitality to Lady Nicotine.

One o'clock struck. Downstairs there was a sound of closing and locking doors. Frank pulled down the green shades of the front windows carefully. Rooney went below in the dark hall and stood at the front door, his cigarette cached in the hollow of his hand. Thenceforth whoever might seek admittance must present a countenance familiar to Rooney's hawk's eye – the countenance of a true sport.

Cork McManus and the bookbindery girl conversed absorbedly, with their elbows on the table. Their glasses of beer were pushed to one side, scarcely touched, with the foam on them sunken to a thin, white scum. Since the stroke of one the stale pleasures of Rooney's had become renovated and spiced; not by any addition to the list of distractions, but because from that moment the sweets became stolen ones. The flattest glass of beer acquired the tang of illegality; the mildest claret punch struck a knock-out blow at law and order; the harmless and genial company became outlaws, defying authority and rule. For after the stroke of one in such places as Rooney's, where neither bed nor board is to be had, drink may not be set before the thirsty of the city of the four million. It is the law.

'Say,' said Cork McManus, almost covering the table with his eloquent chest and elbows, 'was that dead straight about you workin' in a bookbindery and livin' at home – and just happenin' in here – and – and all that spiel you gave me?'

'Sure it was,' answered the girl with spirit. 'Why, what do you think? Do you suppose I'd lie to you? Go down to the shop and ask 'em. I handed it to you on the level.'

'On the dead level?' said Cork. 'That's the way I want it; because –'

'Because what?'

'I throw up my hands,' said Cork. 'You've got me goin'. You're the girl I've been lookin' for. Will you keep company with me, Ruby?'

'Would you like me to – Eddie?'

'Surest thing. But I wanted a straight story about – about yourself, you know. When a fellow has a girl – a steady girl – she's got to be all right, you know. She's got to be straight goods.'

'You'll find I'll be straight goods, Eddie.'

'Of course you will. I believe what you told me. But you can't blame me for wantin' to find out. You don't see many girls smokin' cigarettes in a place like Rooney's after midnight that are like you.'

The girl flushed a little and lowered her eyes. 'I see that now,' she said meekly. 'I didn't know how bad it looked. But I won't do it any more. And I'll go straight home every night and stay there. And I'll give up cigarettes if you say so, Eddie – I'll cut 'em out from this minute on.'

Cork's air became judicial, proprietary, condemnatory, yet sympathetic. 'A lady can smoke,' he decided slowly, 'at times and places. Why? Because it's being a lady that helps her to pull it off.'

'I'm going to quit. There's nothing to it,' said the girl. She flicked the stub of her cigarette to the floor.

'At times and places,' repeated Cork. 'When I call round for you of evenin's we'll hunt out a dark bench in Stuyvesant Square and have a puff or two. But no more Rooney's at one o'clock – see?'

'Eddie, do you really like me?' The girl searched his hard but frank features eagerly with anxious eyes.

'On the dead level.'

'When are you coming to see me – where I live?'

'Thursday – day after to-morrow evenin'. That suit you?'

'Fine. I'll be ready for you. Come about seven. Walk to the door with me to-night and I'll show you where I live. Don't forget, now. And don't you go to see any other girls before then, mister! I bet you will, though.'

'On the dead level,' said Cork, 'you make 'em all look like rag-dolls to me. Honest, you do. I know when I'm suited. On the dead level, I do.'

Against the front door downstairs repeated heavy blows were delivered. The loud crashes resounded in the room above. Only a trip-hammer or a policeman's boot could have been the author of those sounds. Rooney jumped like a bullfrog to a corner of the room, turned off the electric lights and hurried swiftly below. The room was left utterly dark except for the winking, red glow of cigars and cigarettes. A second volley of crashes came up from the assaulted door. A little, rustling, murmuring panic moved among the besieged guests. Frank, cool, smooth, reassuring, could be seen in the rosy glow of the burning tobacco, going from table to table.

'All keep still!' was his caution. 'Don't talk or make any noise! Everything will be all right. Now, don't feel the slightest alarm. We'll take care of you all.'

Ruby felt across the table until Cork's firm hand closed upon hers. 'Are you afraid, Eddie?' she whispered. 'Are you afraid you'll get a free ride?'

'Nothin' doin' in the teeth-chatterin' line,' said Cork. 'I guess Rooney's been slow with his envelope. Don't you worry, girly; I'll look out for you all right.'

Yet Mr McManus's ease was only skin-and-muscle deep. With the police looking everywhere for Buck Malone's assailant, and with Corrigan still on the ocean wave, he felt that to be caught in a police raid would mean an ended career for him. And just when he had met Ruby, too! He wished he had remained in the high rear room of the true Capulet reading the pink extras.

Rooney seemed to have opened the front door below and engaged the police in conference in the dark hall. The wordless, low growl of their voices came up the stairway. Frank made a wireless news station of himself at the upper door. Suddenly he closed the door, hurried to the extreme rear of the room and lighted a dim gas-jet.

'This way, everybody,' he called sharply. 'In a hurry, but no noise, please!'

The guests crowded in confusion to the rear. Rooney's lieutenant swung open a panel in the wall, overlooking the back yard, revealing a ladder placed already for the escape.

'Down and out, everybody!' he commanded. 'Ladies first! Less talking, please! Don't crowd. There's no danger.'

Among the last, Cork and Ruby waited their turn at the open panel. Suddenly she swept him aside and clung to his arm fiercely.

'Before we go out,' she whispered in his ear – 'before anything happens, tell me again, Eddie, do you – do you really like me?'

'On the dead level,' said Cork, holding her close with one arm, 'when it comes to you, I'm all in.'

When they turned they found they were lost and in darkness. The last of the fleeing customers had descended. Half-way across the yard they bore the ladder, stumbling, giggling, hurrying to place it against an adjoining low building over the roof of which lay their only route to safety.

'We may as well sit down,' said Cork grimly. 'Maybe Rooney will stand the cops off, anyhow.'

They sat at a table; and their hands came together again.

A number of men then entered the dark room, feeling their way about. One of them, Rooney himself, found the switch and turned on the electric light. The other man was a cop of the old régime – a big cop, a thick cop, a fuming abrupt cop – not a pretty cop. He went up to the pair at the table and sneered familiarly at the girl.

'What are youse doin' in here?' he asked.

'Dropped in for a smoke,' said Cork mildly.

'Had any drinks?'

'Not later than one o'clock.'

'Get out – quick!' ordered the cop. Then, 'Sit down!' he countermanded.

He took off Cork's hat roughly and scrutinized him shrewdly. 'Your name's McManus.'

'Bad guess,' said Cork. 'It's Peterson.'

'Cork McManus, or something like that,' said the cop. 'You put a knife into a man in Dutch Mike's saloon a week ago.'

'Aw, forget it!' said Cork, who perceived a shade of doubt in the officer's tones. 'You've got my mug mixed with somebody else's.'

'Have I? Well, you'll come to the station with me, anyhow, and be looked over. The description fits you all right.' The cop twisted his fingers under Cork's collar. 'Come on!' he ordered roughly.

Cork glanced at Ruby. She was pale, and her thin nostrils quivered. Her quick eye glanced from one man's face to the other's as they spoke or moved. What hard luck! Cork was thinking – Corrigan on the briny; and Ruby met and lost almost within an hour! Somebody at the police-station would recognize him, without a doubt. Hard luck!

But suddenly the girl sprang up and hurled herself with both arms extended against the cop. His hold on Cork's collar was loosened and he stumbled back two or three paces.

'Don't go so fast, Maguire!' she cried in shrill fury. 'Keep your hands off my man! You know me, and you know I'm givin' you good advice. Don't you touch him again! He's not the guy you are lookin' for – I'll stand for that.'

'See here, Fanny,' said the cop, red and angry, 'I'll take you, too, if you don't look out! How do you know this ain't the man I want? What are you doing in here with him?'

'How do I know?' said the girl, flaming red and white by turns. 'Because I've known him a year. He's mine. Oughtn't I to know? And what am I doin' here with him? That's easy.'

She stooped low and reached down somewhere into a swirl of

flirted draperies, heliotrope and black. An elastic snapped, she threw on the table toward Cork a folded wad of bills. The money slowly straightened itself with little leisurely jerks.

'Take that, Jimmy, and let's go,' said the girl. 'I'm declaring the usual dividends, Maguire,' she said to the officer. 'You had your usual five-dollar graft at the usual corner at ten.'

'A lie!' said the cop, turning purple. 'You go on my beat again and I'll arrest you every time I see you.'

'No you won't,' said the girl. 'And I'll tell you why. Witnesses saw me give you the money to-night, and last week, too. I've been getting fixed for you.'

Cork put the wad of money carefully into his pocket, and said: 'Come on, Fanny; let's have some chop suey before we go home.'

'Clear out, quick, both of you, or I'll –'

The cop's bluster trailed away into inconsequentiality.

At the corner of the street the two halted. Cork handed back the money without a word. The girl took it and slipped it slowly into her hand-bag. Her expression was the same she had worn when she entered Rooney's that night – she looked upon the world with defiance, suspicion, and sullen wonder.

'I guess I might as well say good-bye here,' she said dully. 'You won't want to see me again, of course. Will you – shake hands – Mr McManus?'

'I mightn't have got wise if you hadn't give the snap away,' said Cork. 'Why did you do it?'

'You'd have been pinched if I hadn't. That's why. Ain't that reason enough?' Then she began to cry. 'Honest, Eddie, I was goin' to be the best girl in the world. I hated to be what I am; I hated men: I was ready almost to die when I saw you. And you seemed different from everybody else. And when I found you liked me, too, why, I thought I'd make you believe I was good, and I was goin' to be good. When you asked to come to my house and see me, why, I'd have died rather than do anything wrong after that. But what's the use of talking about it? I'll say good-bye, if you will, Mr McManus.'

Cork was pulling at his ear. 'I knifed Malone,' said he. 'I was the one the cop wanted.'

'Oh, that's all right,' said the girl listlessly. 'It didn't make any difference about that.'

'That was all hot air about Wall Street. I don't do nothin' but hang out with a tough gang on the East Side.'

'That was all right, too,' repeated the girl. 'It didn't make any difference.'

Cork straightened himself, and pulled his hat down low. 'I could get a job at O'Brien's,' he said aloud, but to himself.

'Good-bye,' said the girl.

'Come on,' said Cork, taking her arm. 'I know a place.'

Two blocks away he turned with her up the steps of a red-brick house facing a little park.

'What house is this?' she asked, drawing back. 'Why are you going in there?'

A street lamp shone brightly in front. There was a brass name-plate on one side of the closed front doors. Cork drew her firmly up the steps. 'Read that,' said he.

She looked at the name on the plate, and gave a cry between a moan and a scream. 'No, no, no, Eddie! Oh, my God, no! I won't let you do that – not now! Let me go! You shan't do that! You can't – you mustn't! Not after you know! No, no! Come away quick! Oh, my God! Please, Eddie, come!'

Half fainting, she reeled, and was caught in the bend of his arm. Cork's right hand felt for the electric button and pressed it long.

Another cop – how quickly they scent trouble when trouble is on the wing! – came along, saw them, and ran up the steps. 'Here! What are you doing with that girl?' he called gruffly.

'She'll be all right in a minute,' said Cork. 'It's a straight deal.'

'Reverend Jeremiah Jones,' read the cop from the door-plate with true detective cunning.

'Correct,' said Cork. 'On the dead level, we're going to get married.'

THE MOMENT OF VICTORY

Ben Granger is a war veteran aged twenty-nine – which should enable you to guess the war. He is also principal merchant and postmaster of Cadiz, a little town over which the breezes from the Gulf of Mexico perpetually blow.

Ben helped to hurl the Don from his stronghold in the Greater Antilles; and then, hiking across half the world, he marched as a corporal-usher up and down the blazing tropic aisles of the open-air college in which the Filipino was schooled. Now, with his bayonet beaten into a cheese slicer, he rallies his corporal's guard of cronies in the shade of his well-whittled porch, instead of in the matted jungles of Mindanao. Always have his interest and choice been for deeds rather than for words; but the consideration and digestion of motives is not beyond him, as this story, which is his, will attest.

'What is it,' he asked me one moonlit eve, as we sat among his boxes and barrels, 'that generally makes men go through dangers, and fire, and trouble, and starvation, and battle, and such recourses? What does a man do it for? Why does he try to outdo his fellow-humans, and be braver and stronger and more daring and showy than even his best friends are? What's his game? What does he expect to get out of it? He don't do it just for the fresh air and exercise. What would you say, now, Bill, that an ordinary man expects, generally speaking, for his efforts along the line of ambition and extraordinary hustling in the market-places, forums, shooting-galleries, lyceums, battlefields, links, cinder-paths, and arenas of the civilized and vice versa places of the world?'

'Well, Ben,' said I, with judicious seriousness, 'I think we might safely limit the number of motives of a man who seeks fame to three – to ambition, which is a desire for popular applause; to avarice, which looks to the material side of success; and to love of some woman whom he either possesses or desires to possess.'

Ben pondered over my words while a mocking-bird on the top

of a mesquite by the porch trilled a dozen bars.

'I reckon,' said he, 'that your diagnosis about covers the case according to the rules laid down in the copybooks and historical readers. But what I had in mind was the case of Willie Robbins, a person I used to know. I'll tell you about him before I close up the store, if you don't mind listening.

'Willie was one of our social set up in San Augustine. I was clerking there then for Brady & Murchison, wholesale dry-goods and ranch supplies. Willie and I belonged to the same german club and athletic association and military company. He played the triangle in our serenading and quartet crowd that used to ring the welkin three nights a week somewhere in town.

'Willie jibed with his name considerable. He weighed about as much as a hundred pounds of veal in his summer suitings, and he had a "Where-is-Mary?" expression on his features so plain that you could almost see the wool growing on him.

'And yet you couldn't fence him away from the girls with barbed wire. You know that kind of young fellows – a kind of a mixture of fools and angels – they rush in and fear to tread at the same time; but they never fail to tread when they get the chance. He was always on hand when "a joyful occasion was had," as the morning paper would say, looking as happy as a king full, and at the same time as uncomfortable as a raw oyster served with sweet pickles. He danced like he had hind hobbles on; and he had a vocabulary of about three hundred and fifty words that he made stretch over four germans a week, and plagiarized from to get him through two ice-cream suppers and a Sunday-night call. He seemed to me to be a sort of a mixture of Maltese kitten, sensitive plant, and a member of a stranded "Two Orphans" company.

'I'll give you an estimate of his physiological and pictorial makeup and then I'll stick spurs into the sides of my narrative.

'Willie inclined to the Caucasian in his colouring and manner of style. His hair was opalescent and his conversation fragmentary. His eyes were the same blue shade as the china dog's on the right-hand corner of your Aunt Ellen's mantelpiece. He took things as they came, and I never felt any hostility against him. I let him live, and so did others.

'But what does this Willie do but coax his heart out of his boots and lose it to Myra Allison, the liveliest, brightest, keenest, smartest, and prettiest girl in San Augustine. I tell you, she had the blackest eyes, the shiniest curls, and the most tantalizing – Oh, no, you're off – I wasn't a victim. I might have been, but I knew better. I kept out. Joe Granberry was It from the start. He had everybody else beat a couple of leagues and thence east to a stake and mound. But, anyhow, Myra was a nine-pound, full-merino, fall-clip fleece, sacked and loaded on a four-horse team for San Antone.

'One night there was an ice-cream sociable at Mrs Colonel Spraggins', in San Augustine. We fellows had a big room upstairs opened up for us to put our hats and things in, and to comb our hair and put on the clean collars we brought along inside the sweatbands of our hats – in short, a room to fix up in just like they have everywhere at high-toned doings. A little farther down the hall was the girls' room, which they used to powder up in, and so forth. Downstairs we – that is, the San Augustine Social Cotillion and Merrymakers' Club – had a stretcher put down in the parlour where our dance was going on.

'Willie Robbins and me happened to be up in our – cloak-room, I believe we called it – when Myra Allison skipped through the hall on her way downstairs from the girls' room. Willie was standing before the mirror, deeply interested in smoothing down the blond grass-plot on his head, which seemed to give him lots of trouble. Myra was always full of life and devilment. She stopped and stuck her head in our door. She certainly was good-looking. But I knew how Joe Granberry stood with her. So did Willie; but he kept on ba-a-a-ing after her and following her around. He had a system of persistence that didn't coincide with pale hair and light eyes.

'"Hello, Willie!" says Myra. "What are you doing to yourself in the glass?"

'"I'm trying to look fly," says Willie.

'"Well, you never could *be* fly," says Myra with her special laugh, which was the provokingest sound I ever heard except the rattle of an empty canteen against my saddle-horn.

'I looked around at Willie after Myra had gone. He had a kind of lily-white look on him which seemed to show that her remark had, as you might say, disrupted his soul. I never noticed anything in what she said that sounded particularly destructive to a man's ideas of self-consciousness; but he was set back to an extent you could scarcely imagine.

'After we went downstairs with our clean collars on, Willie never went near Myra again that night. After all, he seemed to be a diluted kind of skim-milk sort of a chap, and I never wondered that Joe Granberry beat him out.

'The next day the battleship *Maine* was blown up, and then pretty soon somebody – I reckon it was Joe Bailey, or Ben Tillman, or maybe the Government – declared war against Spain.

'Well, everybody south of Mason & Hamlin's line knew that the North by itself couldn't whip a whole country the size of Spain. So the Yankees commenced to holler for help, and the Johnny Rebs answered the call. "We're coming, Father William, a hundred thousand strong – and then some," was the way they sang it. And the old party lines drawn by Sherman's march and the Ku-Klux and nine-cent cotton and the Jim Crow street-car ordinances faded away. We became one undivided country, with no North, very little East, a good-sized chunk of West, and a South that loomed up as big as the first foreign label in a new eight-dollar suit-case.

'Of course the dogs of war weren't a complete pack without a yelp from the San Augustine Rifles, Company D, of the Fourteenth Texas Regiment. Our company was among the first to land in Cuba and strike terror into the hearts of the foe. I'm not going to give you a history of the war; I'm just dragging it in to fill out my story about Willie Robbins, just as the Republican party dragged it in to help out the election in 1898.

'If anybody ever had heroitis, it was that Willie Robbins. From the minute he set foot on the soil of the tyrants of Castile he seemed to engulf danger as a cat laps up cream. He certainly astonished every man in our company, from the captain up. You'd have expected him to gravitate naturally to the job of an orderly to the colonel, or typewriter in the commissary – but not any. He created the part of the flaxen-haired boy hero who lives and gets back home with the goods, instead of dying with an important despatch in his hands at his colonel's feet.

'Our company got into a section of Cuban scenery where one of the messiest and most unsung portions of the campaign occurred. We were out every day capering around in the bushes, and having little skirmishes with the Spanish troops that looked more like kind of tired-out feuds than anything else. The war was a joke to us, and of no interest to them. We never could see it any other way than as a howling farce-comedy that the San Augustine Rifles were actually fighting to uphold the Stars and Stripes. And the blamed little señors didn't get enough pay to make them care whether they were patriots or traitors. Now and then somebody would get killed. It seemed like a waste of life to me. I was at Coney Island when I went to New York once, and one of them down-hill skidding apparatuses they call "roller-coasters" flew the track and killed a man in a brown sack-suit. Whenever the Spaniards shot one of our men it struck me as just about as unnecessary and regrettable as that was.

'But I'm dropping Willie Robbins out of the conversation.

'He was out for bloodshed, laurels, ambition, medals, recommendations, and all other forms of military glory. And he didn't seem to be afraid of any of the recognized forms of military danger, such as Spaniards, cannon-balls, canned beef, gunpowder, or nepotism. He went forth with his pallid hair and china-blue eyes and ate up Spaniards like you would sardines *à la* canopy. Wars and rumbles of wars never flustered him. He would stand guard-duty, mosquitoes, hard-tack, treat, and fire with equally perfect unanimity. No blondes in history ever come in comparison distance of him except the Jack of Diamonds and Queen Catherine of Russia.

'I remember, one time, a little *caballard* of Spanish men sauntered out from behind a patch of sugar-cane and shot Bob Turner, the first sergeant of our company, while we were eating dinner. As required by the army regulations, we fellows went through the usual tactics of falling into line, saluting the enemy, and loading and firing, kneeling.

'That wasn't the Texas way of scrapping; but, being a very important addendum and annex to the regular army, the San Augustine Rifles had to conform to the red-tape system of getting even.

'By the time we had got out our *Upton's Tactics*, turned to page fifty-seven, said "one – two – three – one – two – three" a couple of times, and got blank cartridges into our Springfields, the Spanish outfit had smiled repeatedly, rolled and lit cigarettes by squads and walked away contemptuously.

'I went straight to Captain Floyd, and says to him: "Sam, I don't think this war is a straight game. You know as well as I do that Bob Turner was one of the whitest fellows that ever threw a leg over a saddle, and now these wire-pullers in Washington have fixed his clock. He's politically and ostensibly dead. It ain't fair. Why should they keep this thing up? If they want Spain licked, why don't they turn the San Augustine Rifles and Joe Seely's ranger company and a carload of West Texas deputy-sheriffs on to these Spaniards, and let us exonerate them from the face of the earth? I never did," says I, "care much about fighting by the Lord Chesterfield ring rules. I'm going to hand in my resignation and go home if anybody else I am personally acquainted with gets hurt in this war. If you can get somebody in my place, Sam," says I, "I'll quit the first of next week. I don't want to work in any army that don't give its help a chance. Never mind my wages," says I; "let the Secretary of the Treasury keep 'em."

'"Well, Ben," says the captain to me, "your allegations and estimations of the tactics of war, government, patriotism, guard-mounting, and democracy are all right. But I've looked into the system of international arbitration and the ethics of justifiable slaughter a little closer, maybe, than you have. Now, you can hand in your resignation the first of next week if you are so minded. But if you do," says Sam, "I'll order a corporal's guard to take you over by that limestone bluff on the creek and shoot enough lead into you to ballast a submarine airship. I'm captain of this company, and I've swore allegiance to the Amalgamated States regardless of sectional, secessional, and Congressional differences. Have you got any smoking-tobacco?" winds up Sam. "Mine got wet when I swum the creek this morning."

'The reason I drag all this *non ex parte* evidence in is because Willie Robbins was standing there listening to us. I was a second sergeant and he was a private then, but among us Texans and Westerners there never was as much tactics and subordination as there was in the regular army. We never called our captain anything but "Sam" except when there was a lot of major-generals and admirals around, so as to preserve the discipline.

'And says Willie Robbins to me, in a sharp construction of voice much unbecoming to his light hair and previous record:

'"You ought to be shot, Ben, for emitting any such sentiments. A man that won't fight for his country is worse than a horse-thief. If I was the cap, I'd put you in the guard-house for thirty days on round steak and tamales. War," says Willie, "is great and glorious. I didn't know you were a coward."

'"I'm not," says I. "If I was, I'd knock some of the pallidness off of your marble brow. I'm lenient with you," I says, "just as I am with the Spaniards, because you have always reminded me of something with mushrooms on the side. Why, you little Lady of Shalott," says I, "you underdone leader of cotillions, you glassy fashion and moulded form, you whitepine soldier made in the Cisalpine Alps in Germany for the late New-Year trade, do you know of whom you are talking to? We've been in the same social circle," says I, "and I've put up with you because you seemed so meek and self-unsatisfying. I don't understand why you have so sudden taken a personal interest in chivalrousness and murder. Your nature's undergone a complete revelation. Now, how is it?"

'"Well, you wouldn't understand, Ben," says Willie, giving one of his refined smiles and turning away.

'"Come back here!" says I, catching him by the tail of his khaki coat. "You've made me kind of mad in spite of the aloofness in which I have heretofore held you. You are out for making a success in this hero business, and I believe I know what for. You are doing it either because you are crazy or because you expect to catch some girl by it. Now, if it's a girl, I've got something here to show you."

'I wouldn't have done it, but I was plumb mad. I pulled a San Augustine paper out of my hip-pocket, and showed him an item. It was a half a column about the marriage of Myra Allison and Joe Granberry.

'Willie laughed, and I saw I hadn't touched him.

'"Oh," says he, "everybody knew that was going to happen. I heard about that a week ago." And then he gave me the laugh again.

'"All right," says I. "Then why do you so recklessly chase the bright rainbow of fame? Do you expect to be elected President, or do you belong to a suicide club?"

'And then Captain Sam interferes.

'"You gentlemen quit jawing and go back to your quarters," says he, "or I'll have you escorted to the guard-house. Now, scat, both of you! Before you go, which one of you has got any chewing-tobacco?"

'"We're off, Sam," says I. "It's supper-time, anyhow. But what do you think of what we was talking about? I've noticed you throwing out a good many grappling-hooks for this here balloon called fame – What's ambition, anyhow? What does a man risk his life day after day for? Do you know of anything he gets in the end that can pay him for the trouble? I want to go back home," says I. "I don't care whether Cuba sinks or swims, and I don't give a pipeful of rabbit tobacco whether Queen Sophia Christina or Charlie Culberson rules these fairy isles; and I don't want my name on any list except the list of survivors. But I've noticed you, Sam," says I, "seeking the bubble notoriety in the cannon's larynx a number of times. Now, what do you do it for? Is it ambition, business, or some freckle-faced Phœbe at home that you are heroing for?"

'"Well, Ben," says Sam, kind of hefting his sword out from between his knees, "as your superior officer I could court-martial you for attempted cowardice and desertion. But I won't. And I'll tell you why I'm trying for promotion and the usual honours of war and conquest. A major gets more pay than a captain, and I need the money."

'"Correct for you!" says I. "I can understand that. Your system of fame-seeking is rooted in the deepest soil of patriotism. But I can't comprehend," says I, "why Willie Robbins, whose folks at home are well off, and who used to be as meek and undesirous of notice as a cat with cream on his whiskers, should all at once develop into a warrior bold with the most fire-eating kind of proclivities. And the girl in his case seems to have been eliminated by marriage to another fellow. I reckon," says I, "it's a plain case of just common ambition. He wants his name, maybe, to go thundering down the coroners of time. It must be that."

'Well, without itemizing his deeds, Willie sure made good as a hero. He simply spent most of his time on his knees begging our captain to send him on forlorn hopes and dangerous scouting expeditions. In every fight he was the first man to mix it at close quarters with the Don Alfonsos. He got three or four bullets planted in various parts of his autonomy. Once he went off with a detail of eight men and captured a whole company of Spanish. He kept Captain Floyd busy writing out recommendations of his bravery to send in to headquarters; and he began to accumulate medals for all kinds of things – heroism and target-shooting and valour and tactics and uninsubordination, and all the little accomplishments that look good to the third assistant secretaries of the War Department.

'Finally, Cap Floyd got promoted to be a major-general, or a knight commander of the main herd, or something like that. He pounded around on a white horse, all desecrated up with gold-leaf and hen-feathers and a Good Templar's hat, and wasn't allowed by the regulations to speak to us. And Willie Robbins was made captain of our company.

'And maybe he didn't go after the wreath of fame then! As far as I could see it was him that ended the war. He got eighteen of us boys – friends of his, too – killed in battles that he stirred up himself and that didn't seem to me necessary at all. One night he took twelve of us and waded through a little rill about a hundred and ninety yards wide, and climbed a couple of mountains, and sneaked through a mile of neglected shrubbery and a couple of rock-quarries and into a rye-straw village, and captured a Spanish general named, as they said, Benny Veedus. Benny seemed to me hardly worth the trouble, being a blackish man without shoes or cuffs, and anxious to surrender and throw himself on the commissary of his foe.

'But that job gave Willie the big boost he wanted. The San Augustine *News* and the Galveston, St Louis, New York, and Kansas City papers printed his picture and columns of stuff about him. Old San Augustine simply went crazy over its "gallant son." The *News* had an editorial tearfully begging the Government to call off the regular army and the national guard, and let Willie carry on the rest of the war single-handed. It said that a refusal to do so would be regarded as a proof that the Northern jealousy of the South was still as rampant as ever.

'If the war hadn't ended pretty soon, I don't know to what heights of gold braid and encomiums Willie would have climbed; but it did. There was a secession of hostilities just three days after he was appointed a colonel, and got in three more medals by registered mail, and shot two Spaniards while they were drinking lemonade in an ambuscade.

'Our company went back to San Augustine when the war was over. There wasn't anywhere else for it to go. And what do you think? The old town notified us in print, by wire cable, special delivery, and a nigger named Saul sent on a grey mule to San Antone, that they was going to give us the biggest blow-out, complimentary, alimentary, and elementary, that ever disturbed the kildees on the sandflats outside of the immediate contiguity of the city.

'I say "we," but it was all meant for ex-Private, Captain *de facto*, and Colonel-elect Willie Robbins. The town was crazy about him. They notified us that the reception they were going to put up would make the Mardi Gras in New Orleans look like an afternoon tea in Bury St Edmunds with a curate's aunt.

'Well, the San Augustine Rifles got back home on schedule time. Everybody was at the depot giving forth Roosevelt-Democrat – they used to be called Rebel – yells. There was two brass-bands, and the mayor, and schoolgirls in white frightening the street-car horses by throwing Cherokee roses in the streets, and – well, maybe you've seen a celebration by a town that was inland and out of water.

'They wanted Brevet-Colonel Willie to get into a carriage and be drawn by prominent citizens and some of the city aldermen to the armoury, but he stuck to his company and marched at the head of it up to Sam Houston Avenue. The buildings on both sides was covered with flags and audiences, and everybody hollered "Robbins!" or "Hello, Willie!" as we marched up in files of fours. I never saw a illustriouser-looking human in my life than Willie was. He had at least seven or eight medals and diplomas and decorations on the breast of his khaki coat; he was sunburnt the colour of a saddle, and he certainly done himself proud.

'They told us at the depot that the courthouse was to be illuminated at half-past seven, and there would be speeches and chili-con-carne at the Palace Hotel. Miss Delphine Thompson was to read an original poem by James Whitcomb Ryan, and Constable Hooker had promised us a salute of nine guns from Chicago that he had arrested that day.

'After we had disbanded in the armoury, Willie says to me:

'"Want to walk out a piece with me?"

'"Why, yes," says I, "if it ain't so far that we can't hear the tumult and the shouting die away. I'm hungry myself," says I, "and I'm pining for some home grub, but I'll go with you."

'Willie steered me down some side streets till we came to a little white cottage in a new lot with a twenty-by-thirty-foot lawn decorated with brickbats and old barrel-staves.

'"Halt and give the countersign," says I to Willie. "Don't you know this dugout? It's the bird's nest that Joe Granberry built before he married Myra Allison. What you going there for?"

'But Willie already had the gate open. He walked up the brick walk to the steps, and I went with him. Myra was sitting in a rocking-chair on the porch, sewing. Her hair was smoothed back kind of hasty and tied in a knot. I never noticed till then that she had freckles. Joe was at one side of the porch, in his shirt-sleeves, with no collar on, and no signs of a shave, trying to scrape out a hole among the brickbats and tin cans to plant a little fruit-tree in. He looked up but never said a word, and neither did Myra.

'Willie was sure dandy-looking in his uniform, with medals

strung on his breast and his new gold-handled sword. You'd never have taken him for the little white-headed snipe that the girls used to order about and make fun of. He just stood there for a minute, looking at Myra with a peculiar little smile on his face; and then he says to her, slow, and kind of holding on to his words with his teeth:

'"*Oh, I don't know. Maybe I could if I tried!*"

'That was all that was said. Willie raised his hat, and we walked away.

'And, somehow, when he said that, I remembered, all of a sudden, the night of that dance and Willie brushing his hair before the looking-glass, and Myra sticking her head in the door to guy him.

'When we got back to Sam Houston Avenue, Willie says:

'"Well, so long, Ben. I'm going down home and get off my shoes and take a rest."

'"You?" says I. "What's the matter with you? Ain't the court-house jammed with everybody in town waiting to honour the hero? And two brass-bands, and recitations and flags and jags, and grub to follow waiting for you?"

'Willie sighs.

'"All right, Ben," says he. "Darned if I didn't forget all about that."

'And that's why I say,' concluded Ben Grainger, 'that you can't tell where ambition begins any more than you can tell where it is going to wind up.'

THE LAST OF THE
TROUBADOURS

Inexorably Sam Galloway saddled his pony. He was going away from the Rancho Altito at the end of a three-months' visit. It is not to be expected that a guest should put up with wheat coffee and biscuits yellow-streaked with saleratus for longer than that. Nick Napoleon, the big negro man cook, had never been able to make good biscuits. Once before, when Nick was cooking at the Willow Ranch, Sam had been forced to fly from his *cuisine*, after only a six-weeks' sojourn.

On Sam's face was an expression of sorrow, deepened with regret and slightly tempered by the patient forgiveness of a connoisseur who cannot be understood. But very firmly and inexorably he buckled his saddle-cinches, looped his stake-rope and hung it to his saddle-horn, tied his slicker and coat on the cantle, and looped his quirt on his right wrist. The Merrydews (householders of the Rancho Altito), men, women, children, and servants, vassals, visitors, employés, dogs, and casual callers were grouped in the 'gallery' of the ranch house, all with faces set to the tune of melancholy and grief. For, as the coming of Sam Galloway to any ranch, camp, or cabin between the rivers Frio and Bravo del Norte aroused joy, so his departure caused mourning and distress.

And then, during absolute silence, except for the bumping of a hind elbow of a hound dog as he pursued a wicked flea, Sam tenderly and carefully tied his guitar across his saddle on top of his slicker and coat. The guitar was in a green duck bag; and if you catch the significance of it, it explains Sam.

Sam Galloway was the Last of the Troubadours. Of course you know about the troubadours. The encyclopædia says they flourished between the eleventh and the thirteenth centuries. What they flourished doesn't seem clear – you may be pretty sure it wasn't a sword: maybe it was a fiddlebow, or a forkful of spaghetti, or a lady's scarf. Anyhow, Sam Galloway was one of 'em.

Sam put on a martyred expression as he mounted his pony. But the expression on his face was hilarious compared with the one on his pony's. You see, a pony gets to know his rider mighty well, and it is not unlikely that cow ponies in pastures and at hitching racks had often guyed Sam's pony for being ridden by a guitar player instead of by a rollicking, cussing, all-wool cowboy. No man is a hero to his saddle-horse. And even an escalator in a department store might be excused for tripping up a troubadour.

Oh, I know I'm one; and so are you. You remember the stories you memorize and the card tricks you study and that little piece on the piano – how does it go – ti-tum-te-tum-ti-tum – those little Arabian Ten Minute Entertainments that you furnish when you go up to call on your rich Aunt Jane. You should know that *omnæ personæ in tres partes divisæ sunt*. Namely: Barons, Troubadours, and Workers. Barons have no inclination to read such folderol as this; and Workers have no time: so I know you must be a Troubadour, and that you will understand Sam Galloway. Whether we sing, act, dance, write, lecture, or paint, we are only troubadours; so let us make the worst of it.

The pony with the Dante Alighieri face, guided by the pressure of Sam's knees, bore that wandering minstrel sixteen miles southeastward. Nature was in her most benignant mood. League after league of delicate, sweet flowerets made fragrant the gently undulating prairie. The east wind tempered the spring warmth; wool-white clouds flying in from the Mexican Gulf hindered the direct rays of the April sun. Sam sang songs as he rode. Under his pony's bridle he had tucked some sprigs of chaparral to keep away the deer flies. Thus crowned, the long-faced quadruped looked more Dantesque than before, and, judging by his countenance, seemed to think of Beatrice.

Straight as topography permitted, Sam rode to the sheep ranch of old man Ellison. A visit to a sheep ranch seemed to him desirable just then. There had been too many people, too much noise, argument, competition, confusion at Rancho Altito. He had never conferred upon old man Ellison the favour of sojourning at his ranch; but he knew he would be welcome. The troubadour is his own passport everywhere. The Workers in the castle let down the drawbridge to him, and the Baron sets him at his left hand at table in the banquet hall. There ladies smile upon him and applaud his songs and stories, while the Workers bring boars' heads and flagons. If the Baron nods once or twice in his carved oaken chair, he does not do it maliciously.

Old man Ellison welcomed the troubadour flatteringly. He had often heard praises of Sam Galloway from other ranchmen who had been complimented by his visits, but had never aspired to such an honour for his own humble barony. I say barony because old man Ellison was the Last of the Barons. Of course, Bulwer-Lytton lived too early to know him, or he wouldn't have conferred that sobriquet upon Warwick. In life it is the duty and the function of the Baron to provide work for the Workers and lodging and shelter for the Troubadours.

Old man Ellison was a shrunken old man, with a short, yellow-white beard and a face lined and seamed by past-and-gone smiles. His ranch was a little two-room box house in a grove of hackberry trees in the lonesomest part of the sheep country. His household consisted of a Kiowa Indian man cook, four hounds, a pet sheep, and a half-tamed coyote chained to a fence-post. He owned 3,000 sheep, which he ran on two sections of leased land and many thousands of acres neither leased nor owned. Three or four times a year someone who spoke his language would ride up to his gate and exchange a few bald ideas with him. Those were red-letter days to old man Ellison. Then in what illuminated, embossed, and gorgeously decorated capitals must have been written the day on which a troubadour – a troubadour who, according to the encyclopædia, should have flourished between the eleventh and the thirteenth centuries – drew rein at the gates of his baronial castle!

Old man Ellison's smiles came back and filled his wrinkles when he saw Sam. He hurried out of the house in his shuffling, limping way to greet him.

'Hallo, Mr Ellison,' called Sam cheerfully. 'Thought I'd drop over and see you awhile. Notice you've had fine rains on your range. They ought to make good grazing for your spring lambs.'

'Well, well, well,' said old man Ellison. 'I'm mighty glad to see you, Sam. I never thought you'd take the trouble to ride over to as out-of-the-way an old ranch as this. But you're mighty welcome. 'Light. I've got a sack of new oats in the kitchen – shall I bring out a feed for your hoss?'

'Oats for him?' said Sam derisively. 'No, sir-ee. He's as fat as a pig now on grass. He don't get rode enough to keep him in condition. I'll just turn him in the horse pasture with a drag rope on if you don't mind.'

I am positive that never during the eleventh and thirteenth centuries did Baron, Troubadour, and Worker amalgamate as harmoniously as their parallels did that evening at old man Ellison's sheep ranch. The Kiowa's biscuits were light and tasty and his coffee strong. Ineradicable hospitality and appreciation glowed on old man Ellison's weather-tanned face. As for the troubadour, he said to himself that he had stumbled upon pleasant places indeed. A well-cooked, abundant meal, a host whom his lightest attempt to entertain seemed to delight far beyond the merits of the exertion, and the reposeful atmosphere that his sensitive soul at that time craved united to confer upon him a satisfaction and luxurious ease that he had seldom found on his tours of the ranches.

After the delectable supper, Sam untied the green duck bag and took out his guitar. Not by way of payment, mind you – neither Sam Galloway nor any other of the true troubadours are lineal descendants of the late Tommy Tucker. You have read of Tommy Tucker in the works of the esteemed but often obscure Mother Goose. Tommy Tucker sang for his supper. No true troubadour would do that. He would have his supper, and then sing for Art's sake.

Sam Galloway's repertoire comprised about fifty funny stories and between thirty and forty songs. He by no means stopped there. He could talk through twenty cigarettes on any topic that you brought up. And he never sat up when he could lie down; and never stood when he could sit. I am strongly disposed to linger with him, for I am drawing a portrait as well as a blunt pencil and a tattered thesaurus will allow.

I wish you could have seen him: he was small and tough and inactive beyond the power of imagination to conceive. He wore an ultramarine-blue woollen shirt laced down the front with a pearl-grey, exaggerated sort of shoe-string, indestructible brown duck clothes, inevitable high-heeled boots with Mexican spurs, and a Mexican straw sombrero.

That evening Sam and old man Ellison dragged their chairs out under the hackberry trees. They lighted cigarettes, and the troubadour gaily touched his guitar. Many of the songs he sang were weird, melancholy, minor-keyed *canciones* that he had learned from the Mexican sheep herders and *vaqueros*. One, in particular, charmed and soothed the soul of the lonely baron. It was a favourite song of the sheep herders, beginning 'Huile, huile, palomita,' which being translated means, 'Fly, fly, little dove.' Sam sang it for old man Ellison many times that evening.

The troubadour stayed on at the old man's ranch. There was peace and quiet and appreciation there such as he had not found in the noisy camps of the cattle kings. No audience in the world could have crowned the work of poet, musician, or artist with more worshipful and unflagging approval than that bestowed upon his efforts by old man Ellison. No visit by a royal personage to a humble wood-chopper or peasant could have been received with more flattering thankfulness and joy.

On a cool, canvas-covered cot in the shade of the hackberry trees, Sam Galloway passed the greater part of his time. There he rolled his brown-paper cigarettes, read such tedious literature as the ranch afforded, and added to his repertoire of improvisations that he played so expertly on his guitar. To him, as a slave ministering to a great lord, the Kiowa brought cool water from the red jar hanging under the brush shelter, and food when he called for it. The prairie zephyrs fanned him mildly; mocking-birds at morn and eve competed with, but scarce equalled, the sweet melodies of his lyre; a perfumed stillness seemed to fill all his world. While old man Ellison was pottering among his flocks of sheep on his mile-an-hour pony, and while the Kiowa took his siesta in the burning sunshine at the end of the kitchen, Sam would lie on his cot thinking what a happy world he lived in, and how kind it is to the ones whose mission in life it is to give entertainment and pleasure. Here he had food and lodging as good as he had ever longed for; absolute immunity from care or exertion or strife; an endless welcome, and a host whose delight at the sixteenth repetition of a song or a story was as keen as at its initial giving. Was there ever a troubadour of old who struck upon as royal a castle in his wanderings ? While he lay thus, meditating upon his blessings, little brown cottontails would shyly frolic through the yard; a covey of white-topknotted blue quail would run past, in single file, twenty yards away; a paisano bird, out hunting for tarantulas, would hop upon the fence and salute him with sweeping flourishes of its long tail. In the eighty-acre horse pasture the pony with the Dantesque face grew fat and almost smiling. The troubadour was at the end of his wanderings.

Old man Ellison was his own vaciero. That means that he supplied his sheep camps with wood, water, and rations by his own labours instead of hiring a *vaciero*. On small ranches it is often done.

One morning he started for the camp of Incarnación Felipe de la Cruz y Monte Piedras (one of his sheep herders) with the week's usual rations of brown beans, coffee, meal, and sugar. Two miles away on the trail from Fort Ewing he met, face to face, a terrible being called King James, mounted on a fiery, prancing, Kentucky-bred horse.

King James's real name was James King; but people reversed it because it seemed to fit him better, and also because it seemed to please his majesty. King James was the biggest cattleman between the Alamo plaza in San Antone and Bill Hopper's saloon in Brownsville. Also he was the loudest and most offensive bully and braggart and bad man in south-west Texas. And he always made good whenever he bragged; and the more noise he made the more dangerous he was. In the story papers it is always the quiet, mild-mannered man with light-blue eyes and a low voice who turns out to be really dangerous; but in real life and in this story such is not the case. Give me my choice between assaulting a large, loudmouthed rough-houser and an inoffensive stranger with blue eyes sitting quietly in a corner, and you will see something doing in the corner every time.

King James, as I intended to say earlier, was a fierce, two-hundred-pound, sunburned, blond man, as pink as an October strawberry, and with two horizontal slits under shaggy red eyebrows for eyes. On that day he wore a flannel shirt that was tan-coloured, with the exception of certain large areas which were darkened by transudations due to the summer sun. There seemed to be other clothing and garnishings about him, such as brown duck trousers stuffed into immense boots, and red handkerchiefs and revolvers; and a shot-gun laid across his saddle and a leather belt with millions of cartridges shining in it – but your mind skidded off such accessories; what held your gaze was just the two little horizontal slits that he used for eyes.

This was the man that old man Ellison met on the trail; and when you count up in the baron's favour that he was sixty-five and weighed ninety-eight pounds and had heard of King James's record and that he (the baron) had a hankering for the *vita simplex* and had no gun with him and wouldn't have used it if he had, you can't censure him if I tell you that the smiles with which the troubadour had filled his wrinkles went out of them and left them plain wrinkles again. But he was not the kind of baron that flies from danger. He reined in the mile-an-hour pony (no difficult feat), and saluted the formidable monarch.

King James expressed himself with royal directness.

'You're that old snoozer that's running sheep on this range, ain't you ?' said he. 'What right have you got to do it? Do you own any land, or lease any?'

'I have two sections leased from the state,' said old man Ellison mildly.

'Not by no means you haven't,' said King James. 'Your lease expired yesterday; and I had a man at the land office on the minute to take it up. You don't control a foot of grass in Texas. You sheep men have got to git. Your time's up. It's a cattle country, and there ain't any room in it for snoozers. This range you've got your sheep on is mine. I'm putting up a wire fence, forty by sixty miles; and if there's a sheep inside of it when it's done it'll be a dead one. I'll give you a week to move yours away. If they ain't gone by then, I'll send six men over here with Winchesters to make mutton out of the whole lot. And if I find you here at the same time this is what you'll get.'

King James patted the breech of his shot-gun warningly.

Old man Ellison rode on to the camp of Incarnación. He sighed many times, and the wrinkles in his face grew deeper. Rumours that the old order was about to change had reached him before. The end of Free Grass was in sight. Other troubles, too, had been accumulating upon his shoulders. His flocks were decreasing instead of growing; the price of wool was declining at every clip; even Bradshaw, the storekeeper at Frio City, at whose store he bought his ranch supplies, was dunning him for his last six months' bill and threatening to cut him off. And so this last greatest calamity suddenly dealt out to him by the terrible King James was a crusher.

When the old man got back to the ranch at sunset he found Sam Galloway lying on his cot, propped against a roll of blankets and wool sacks, fingering his guitar.

'Hallo, Uncle Ben,' the troubadour called cheerfully. 'You rolled in early this evening. I been trying a new twist on the Spanish Fandango to-day. I just about got it. Here's how she goes – listen.'

'That's fine, that's mighty fine,' said old man Ellison, sitting on the kitchen step and rubbing his white Scotch-terrier whiskers. 'I reckon you've got all the musicians beat east and west, Sam, as far as the roads are cut out.'

'Oh, I don't know,' said Sam reflectively. 'But I certainly do get there on variations. I guess I can handle anything in five flats about as well as any of 'em. But you look kind of fagged out, Uncle Ben – ain't you feeling right well this evening?'

'Little tired; that's all, Sam. If you ain't played yourself out, let's have that Mexican piece that starts off with "*Huile, huile, palomita.*" It seems that that song always kind of soothes and comforts me after I've been riding far or anything bothers me.'

'Why, *seguramente, señor,*' said Sam. 'I'll hit her up for you as often as you like. And before I forget about it, Uncle Ben, you want to jerk Bradshaw up about them last hams he sent us. They're just a little bit strong.'

A man sixty-five years old, living on a sheep ranch and beset by a complication of disasters, cannot successfully and continuously dissemble. Moreover, a troubadour has eyes quick to see unhappiness in others around him – because it disturbs his own ease. So, on the next day, Sam again questioned the old man about his air of sadness and abstraction. Then old man Ellison told him the story of King James's threats and orders and that pale melancholy and red ruin appeared to have marked him for their own. The troubadour took the news thoughtfully. He had heard much about King James.

On the third day of the seven days of grace allowed him by the autocrat of the range, old man Ellison drove his buckboard to Frio City to fetch some necessary supplies for the ranch. Bradshaw was hard but not implacable. He divided the old man's order by two, and let him have a little more time. One article secured was a new, fine ham for the pleasure of the troubadour.

Five miles out of Frio City on his way home the old man met King James riding into town. His majesty could never look anything but fierce and menacing, but to-day his slits of eyes appeared to be a little wider than they usually were.

'Good day,' said the king gruffly. 'I've been wanting to see you. I hear it said by a cowman from Sandy yesterday that you was from Jackson County, Mississippi, originally. I want to know if that's a fact.'

'Born there,' said old man Ellison, 'and raised there till I was twenty-one.'

'This man says,' went on King James, 'that he thinks you was related to the Jackson County Reeveses. Was he right?'

'Aunt Caroline Reeves,' said the old man, 'was my half-sister.'

'She was my aunt,' said King James. 'I run away from home when I was sixteen. Now, let's re-talk over some things that we discussed a few days ago. They call me a bad man; and they're only half right. There's plenty of room in my pasture for your bunch of sheep and their increase for a long time to come. Aunt Caroline used to cut out sheep in cake dough and bake 'em for me. You keep your sheep where they are, and use all the range you want. How's your finances?'

The old man related his woes in detail, dignifiedly, with restraint and candour.

'She used to smuggle extra grub into my school basket – I'm speaking of Aunt Caroline,' said King James. 'I'm going over to Frio City to-day, and I'll ride back by your ranch to-morrow. I'll draw $2,000 out of the bank there and bring it over to you; and I'll tell Bradshaw to let you have everything you want on credit. You are bound to have heard the old saying at home that the Jackson County Reeveses and Kings would stick closer by each other than chestnut burrs. Well, I'm a King yet whenever I run across a Reeves. So you look out for me along about sundown to-morrow, and don't worry about nothing. Shouldn't wonder if the dry spell don't kill out the young grass.'

Old man Ellison drove happily ranchward. Once more the smiles filled out his wrinkles. Very suddenly, by the magic of kinship and the good that lies somewhere in all hearts, his troubles had been removed.

On reaching the ranch he found that Sam Galloway was not there. His guitar hung by its buckskin string to a hackberry limb, moaning as the gulf breeze blew across its masterless strings.

The Kiowa endeavoured to explain.

'Sam, he catch pony,' said he, 'and say he ride to Frio City. What for no can damn sabe. Say he come back to-night. Maybe so. That all.'

As the first stars came out the troubadour rode back to his haven. He pastured his pony and went into the house, his spurs jingling martially.

Old man Ellison sat at the kitchen table, having a tin cup of before-supper coffee. He looked contented and pleased.

'Hallo, Sam,' said he, 'I'm darned glad to see ye back. I don't know how I managed to get along on this ranch, anyhow, before ye dropped in to cheer things up. I'll bet ye've been skylarking around with some of them Frio City gals, now, that's kept ye so late.'

And then old man Ellison took another look at Sam's face and saw that the minstrel had changed to the man of action.

And while Sam is unbuckling from his waist old man Ellison's six-shooter, that the latter had left behind when he drove to town, we may well pause to remark that anywhere and whenever a troubadour lays down the guitar and takes up the sword trouble is sure to follow. It is not the expert thrust of Athos nor the cold skill of Aramis nor the iron wrist of Porthos that we have to fear – it is the Gascon's fury – the wild and unacademic attack of the troubadour – the sword of D'Artagnan.

'I done it,' said Sam. 'I went over to Frio City to do it. I couldn't let him put the skibunk on you, Uncle Ben. I met him in Summers's saloon. I knowed what to do. I said a few things to him that nobody else heard. He reached for his gun first – half a dozen fellows saw him do it – but I got mine unlimbered first. Three doses I gave him – right around the lungs, and a saucer could have covered up all of 'em. He won't bother you no more.'

'This – is – King – James – you speak – of?' asked old man Ellison, while he sipped his coffee.

'You bet it was. And they took me before the county judge; and the witnesses what saw him draw his gun first was all there. Well, of course, they put me under $300 bond to appear before the court, but there was four or five boys on the spot ready to sign the bail. He won't bother you no more, Uncle Ben. You ought to have seen how close them bullet holes was together. I reckon playing a guitar as much as I do must kind of limber a fellow's trigger finger up a little, don't you think, Uncle Ben?'

Then there was a little silence in the castle, except for the spluttering of a venison steak that the Kiowa was cooking.

'Sam,' said old man Ellison, stroking his white whiskers with a tremulous hand, 'would you mind getting the guitar and playing that "*Huile, huile, palomita*" piece once or twice? It always seems to be kind of soothing and comforting when a man's tired and fagged out.'

There is no more to be said, except that the title of the story is wrong. It should have been called *The Last of the Barons*. There never will be an end to the troubadours; and now and then it does seem that the jingle of their guitars will drown the sound of the muffled blows of the pickaxes and trip-hammers of all the Workers in the world.

THE MEMENTO

Miss Lynnette D'Armande turned her back on Broadway. This was but tit for tat, because Broadway had often done the same thing to Miss D'Armande. Still, the 'tats' seemed to have it, for the ex-leading lady of the 'Reaping the Whirlwind' Company had everything to ask of Broadway, while there was no vice versa.

So Miss Lynnette D'Armande turned the back of her chair to her window that overlooked Broadway, and sat down to stitch in time the lisle-thread heel of a black silk stocking. The tumult and glitter of the roaring Broadway beneath her window had no charm for her; what she greatly desired was the stifling air of a dressing-room on that fairyland street and the roar of an audience gathered in that capricious quarter. In the meantime, those stockings must not be neglected. Silk does wear out so, but – after all, isn't it just the only goods there is?

The Hotel Thalia looks on Broadway as Marathon looks on the sea. It stands like a gloomy cliff above the whirlpool where the tides of two great thoroughfares clash. Here the player-bands gather at the end of their wanderings, to loosen the buskin and dust the sock. Thick in the streets around it are booking-offices, theatres, agents, schools, and the lobster-palaces to which those thorny paths lead.

Wandering through the eccentric halls of the dim and fusty Thalia, you seem to have found yourself in some great ark or caravan about to sail, or fly, or roll away on wheels. About the house lingers a sense of unrest, of expectation, of transientness, even of anxiety and apprehension. The halls are a labyrinth. Without a guide you wander like a lost soul in a Sam Lloyd puzzle.

Turning any corner, a dressing-sack or a *cul-de-sac* may bring you up short. You meet alarming tragedians stalking in bath-robes in search of rumoured bath-rooms. From hundreds of rooms come the buzz of talk, scraps of new and old songs, and the ready laughter of the convened players.

Summer has come; their companies have disbanded, and they

take their rest in their favourite caravansary, while they besiege the managers for engagements for the coming season.

At this hour of the afternoon the day's work of tramping the rounds of the agents' offices is over. Past you, as you ramble distractedly through the mossy halls, flit audible visions of houris, with veiled, starry eyes, flying tag-ends of things, and a swish of silk, bequeathing to the dull hallways an odour of gaiety and a memory of *frangipani*. Serious young comedians, with versatile Adam's apples, gather in doorways and talk of Booth. Far-reaching from somewhere comes the smell of ham and red cabbage, and the crash of dishes on the American plan.

The indeterminate hum of life in the Thalia is enlivened by the discreet popping – at reasonable and salubrious intervals – of beer-bottle corks. Thus punctuated, life in the genial hostel scans easily – the comma being the favourite mark, semicolons frowned upon, and periods barred.

Miss D'Armande's room was a small one. There was room for her rocker between the dresser and the wash-stand if it were placed longitudinally. On the dresser were its usual accoutrements, plus the ex-leading lady's collected souvenirs of road engagements and photographs of her dearest and best professional friends.

At one of these photographs she looked twice or thrice as she darned, and smiled friendlily.

'I'd like to know where Lee is just this minute,' she said, half-aloud.

If you had been privileged to view the photograph thus flattered, you would have thought at the first glance that you saw the picture of a many-petalled, white flower, blown through the air by a storm. But the floral kingdom was not responsible for that swirl of petalous whiteness.

You saw the filmy, brief skirt of Miss Rosalie Ray as she made a complete heels-over-head turn in her wistaria-entwined swing, far out from the stage, high above the heads of the audience. You saw the camera's inadequate representation of the graceful, strong kick, with which she, at this exciting moment, sent flying, high and far, the yellow silk garter that each evening spun from her agile limb and descended upon the delighted audience below.

You saw, too, amid the black-clothed, mainly masculine patrons of select vaudeville a hundred hands raised with the hope of staying the flight of the brilliant aerial token.

Forty weeks of the best circuits this act had brought Miss Rosalie Ray for each of two years. She did other things during her twelve minutes – a song and dance, imitations of two or three actors who are but imitations of themselves, and a balancing feat with a step-ladder and feather-duster; but when the blossom-decked swing was let down from the flies, and Miss Rosalie sprang smiling into the seat, with the golden circlet conspicuous in the place whence it was soon to slide and become a soaring and coveted guerdon – then it was that the audience rose in its seat as a single man – or presumably so – and endorsed the speciality that made Miss Ray's name a favourite in the booking-offices.

At the end of the two years Miss Ray suddenly announced to her dear friend, Miss D'Armande, that she was going to spend the summer at an antediluvian village on the north shore of Long Island, and that the stage would see her no more.

Seventeen minutes after Miss Lynnette D'Armande had expressed her wish to know the whereabouts of her old chum, there were sharp raps at her door.

Doubt not that it was Rosalie Ray. At the shrill command to enter she did so, with something of a tired flutter, and dropped a heavy handbag on the floor. Upon my word, it was Rosalie, in a loose, travel-stained automobileless coat, closely tied brown veil with yard-long flying ends, grey walking-suit and tan Oxfords with lavender over-gaiters.

When she threw off her veil and hat, you saw a pretty enough face, now flushed and disturbed by some unusual emotion, and restless, large eyes with discontent marring their brightness. A heavy pile of dull auburn hair, hastily put up, was escaping in crinkly waving strands and curling small locks from the confining combs and pins.

The meeting of the two was not marked by the effusion vocal, gymnastical, osculatory, and catechetical that distinguishes the greetings of their unprofessional sisters in society. There was a brief clinch, two simultaneous labial dabs, and they stood on the same footing of the old days. Very much like the short salutations of soldiers or of travellers in foreign wilds are the welcomes between the strollers at the corners of their criss-cross roads.

'I've got the hall-room two flights up above yours,' said Rosalie, 'but I came straight to see you before going up. I didn't know you were here till they told me.'

'I've been in since the last of April,' said Lynnette. 'And I'm going on the road with a "Fatal Inheritance" Company. We open next week in Elizabeth. I thought you'd quit the stage, Lee. Tell me about yourself.'

Rosalie settled herself with a skilful wriggle on the top of Miss D'Armande's wardrobe trunk, and leaned her head against the papered wall. From long habit, thus can peripatetic leading ladies and their sisters make themselves as comfortable as though the deepest arm-chairs embraced them.

'I'm going to tell you, Lynn,' she said, with a strangely sardonic and yet carelessly resigned look on her youthful face. 'And then to-morrow I'll strike the old Broadway trail again, and wear some more paint off the chairs in the agents' offices. If anybody had told me any time in the last three months up to four o'clock this afternoon that I'd ever listen to that "Leave-your-name-and-address" rot of the booking bunch again, I'd have given 'em the real Mrs Fiske laugh. Loan me a handkerchief, Lynn. Gee! but those Long Island trains are fierce. I've got enough soft coal cinders on my face to go on and play *Topsy* without using the cork. And, speaking of corks – got anything to drink, Lynn?'

Miss D'Armande opened a door of the wash-stand and took out a bottle.

'There's nearly a pint of Manhattan. There's a cluster of carnations in the drinking-glass, but –'

'Oh, pass the bottle. Save the glass for company. Thanks! That hits the spot. The same to you. My first drink in three months!

'Yes, Lynn, I quit the stage at the end of last season. I quit it because I was sick of the life. And especially because my heart and soul were sick of men – of the kind of men we stage people have to be up against. You know what the game is to us – it's a fight against 'em all the way down the line, from the manager who wants us to try his new motor-car to the bill-posters who want to call us by our front names.

'And the men we have to meet after the show are the worst of all. The stage-door kind, and the manager's friends who take us to supper, and show their diamonds, and talk about seeing "Dan" and "Dave" and "Charlie" for us. They're beasts, and I hate 'em.

'I tell you, Lynn, it's the girls like us on the stage that ought to be pitied. It's girls from good homes that are honestly ambitious and work hard to rise in the profession, but never do get there. You hear a lot of sympathy sloshed around on chorus girls and their fifteen dollars a week. Piffle! There ain't a sorrow in the chorus that a lobster cannot heal.

'If there's any tears to shed, let 'em fall for the actress that gets a salary of from thirty to forty-five dollars a week for taking a leading part in a bum show. She knows she'll never do any better; but she hangs on for years, hoping for the "chance" that never comes.

'And the fool plays we have to work in! Having another girl roll you around the stage by the hind legs in a "Wheelbarrow Chorus" in a musical comedy is dignified drama compared with the idiotic things I've had to do in the thirty-centers.

'But what I hated most was the men – the men leering and blathering at you across tables, trying to buy you with Würzburger or Extra Dry, according to their estimate of your price. And the men in the audiences, clapping, yelling, snarling, crowding, writhing, gloating – like a lot of wild beasts, with their eyes fixed on you, ready to eat you up if you come in reach of their claws. Oh, how I hate 'em!

'Well, I'm not telling you much about myself, am I, Lynn?

'I had two hundred dollars saved up, and I cut the stage the first of the summer. I went over on Long Island, and found the sweetest little village that ever was, called Soundport, right on the water. I was going to spend the summer there, and study up on elocution, and try to get a class in the fall. There was an old widow lady with a cottage near the beach who sometimes rented a room or two just for company, and she took me in. She had another boarder, too – the Reverend Arthur Lyle.

'Yes, he was the head-liner. You're on, Lynn. I'll tell you all of it in a minute. It's only a one-act play.

'The first time he walked on, Lynn, I felt myself going; the first lines he spoke, he had me. He was different from the men in audiences. He was tall and slim, and you never heard him come in the room, but you *felt* him. He had a face like a picture of a knight – like one of that Round Table bunch – and a voice like a 'cello solo. And his manners!

'Lynn, if you'd take John Drew in his best drawing-room scene and compare the two you'd have John arrested for disturbing the peace.

'I'll spare you the particulars; but in less than a month Arthur and I were engaged. He preached at a little one-night stand of a Methodist church. There was to be a parsonage the size of a lunch-wagon, and hens and honeysuckles when we were married.

Arthur used to preach to me a good deal about Heaven, but he never could get my mind quite off those honeysuckles and hens.

'No; I didn't tell him I'd been on the stage. I hated the business and all that went with it; I'd cut it out for ever, and I didn't see any use of stirring things up. I was a good girl, and I didn't have anything to confess, except being an elocutionist, and that was about all the strain my conscience would stand.

'Oh, I tell you, Lynn, I was happy. I sang in the choir and attended the sewing society, and recited that "Annie Laurie" thing with the whistling stunt in it, "in a manner bordering upon the professional," as the weekly village paper reported it. And Arthur and I went rowing, and walking in the woods, and clamming, and that poky little village seemed to me the best place in the world. I'd have been happy to live there always, too, if –

'But one morning old Mrs Gurley, the widow lady, got gossipy while I was helping her string beans on the back porch, and began to gush information, as folks who rent out their rooms usually do. Mr Lyle was her idea of a saint on earth – as he was mine, too. She went over all his virtues and graces, and wound up by telling me that Arthur had had an extremely romantic love-affair, not long before, that had ended unhappily. She didn't seem to be on to the details, but she knew that he had been hit pretty hard. He was paler and thinner, she said, and he had some kind of a remembrance or keepsake of the lady in a little rosewood box that he kept locked in his desk drawer in his study.

'"Several times," says she, "I've seen him gloomerin' over that box of evenings, and he always locks it up right away if anybody comes into the room."

'Well, you can imagine how long it was before I got Arthur by the wrist and led him down stage and hissed in his ear.

'That same afternoon we were lazying around in a boat among the water-lilies at the edge of the bay.

'"Arthur," says I, "you never told me you'd had another love-affair. But Mrs Gurley did," I went on, to let him know I knew. I hate to hear a man lie.

'"Before you came," says he, looking me frankly in the eye, "there was a previous affection – a strong one. Since you know of it, I will be perfectly candid with you."

'"I am waiting," says I.

'"My dear Ida," says Arthur – of course, I went by my real name while I was in Soundport – "this former affection was a spiritual one, in fact. Although the lady aroused my deepest sentiments, and was, as I thought, my ideal woman, I never met her, and never spoke to her. It was an ideal love. My love for you, while no less ideal, is different. You wouldn't let that come between us.'

'"Was she pretty?" I asked.

'"She was very beautiful," said Arthur.

'"Did you see her often?" I asked.

'"Something like a dozen times," says he.

'"Always from a distance?" says I.

'"Always from quite a distance," says he.

'"And you loved her?" I asked.

'"She seemed my ideal of beauty and grace – and soul," says Arthur.

'"And this keepsake that you keep under lock and key, and moon over at times, is that a remembrance from her?"

'"A memento," says Arthur, "that I have treasured."

'"Did she send it to you?"

'"It came to me from her," says he.

'"In a roundabout way?" I asked.

'"Somewhat roundabout," says he, "and yet rather direct."

'"Why didn't you ever meet her?" I asked. "Were your positions in life so different?"

'"She was far above me," says Arthur. "Now, Ida," he goes on, "this is all of the past. You're not going to be jealous, are you?"

'"Jealous!" says I. "Why, man, what are you talking about? It makes me think ten times as much of you as I did before I knew about it."

'And it did, Lynn – if you can understand it. That ideal love was a new one on me, but it struck me as being the most beautiful and glorious thing I'd ever heard of. Think of a man loving a woman he'd never even spoken to, and being faithful just to what his mind and heart pictured her. Oh, it sounded great to me. The men I'd always known come at you with either diamonds, knock-out-drops or a raise of salary – and their ideals! – well, we'll say no more.

'Yes, it made me think more of Arthur than I did before. I couldn't be jealous of that far-away divinity that he used to worship, for I was going to have him myself. And I began to look upon him as a saint on earth, just as old lady Gurley did.

'About four o'clock this afternoon a man came to the house for Arthur to go and see somebody that was sick among his church bunch. Old lady Gurley was taking her afternoon snore on a couch, so that left me pretty much alone.

'In passing by Arthur's study I looked in, and saw his bunch of keys hanging in the drawer of his desk, where he'd forgotten 'em. Well, I guess we're all to the Mrs Bluebeard now and then, ain't we, Lynn? I made up my mind I'd have a look at that memento he kept so secret. Not that I cared what it was – it was just curiosity.

'While I was opening the drawer I imagined one or two things it might be. I thought it might be a dried rosebud she'd dropped down to him from a balcony, or maybe a picture of her he'd cut out of a magazine, she being so high up in the world.

'I opened the drawer, and there was the rosewood casket about the size of a gent's collar box. I found the little key in the bunch that fitted it and unlocked it and raised the lid.

'I took one look at that memento, and then I went to my room and packed my trunk. I threw a few things into my grip, gave my hair a flirt or two with a side-comb, put on my hat, and went in and gave the old lady's foot a kick. I'd tried awfully hard to use proper and correct language while I was there for Arthur's sake, and I had the habit down pat, but it left me then.

'"Stop sawing gourds," says I, "and sit up and take notice. The ghost's about to walk. I'm going away from here, and I owe you eight dollars. The expressman will call for my trunk."

'I handed her the money.

'"Dear me, Miss Crosby!" says she. "Is anything wrong? I thought you were pleased here. Dear me, young women are so hard to understand, and so different from what you expect 'em to be."

'"You're damn right," says I. "Some of 'em are. But you can't say that about men. *When you know one man you know 'em all!* That settles the human-race question."

'And then I caught the four-thirty-eight, soft-coal unlimited; and here I am.'

'You didn't tell me what was in the box, Lee,' said Miss D'Armande anxiously.

'One of those yellow silk garters that I used to kick off my leg into the audience during that old vaudeville swing act of mine. Is there any of the cocktail left, Lynn?'

THE MAN HIGHER UP

Across our two dishes of spaghetti, in a corner of Provenzano's restaurant, Jeff Peters was explaining to me the three kinds of graft.

Every winter Jeff comes to New York to eat spaghetti, to watch the shipping in East River from the depths of his chinchilla overcoat, and to lay in a supply of Chicago-made clothing at one of the Fulton Street stores. During the other three seasons he may be found farther west – his range is from Spokane to Tampa. In his profession he takes a pride which he supports and defends with a serious and unique philosophy of ethics. His profession is no new one. He is an incorporated, uncapitalized, unlimited asylum for the reception of the restless and unwise dollars of his fellow-men.

In the wilderness of stone in which Jeff seeks his annual lonely holiday he is glad to palaver of his many adventures, as a boy will whistle after sundown in a wood. Wherefore, I mark on my calendar the time of his coming, and open a question of privilege at Provenzano's concerning the little wine-stained table in the corner between the rakish rubber plant and the framed palazzio della something on the wall.

'There are two kinds of grafts,' said Jeff, 'that ought to be wiped out by law. I mean Wall Street speculation, and burglary.'

'Nearly everybody will agree with you as to one of them,' said I, with a laugh.

'Well, burglary ought to be wiped out too,' said Jeff; and I wondered whether the laugh had been redundant.

'About three months ago,' said Jeff, 'it was my privilege to become familiar with a sample of each of the aforesaid branches of illegitimate art. I was *sine qua grata* with a member of the housebreakers' union and one of the John D. Napoleons of finance at the same time.'

'Interesting combination,' said I, with a yawn. 'Did I tell you I bagged a duck and a ground-squirrel at one shot last week over in the Ramapos?' I knew well how to draw Jeff's stories.

'Let me tell you first about these barnacles that clog the wheels of society by poisoning the springs of rectitude with their upas-like eye,' said Jeff, with the pure gleam of the muck-raker in his own.

'As I said, three months ago I got into bad company. There are two times in a man's life when he does this – when he's dead broke, and when he's rich.

'Now and then the most legitimate business runs out of luck. It was out in Arkansas I made the wrong turn at a cross-road, and drives into this town of Peavine by mistake. It seems I had already assaulted and disfigured Peavine the spring of the year before. I had sold $600 worth of young fruit trees there – plums, cherries, peaches, and pears. The Peaviners were keeping an eye on the country road and hoping I might pass that way again. I drove down Main Street as far as the Crystal Palace drug-store before I realized I had committed ambush upon myself and my white horse Bill.

'The Peaviners took me by surprise and Bill by the bridle and began a conversation that wasn't entirely dissociated with the subject of fruit trees. A committee of 'em ran some trace-chains through the armholes of my vest, and escorted me through their gardens and orchards.

'Their fruit trees hadn't lived up to their labels. Most of 'em had turned out to be persimmons and dogwoods, with a grove or two of blackjacks and poplars. The only one that showed any signs of bearing anything was a fine young cottonwood that had put forth a hornet's nest and half of an old corset-cover.

'The Peaviners protracted our fruitless stroll to the edge of town. They took my watch and money on account; and they kept Bill and the wagon as hostages. They said the first time one of them dogwood trees put forth an Amsden's June peach I might come back and get my things. Then they took off the trace-chains and jerked their thumbs in the direction of the Rocky Mountains; and I struck a Lewis and Clark lope for the swollen rivers and impenetrable forests.

'When I regained intellectualness I found myself walking into an unidentified town on the A.,T. & S. F. railroad. The Peaviners hadn't left anything in my pockets except a plug of chewing – they wasn't after my life – and that saved it. I bit off a chunk and sits down on a pile of ties by the track to recogitate my sensations of thought and perspicacity.

'And then along comes a fast freight which slows up a little at the town; and off of it drops a black bundle that rolls for twenty yards in a cloud of dust and then gets up and begins to spit soft coal and interjections. I see it is a young man broad across the face, dressed more for Pullmans than freights, and with a cheerful kind of smile in spite of it all that made Phœbe Snow's job look like a chimney-sweep's.

'"Fall off?" says I.

'"Nunk," says he. "Got off. Arrived at my destination. What town is this?"

'"Haven't looked it up on the map yet," says I. "I got in about five minutes before you did. How does it strike you?"

'"Hard," says he, twisting one of his arms around. "I believe that shoulder – no, it's all right."

'He stoops over to brush the dust off his clothes, when out of his pocket drops a fine, nine-inch burglar's steel jimmy. He picks it up and looks at me sharp, and then grins and holds out his hand.

'"Brother," says he, "greetings. Didn't I see you in Southern Missouri last summer selling coloured sand at half a dollar a teaspoonful to put into lamps to keep the oil from exploding?"

'"Oil," says I, "Never explodes. It's the gas that forms that explodes." But I shake hands with him, anyway.

'"My name's Bill Bassett," says he to me, "and if you'll call it professional pride instead of conceit, I'll inform you that you have the pleasure of meeting the best burglar that ever set a gum-shoe on ground drained by the Mississippi River."

'Well, me and this Bill Bassett sits on the ties and exchanges brags as artists in kindred lines will do. It seems he didn't have a cent, either, and we went into close caucus. He explained why an able burglar sometimes had to travel on freights by telling me that a servant girl had played him false in Little Rock, and he was making a quick get-away.

'"It's part of my business," says Bill Bassett, "to play up the ruffles when I want to make a riffle as Raffles. 'Tis loves that makes the bit go 'round. Show me a house with the swag in it and a pretty parlourmaid, and you might as well call the silver melted down and sold, and me spilling truffles and that Château stuff on the napkin under my chin, while the police are calling it an inside job just because the old lady's nephew teaches a Bible class. I first make an impression on the girl," says Bill, "and when she lets me inside I make an impression on the locks. But this one in Little

Rock done me," says he. "She saw me taking a trolley ride with another girl, and when I came round on the night she was to leave the door open for me it was fast. And I had keys made for the doors upstairs. But, no, sir. She had sure cut off my locks. She was a Delilah," says Bill Bassett.

'It seems that Bill tried to break in anyhow with his jimmy, but the girl emitted a succession of bravura noises like the top-riders of a tally-ho, and Bill had to take all the hurdles between there and the depot. As he had no baggage they tried hard to check his departure, but he made a train that was just pulling out.

'"Well," says Bill Bassett, when we had exchanged memoirs of our dead lives, "I could eat. This town don't look like it was kept under a Yale lock. Suppose we commit some mild atrocity that will bring in temporary expense money. I don't suppose you've brought along any hair tonic or rolled-gold watch-chains, or similar law-defying swindles that you could sell on the plaza to the pikers of the paretic populace, have you?"

'"No," says I, "I left an elegant line of Patagonian diamond earrings and rainy-day sunbursts in my valise at Peavine. But they're to stay there till some of them black-gum trees begin to glut the market with yellow clings and Japanese plums. I reckon we can't count on them unless we take Luther Burbank in for a partner."

'"Very well," says Bassett, "we'll do the best we can. Maybe after dark I'll borrow a hairpin from some lady, and open the Farmers' and Drovers' Marine Bank with it."

'While we were talking, up pulls a passenger train to the depot near by. A person in a high hat gets off on the wrong side of the train and comes tripping down the track towards us. He was a little, fat man with a big nose and rat's eyes, but dressed expensive, and carrying a hand-satchel careful, as if it had eggs or railroad bonds in it. He passes by us and keeps on down the track, not appearing to notice the town.

'"Come on," says Bill Bassett to me, starting after him.

'"Where?" I asks.

'"Lordy!" says Bill, "had you forgot you was in the desert? Didn't you see Colonel Manna drop down right before your eyes? Don't you hear the rustling of General Raven's wings? I'm surprised at you, Elijah."

'We overtook the stranger in the edge of some woods, and, as it was after sundown and in a quiet place, nobody saw us stop him. Bill takes the silk hat off the man's head and brushes it with his sleeve and puts it back.

'"What does this mean, sir?" says the man.

'"When I wore one of these," says Bill, "and felt embarrassed, I always done that. Not having one now, I had to use yours. I hardly know how to begin, sir, in explaining our business with you, but I guess we'll try your pockets first."

'Bill Bassett felt in all of them, and looked disgusted.

'"Not even a watch," he says. "Ain't you ashamed of yourself, you whited sculpture? Going about dressed like a head-waiter, and financed like a Count! You haven't even got, car-fare. What did you do with your transfer?"

'The man speaks up and says he has no assets or valuables of any sort. But Bassett takes his hand-satchel and opens it. Out comes some collars and socks and a half a page of newspaper clipped out. Bill reads the clipping careful, and holds out his hand to the held-up party.

'"Brother," says he, "greetings! Accept the apologies of friends. I am Bill Bassett, the burglar. Mr Peters, you must make the acquaintance of Mr Alfred E. Ricks. Shake hands. Mr Peters," says Bill, "stands about half-way between me and you, Mr Ricks, in the line of havoc and corruption. He always gives something for the money he gets. I'm glad to meet you, Mr Ricks – you and Mr Peters. This is the first time I ever attended a full gathering of the National Synod of Sharks – housebreaking, swindling, and financiering all represented. Please examine Mr Ricks's credentials, Mr Peters."

'The piece of newspaper that Bill Bassett handed me had a good picture of this Ricks on it. It was a Chicago paper, and it had obloquies of Ricks in every paragraph. By reading it over I harvested the intelligence that said alleged Ricks had laid off all that portion of the State of Florida that lies under water into town lots and sold 'em to alleged innocent investors from his magnificently furnished offices in Chicago. After he had taken in a hundred thousand or so dollars one of these fussy purchasers that are always making trouble – (I've had 'em actually try gold watches I've sold 'em with acid) – took a cheap excursion down to the land where it is always just before supper to look at his lot and see if it didn't need a new paling or two on the fence, and market a few lemons in time for the Christmas present trade. He hires a surveyor to find his lot for him. They run the line out and find the flourishing town of Paradise Hollow, so advertised, to be about 40 rods and 16 poles S., 27° E., of the middle of Lake Okeechobee. This man's lot was under thirty-six feet of water, and, besides, had been preempted so long by the alligators and gars that his title looked fishy.

'Naturally, the man goes back to Chicago and makes it as hot for Alfred E. Ricks as the morning after a prediction of snow by the weather bureau. Ricks defied the allegation, but he couldn't deny the alligators. One morning the papers came out with a column about it, and Ricks come out by the fire-escape. It seems the alleged authorities had beat him to the safe-deposit box where he kept his winnings, and Ricks has to westward ho! with only feet-wear and a dozen 15½ English pokes in his shopping bag. He happened to have some mileage left in his book, and that took him as far as the town in the wilderness where he was spilled out on me and Bill Bassett as Elijah III with not a raven in sight for any of us.

'Then this Alfred E. Ricks lets out a squeak that he is hungry, too, and denies the hypothesis that he is good for the value, let alone the price, of a meal. And so, there was the three of us, representing, if we had a mind to draw syllogisms and parabolas, labour and trade and capital. Now, when trade has no capital there isn't a dicker to be made. And when capital has no money there's a stagnation in steak and onions. That put it up to the man with the jimmy.

'"Brother bushrangers," says Bill Bassett, "Never yet, in trouble, did I desert a pal. Hard by, in yon wood, I seem to see unfurnished lodgings. Let us go there and wait till dark."

'There was an old, deserted cabin in the grove, and we three took possession of it. After dark Bill Bassett tells us to wait, and goes out for half an hour. He comes back with a armful of bread and spareribs and pies.

'"Panhandled 'em at a farm-house on Washita Avenue," says he. "Eat, drink and be leary."

'The full moon was coming up bright, so we sat on the floor of the cabin and ate in the light of it. And this Bill Bassett begins to brag.

'"Sometimes," says he, with his mouth full of country produce, "I lose all patience with you people that think you are higher up in the profession than I am. Now, what could either of you have done in the present emergency to set us on our feet again? Could you do it, Ricksy?"

"'I must confess, Mr Bassett,' says Ricks, speaking nearly inaudible out of a slice of pie, "that at this immediate juncture I could not, perhaps, promote an enterprise to relieve the situation. Large operations, such as I direct, naturally require careful preparations in advance. I –"

"'I know, Ricksy,' breaks in Bill Bassett. "You needn't finish. You need $500 to make the first payment on a blonde typewriter, and four roomsful of quartered oak furniture. And you need $500 more for advertising contracts. And you need two weeks' time for the fish to begin to bite. Your line of relief would be about as useful in an emergency as advocating municipal ownership to cure a man suffocated by eighty-cent gas. And your graft ain't much swifter, Brother Peters,' he winds up.

"'Oh,' says I, 'I haven't seen you turn anything into gold with your wand yet, Mr Good Fairy. Most anybody could rub the magic ring for a little left-over victuals.'

"'That was only getting the pumpkin ready,' says Bassett, braggy and cheerful. "The coach and six'll drive up to the door before you know it, Miss Cinderella. Maybe you've got some scheme under your sleeve-holders that will give us a start.'

"'Son,' says I, 'I'm fifteen years older than you are, and young enough yet to take out an endowment policy. I've been broke before. We can see the lights of that town not half a mile away. I learned under Montague Silver, the greatest street man that ever spoke from a wagon. There are hundreds of men walking those streets this moment with grease-spots on their clothes. Give me a gasoline lamp, a dry-goods box, and a two-dollar bar of white castile soap, cut into little –"

"'Where's your two dollars?' snickered Bill Bassett into my discourse. There was no use arguing with that burglar.

"'No,' he goes on; "you're both babes-in-the-wood. Finance has closed the mahogany desk, and trade has put the shutters up. Both of you look to labour to start the wheels going. All right. You admit it. To-night I'll show you what Bill Bassett can do.'

'Bassett tells me and Ricks not to leave the cabin till he comes back, even if it's daylight, and then he starts off toward town, whistling gay.

'This Alfred E. Ricks pulls off his shoes and his coat, lays a silk handkerchief over his hat, and lays down on the floor.

"'I think I will endeavour to secure a little slumber,' he

squeaks. "The day has been fatiguing. Good night, my dear Mr
Peters."

'"My regards to Morpheus," says I. "I think I'll sit up a while."

'About two o'clock, as near as I could guess by my watch in
Peavine, home comes our labouring man and kicks up Ricks, and
calls us to the streak of bright moonlight shining in the cabin door.
Then he spreads out five packages of one thousand dollars each
on the floor, and begins to cackle over the nest-egg like a hen.

'"I'll tell you a few things about that town," says he. "It's
named Rocky Springs, and they're building a Masonic temple,
and it looks like the Democratic candidate for mayor is going to
get soaked by a Pop, and Judge Tucker's wife, who has been down
with pleurisy, is some better. I had a talk on these lilliputian
thesises before I could get a siphon in the fountain of knowledge
that I was after. And there's a bank there called the Lumberman's
Fidelity and Ploughman's Savings Institution. It closed for business yesterday with $23,000 cash on hand. It will open this
morning with $18,000 – all silver – that's the reason I didn't bring
more. There you are, trade and capital. Now, will you be bad?"

'"My young friend," says Alfred E. Ricks, holding up his
hands, "have you robbed this bank? Dear me, dear me!"

'"You couldn't call it that," says Bassett. "'Robbing' sounds
harsh. All I had to do was to find out what street it was on. That
town is so quiet that I could stand on the corner and hear the
tumblers clicking in that safe lock – 'right to 45; left twice to 80;
right once to 60; left to 15' – as plain as the Yale captain giving
orders in the football dialect. Now, boys," says Bassett, "this is
an early rising town. They tell me the citizens are all up and
stirring before daylight. I asked what for, and they said because
breakfast was ready at that time. And what of merry Robin Hood?
It must be Yoicks! and away with the tinkers' chorus. I'll stake
you. How much do you want? Speak up, Capital."

'"My dear young friend," says this ground squirrel of a Ricks,
standing on his hind legs and juggling nuts in his paws, "I have
friends in Denver who would assist me. If I had a hundred dollars
I –"

'Bassett unpins a package of the currency and throws five
twenties to Ricks.

'"Trade, how much?" he says to me.

'"Put your money up, Labour," says I. "I never yet drew upon
honest toil for its hard-earned pittance. The dollars I get are

surplus ones that are burning the pockets of damfools and green-horns. When I stand on a street corner and sell a solid gold diamond ring to a yap for $3.00, I make just $2.60. And I know he's going to give it to a girl in return for all the benefits accruing from a $125.00 ring. His profits are $122.00. Which of us is the biggest faker?"

'"And when you sell a poor woman a pinch of sand for fifty cents to keep her lamp from exploding," says Bassett, "what do you figure her gross earnings to be, with sand at forty cents a ton?"

'"Listen," says I. "I instruct her to keep her lamp clean and well filled. If she does that it can't burst. And with the sand in it she knows it can't, and she don't worry. It's a kind of Industrial Christian Science. She pays fifty cents, and gets both Rockefeller and Mrs Eddy on the job. It ain't everybody that can let the gold-dust twins do their work."

'Alfred E. Ricks all but licks the dust off of Bill Bassett's shoes.

'"My dear young friend," says he, "I will never forget your generosity. Heaven will reward you. But let me implore you to turn from your ways of violence and crime."

'"Mousie," says Bill, "the hole in the wainscoting for yours. Your dogmas and inculcations sound to me like the last words of a bicycle pump. What has your high moral, elevator-service system of pillage brought you to? Penuriousness and want. Even Brother Peters, who insists upon contaminating the art of robbery with theories of commerce and trade, admitted he was on the lift. Both of you live by the gilded rule. Brother Peters," says Bill, "you'd better choose a slice of this embalmed currency. You're welcome."

'I told Bill Bassett once more to put his money in his pocket. I had never had the respect for burglary that some people have. I always gave something for the money I took, even if it was only some little trifle for a souvenir to remind 'em not to get caught again.

'And then Alfred E. Ricks grovels at Bill's feet again, and bids us adieu. He says he will have a team at a farm-house, and drive to the station below, and take the train for Denver. It salubrified the atmosphere when that lamentable bollworm took his departure. He was a disgrace to every non-industrial profession in the country. With all his big schemes and fine offices he had wound up unable even to get an honest meal except by the kindness of a strange and maybe unscrupulous burglar. I was glad to see him go, though I felt a little sorry for him, now that he was ruined for ever. What could such a man do without a big capital to work with? Why, Alfred E. Ricks, as we left him, was as helpless as a turtle on its back. He couldn't have worked a scheme to beat a little girl out of a penny slate-pencil.

'When me and Bill Bassett was left alone I did a little sleight-of-mind turn in my head with a trade secret at the end of it. Thinks I, I'll show this Mr Burglar Man the difference between business and labour. He had hurt some of my professional and self-adulation by casting his Persians upon commerce and trade.

'"I won't take any of your money as a gift, Mr Bassett," says I to him, "but if you'll pay my expenses as a travelling companion until we get out of the danger zone of the immoral deficit you have caused in this town's finances tonight, I'll be obliged."

'Bill Bassett agreed to that, and we hiked westward as soon as we could catch a safe train.

'When we got to a town in Arizona called Los Perros I suggested that we once more try our luck on terra-cotta. That was the home of Montague Silver, my old instructor, now retired from business. I knew Monty would stake me to web money if I could show him a fly buzzing 'round in the locality. Bill Bassett said all towns looked alike to him as he worked mainly in the dark. So we got off the train in Los Perros, a fine little town in the silver region.

'I had an elegant little sure thing in the way of a commercial slungshot that I intended to hit Bassett behind the ear with. I wasn't going to take his money while he was asleep, but I was going to leave him with a lottery ticket that would represent in experience to him $4,755 – I think that was the amount he had when we got off the train. But the first time I hinted to him about an investment, he turns on me and disencumbers himself of the following terms and expressions.

'"Brother Peters," says he, "it ain't a bad idea to go into an enterprise of some kind, as you suggest. I think I will. But if I do it will be such a cold proposition that nobody but Robert E. Peary and Charlie Fairbanks will be able to sit on the board of directors."

'"I thought you might want to turn your money over," says I

'"I do," says he, "frequently. I can't sleep on one side all night I'll tell you, Brother Peters," says he, "I'm going to start a poker room. I don't seem to care for the humdrum in swindling, such a peddling egg-beaters and working off breakfast food on Barnum and Bailey for sawdust to strew in their circus rings. But the gambling business," says he, "from the profitable side of the table is a good compromise between swiping silver spoons and selling pen-wipers at a Waldorf-Astoria charity bazaar."

'"Then," says I, "Mr Bassett, you don't care to talk over my little business proposition?"

'"Why," says he, "do you know, you can't get a Pasteur institute to start up within fifty miles of where I live. I bite so seldom."

'So, Bassett rents a room over a saloon and looks around for some furniture and chromos. The same night I went to Monty Silver's house, and he let me have $200 on my prospects. Then I went to the only store in Los Perros that sold playing cards and bought every deck in the house. The next morning when the store opened I was there bringing all the cards back with me. I said that my partner that was going to back me in the game had changed his mind; and I wanted to sell the cards back again. The store-keeper took 'em at half price.

'Yes, I was seventy-five dollars loser up to that time. But while I had the cards that night I marked every one in every deck. That was labour. And then trade and commerce had their innings, and the bread I had cast upon the waters began to come back in the form of cottage pudding with wine sauce.

'Of course I was among the first to buy chips at Bill Bassett's game. He had bought the only cards there was to be had in town, and I knew the back of every one of them better than I know the back of my head when the barber shows me my haircut in the two mirrors.

'When the game closed I had the five thousand and a few odd dollars, and all Bill Bassett had was the wanderlust and a black cat he had bought for a mascot. Bill shook hands with me when I left.

'"Brother Peters," says he, "I have no business being in business. I was preordained to labour. When a No. 1 burglar tries to make a James out of his jimmy he perpetrates an improfundity. You have a well-oiled and efficacious system of luck at cards," says he. "Peace go with you." And I never afterward sees Bill Bassett again.'

'Well, Jeff,' said I, when the Autolycan adventurer seemed to have divulged the gist of his tale, 'I hope you took care of the money. That would be a respecta – that is a considerable working capital if you should choose some day to settle down to some sort of regular business.'

'Me ?' said Jeff virtuously. 'You can bet I've taken care of that five thousand.'

He tapped his coat over the region of his chest exultantly.

'Gold mining stock,' he explained, 'every cent of it. Shares par value one dollar. Bound to go up 500 per cent. within a year. Non-assessable. The Blue Gopher Mine. Just discovered a month ago. Better get in yourself if you've any spare dollars on hand.'

'Sometimes,' said I, 'these mines are not –'

'Oh, this one's solid as an old goose,' said Jeff. 'Fifty thousand dollars' worth of ore in sight, and 10 per cent. monthly earnings guaranteed.'

He drew a long envelope from his pocket and cast it on the table.

'Always carry it with me,' said he. 'So the burglar can't corrupt or the capitalist break in and water it.'

I looked at the beautifully engraved certificate of stock.

'In Colorado, I see,' said I. 'And, by the way, Jeff, what was the name of the little man who went to Denver – the one you and Bill met at the station?'

'Alfred E. Ricks,' said Jeff, 'was the toad's designation.'

'I see,' said I, 'the president of this mining company signs himself A. L. Fredericks. I was wondering –'

'Let me see that stock,' said Jeff quickly, almost snatching it from me.

To mitigate, even though slightly, the embarrassment I summoned the waiter and ordered another bottle of the Barbera. I thought it was the least I could do.

A MUNICIPAL REPORT

East is East, and West is San Francisco, according to Californians. Californians are a race of people; they are not merely inhabitants of a State. They are the Southerners of the West. Now, Chicagoans are no less loyal to their city; but when you ask them why, they stammer and speak of lake fish and the new Odd Fellows Building. But Californians go into detail.

Of course they have, in the climate, an argument that is good for half an hour while you are thinking of your coal bills and heavy underwear. But as soon as they come to mistake your silence for conviction, madness comes upon them, and they picture the city of the Golden Gate as the Bagdad of the New World. So far, as a matter of opinion, no refutation is necessary. But, dear cousins all (from Adam and Eve descended), it is a rash one who will lay his finger on the map and say: 'In this town there can be no romance – what could happen here?' Yes, it is a bold and rash deed to challenge in one sentence history, romance, and Rand and McNally.

NASHVILLE. – A city, port of delivery, and the capital of the State of Tennessee, is on the Cumberland River and on the N.C. & St L. and the L. & N. railroads. This city is regarded as the most important educational centre in the South.

I stepped off the train at 8 p.m. Having searched the thesaurus in vain for adjectives, I must, as a substitution, hie me to comparison in the form of a recipe.

Take of London fog 30 parts; malaria 10 parts; gas leaks 20 parts; dewdrops, gathered in a brickyard at sunrise, 25 parts; odour of honeysuckle 15 parts. Mix.

The mixture will give you an approximate conception of a Nashville drizzle. It is not so fragrant as a moth-ball nor as thick as pea-soup; but 'tis enough – 'twill serve.

I went to an hotel in a tumbril. It required strong self-suppression for me to keep from climbing to the top of it and giving an imitation of Sydney Carton. The vehicle was drawn by beasts of a bygone era and driven by something dark and emancipated.

I was sleepy and tired, so when I got to the hotel I hurriedly paid it the fifty cents it demanded (with approximate lagniappe, I assure you). I knew its habits; and I did not want to hear it prate about its old 'marster' or anything that happened 'befo' de wah.'

The hotel was one of the kind described as 'renovated.' That means $20,000 worth of new marble pillars, tiling, electric lights and brass cuspidors in the lobby, and a new L. & N. time-table and a lithograph of Lookout Mountain in each one of the great rooms above. The management was without reproach, the attention full of exquisite Southern courtesy, the service as slow as the progress of a snail and as good-humoured as Rip Van Winkle. The food was worth travelling a thousand miles for. There is no other hotel in the world where you can get such chicken livers *en brochette*.

At dinner I asked a negro waiter if there was anything doing in town. He pondered gravely for a minute, and then replied: 'Well, boss, I don't really reckon there's anything at all doin' after sundown.'

Sundown had been accomplished; it had been drowned in the drizzle long before. So that spectacle was denied me. But I went forth upon the streets in the drizzle to see what might be there.

It is built on undulating grounds; and the streets are lighted by electricity at a cost of $32,470 per annum.

As I left the hotel there was a race riot. Down upon me charged a company of freedmen, or Arabs, or Zulus, armed with – no, I saw with relief that they were not rifles, but whips. And I saw dimly a caravan of black, clumsy vehicles; and at the reassuring shouts, 'Kyar you anywhere in the town, boss, fuh fifty cents,' I reasoned that I was merely a 'fare' instead of a victim.

I walked through long streets, all leading uphill. I wondered how those streets ever came down again. Perhaps they didn't until they were 'graded.' On a few of the 'main streets' I saw lights in stores here and there; saw street-cars go by conveying worthy burghers hither and yon; saw people pass engaged in the art of conversation, and heard a burst of semi-lively laughter issuing

from a soda-water and ice-cream parlour. The streets other than
'main' seemed to have enticed upon their borders houses conse-
crated to peace and domesticity. In many of them lights shone
behind discreetly drawn window shades; in a few pianos tinkled
orderly and irreproachable music. There was, indeed, little 'doing.'
I wished I had come before sundown. So I returned to my hotel.

In November, 1864, the Confederate General Hood advanced against
Nashville, where he shut up a National force under General Thomas.
The latter then sallied forth and defeated the confederates in a terrible
conflict.

All my life I have heard of, admired, and witnessed the fine
markmanship of the South in its peaceful conflicts in the tobacco-
chewing regions. But in my hotel a surprise awaited me. There
were twelve bright, new, imposing, capacious brass cuspidors in
the great lobby, tall enough to be called urns and so wide-mouthed
that the crack pitcher of a lady baseball team should have been
able to throw a ball into one of them at five paces distant. But,
although a terrible battle had raged and was still raging, the enemy
had not suffered. Bright, new, imposing, capacious, untouched,
they stood. But shades of Jefferson Brick! the tile floor – the
beautiful tile floor! I could not avoid thinking of the battle of
Nashville, and trying to draw, as is my foolish habit, some
deductions about hereditary markmanship.

Here I first saw Major (by misplaced courtesy) Wentworth
Caswell. I knew him for a type the moment my eyes suffered from
the sight of him. A rat has no geographical habitat. My old friend,
A. Tennyson, said, as he so well said almost everything:

> 'Prophet, curse me the blabbing lip,
> And curse me the British vermin, the rat.'

Let us regard the word 'British' as interchangeable *ad lib*. A rat
is a rat.

This man was hunting about the hotel lobby like a starved dog
that had forgotten where he had buried a bone. He had a face of
great acreage, red, pulpy, and with a kind of sleepy massiveness
like that of Buddha. He possessed one single virtue – he was very
smoothly shaven. The mark of the beast is not indelible upon a
man until he goes about with a stubble. I think that if he had not
used his razor that day I would have repulsed his advances, and
the criminal calendar of the world would have been spared the
addition of one murder.

I happened to be standing within five feet of a cuspidor when
Major Caswell opened fire upon it. I had been observant enough
to perceive that the attacking force was using Gatlings instead of
squirrel rifles; so I side-stepped so promptly that the major seized
the opportunity to apologize to a non-combatant. He had the
blabbing lip. In four minutes he had become my friend and had
dragged me to the bar.

I desire to interpolate here that I am a Southerner. But I am not
one by profession or trade. I eschew the string tie, the slouch hat,
the Prince Albert, the number of bales of cotton destroyed by
Sherman, and plug chewing. When the orchestra plays Dixie I do
not cheer. I slide a little lower on the leather-cornered seat and,
well, order another Würzburger and wish that Longstreet had –
but what's the use?

Major Caswell banged the bar with his fist, and the first gun
at Fort Sumter re-echoed. When he fired the last one at Appomat-
tox I began to hope. But then he began on family trees, and
demonstrated that Adam was only a third cousin of a collateral
branch of the Caswell family. Genealogy disposed of, he took up,
to my distaste, his private family matters. He spoke of his wife,
traced her descent back to Eve, and profanely denied any
possible rumour that she may have had relations in the land of
Nod.

By this time I began to suspect that he was trying to obscure
by noise the fact that he had ordered the drinks, on the chance
that I would be bewildered into paying for them. But when they
were down he crashed a silver dollar loudly upon the bar. Then,
of course, another serving was obligatory. And when I had paid
for that I took leave of him brusquely; for I wanted no more of
him. But before I had obtained my release he had prated loudly
of an income that his wife received, and showed a handful of silver
money.

When I got my key at the desk the clerk said to me courteously:
'If that man Caswell has annoyed you, and if you would like to
make a complaint, we will have him ejected. He is a nuisance, a
loafer, and without any known means of support, although he
seems to have some money most of the time. But we don't seem
to be able to hit upon any means of throwing him out legally.'

'Why, no,' said I, after some reflection; 'I don't see my way
clear to making a complaint. But I would like to place myself on
record as asserting that I do not care for his company. Your town,'

I continued, 'seems to be a quiet one. What manner of entertainment, adventure, or excitement have you to offer to the stranger within your gates?'

'Well, sir,' said the clerk, 'there will be a show here next Thursday. It is – I'll look it up and have the announcement sent up to your room with the ice water. Good night.'

After I went up to my room I looked out of the window. It was only about ten o'clock, but I looked upon a silent town. The drizzle continued, spangled with dim lights, as far apart as currants in a cake sold at the Ladies' Exchange.

'A quiet place,' I said to myself, as my first shoe struck the ceiling of the occupant of the room beneath mine. 'Nothing of the life here that gives colour and variety to the cities in the East and West. Just a good, ordinary, humdrum business town.'

Nashville occupies a foremost place among the manufacturing centres of the country. It is the fifth boot and shoe market in the United States, the largest candy and cracker manufacturing city in the South, and does an enormous wholesale dry goods, grocery and drug business.

I must tell you how I came to be in Nashville, and assure you the digression brings as much tedium to me as it does to you. I was travelling elsewhere on my own business, but I had a commission from a Northern literary magazine to stop over there and establish a personal connection between the publication and one of its contributors, Azalea Adair.

Adair (there was no clue to the personality except the handwriting) had sent in some essays (lost art!) and poems that had made the editors swear approvingly over their one o'clock luncheon. So they had commissioned me to round up said Adair and corner by contract his or her output at two cents a word before some other publisher offered her ten or twenty.

At nine o'clock the next morning, after my chicken livers *en brochette* (try them if you can find that hotel), I strayed out into the drizzle, which was still on for an unlimited run. At the first corner I came upon Uncle Cæsar. He was a stalwart negro older than the pyramids, with grey wool and a face that reminded me of Brutus, and a second afterwards of the late King Cetewayo. He wore the most remarkable coat that I ever had seen or expect to see. It reached to his ankles and had once been a Confederate grey in colours. But rain and sun and age had so variegated it that Joseph's coat, beside it, would have faded to a pale monochrome. I must linger with that coat for it has to do with the story – the story that is so long in coming, because you can hardly expect anything to happen in Nashville.

Once it must have been the military coat of an officer. The cape of it had vanished, but all adown its front it had been frogged and tasselled magnificently. But now the frogs and tassels were gone. In their stead had been patiently stitched (I surmised by some surviving 'black mammy') new frogs made of cunningly twisted common hempen twine. This twine was frayed and dishevelled. It must have been added to the coat as a substitute for vanished splendours, with tasteless but painstaking devotion, for it followed faithfully the curves of the long-missing frogs. And, to complete the comedy and pathos of the garment, all its buttons were gone save one. The second button from the top alone remained. The coat was fastened by other twine strings tied through the button-holes and other holes rudely pierced in the opposite side. There was never such a weird garment so fantastically bedecked and of so many mottled hues. The lone button was the size of a half-dollar, made of yellow horn and sewed on with coarse twine.

This negro stood by a carriage so old that Ham himself might have started a hack line with it after he left the ark with the two animals hitched to it. As I approached he threw open the door, drew out a feather duster, waved it, without using it, and said in deep, rumbling tones:

'Step right in, suh; ain't a speck of dust in it – jus' back from a funeral, suh.'

I inferred that on such gala occasions carriages were given an extra cleaning. I looked up and down the street and perceived that there was little choice among the vehicles for hire that lined the kerb. I looked in my memorandum book for the address of Azalea Adair.

'I want to go to 861 Jessamine Street,' I said, and was about to step into the hack. But for an instant the thick, long, gorilla-like arm of the old negro barred me. On his massive and saturnine face a look of sudden suspicion and enmity flashed for a moment. Then, with quickly returning conviction, he asked blandishingly: 'What are you gwine there for, boss?'

'What is that to you?' I asked a little sharply.

'Nothin', suh, jus' nothin'. Only it's a lonesome kind of part of town and few folks ever has business out there. Step right in. The seats is clean – jes' got back from a funeral, suh.'

A mile and a half it must have been to our journey's end. I could hear nothing but the fearful rattle of the ancient hack over the uneven brick paving; I could smell nothing but the drizzle, now further flavoured with coal smoke and something like a mixture of tar and oleander blossoms. All I could see through the streaming windows were two rows of dim houses.

The city has an area of 10 square miles; 181 miles of streets, of which 137 miles are paved; a system of waterworks that cost $2,000,000, with 77 miles of mains.

Eight-sixty-one Jessamine Street was a decayed mansion. Thirty yards back from the street it stood, outmerged in a splendid grove of trees and untrimmed shrubbery. A row of box bushes overflowed and almost hid the paling fence from sight; the gate was kept closed by a rope noose that encircled the gate-post and the first paling of the gate. But when you got inside you saw that 861 was a shell, a shadow, a ghost of former grandeur and excellence. But in the story, I have not yet got inside.

When the hack had ceased from rattling and the weary quadrupeds came to a rest I handed my jehu his fifty cents with an additional quarter, feeling a glow of conscious generosity as I did so. He refused it.

'It's two dollars, suh,' he said.

'How's that?' I asked. 'I plainly heard you call out at the hotel: "Fifty cents to any part of the town."'

'It's two dollars, suh,' he repeated obstinately. 'It's a long ways from the hotel.'

'It is within the city limits and well within them,' I argued. 'Don't think that you have picked up a greenhorn Yankee. Do you see those hills over there?' I went on, pointing toward the east (I could not see them, myself, for the drizzle); 'well, I was born and raised on their other side. You old fool nigger, can't you tell people from other people when you see 'em?'

The grim face of King Cetewayo softened. 'Is you from the South, suh? I reckon it was them shoes of yourn fooled me. There is somethin' sharp in the toes for a Southern gen'l'man to wear.'

'Then the charge is fifty cents, I suppose?' said I inexorably.

His former expression, a mingling of cupidity and hostility, returned, remained ten minutes, and vanished.

'Boss,' he said, 'fifty cents is right; but I *needs* two dollars, suh; I'm *obleeged* to have two dollars. I ain't *demandin'* it now, suh; after I knows whar you's from; I'm jus' sayin' that I *has* to have two dollars to-night, and business is mighty po'.'

Peace and confidence settled upon his heavy features. He had been luckier than he had hoped. Instead of having picked up a greenhorn, ignorant of rates, he had come upon an inheritance.

'You confounded old rascal,' I said, reaching down into my pocket, 'you ought to be turned over to the police.'

For the first time I saw him smile. He knew; *he knew*; HE KNEW.

I gave him two one-dollar bills. As I handed them over I noticed that one of them had seen parlous times. Its upper right-hand corner was missing, and it had been torn through in the middle, but joined again. A strip of blue tissue-paper, pasted over the split, preserved its negotiability.

Enough of the African bandit for the present: I left him happy, lifted the rope and opened the creaky gate.

The house, as I said, was a shell. A paint-brush had not touched it in twenty years. I could not see why a strong wind should not have bowled it over like a house of cards until I looked again at the trees that hugged it close – the trees that saw the battle of Nashville and still drew their protecting branches around it against storm and enemy and cold.

Azalea Adair, fifty years old, white-haired, a descendant of the cavaliers, as thin and frail as the house she lived in, robed in the cheapest and cleanest dress I ever saw, with an air as simple as a queen's, received me.

The reception-room seemed a mile square, because there was nothing in it except some rows of books, on unpainted, white-pine bookshelves, a cracked, marble-top table, a rag rug, a hairless horsehair sofa and two or three chairs. Yes, there was a picture on the wall, a coloured crayon drawing of a cluster of pansies. I looked around for the portrait of Andrew Jackson and the pine-cone hanging basket, but they were not there.

Azalea Adair and I had conversation, a little of which will be repeated to you. She was a product of the old South, gently nurtured in the sheltered life. Her learning was not broad, but was deep and of splendid originality in its somewhat narrow scope. She had been educated at home, and her knowledge of the world was derived from inference and by inspiration. Of such is the precious, small group of essayists made. While she talked to me, I kept brushing my fingers, trying, unconsciously, to rid them guiltily of the absent dust from the half-calf backs of Lamb, Chaucer, Hazlitt, Marcus Aurelius, Montaigne and Hood. She was exquisite, she was a valuable discovery. Nearly everybody nowadays knows too much – oh, so much too much – of real life.

I could perceive clearly that Azalea Adair was very poor. A house and a dress she had, not much else, I fancied. So, divided between my duty to the magazine and my loyalty to the poets and essayists who fought Thomas in the valley of the Cumberland, I listened to her voice, which was like a harpsichord's, and found that I could not speak of contracts. In the presence of the Nine Muses and the Three Graces one hesitated to lower the topic to two cents. There would have to be another colloquy after I had regained my commercialism. But I spoke of my mission, and three o'clock of the next afternoon was set for the discussion of the business proposition.

'Your town,' I said, as I began to make ready to depart (which is the time for smooth generalities), 'seems to be a quiet, sedate place. A home town, I should say, where few things out of the ordinary ever happen.'

It carries on an extensive trade in stoves and hollow ware with the West and South, and its flouring mills have a daily capacity of more than 2,000 barrels.

Azalea Adair seemed to reflect.

'I have never thought of it that way,' she said, with a kind of sincere intensity that seemed to belong to her. 'Isn't it in the still, quiet places that things do happen? I fancy that when God began to create the earth on the first Monday morning one could have leaned out one's windows and heard the drop of mud splashing from His trowel as He built up the everlasting hills. What did the noisiest project in the world – I mean the building of the tower of Babel – result in finally? A page and a half of Esperanto in the *North American Review*.'

'Of course,' said I platitudinously, 'human nature is the same everywhere; but there is more colour – er – more drama and movement and – er – romance in some cities than in others.'

'On the surface,' said Azalea Adair. 'I have travelled many times around the world in a golden airship wafted on two wings – print and dreams. I have seen (on one of my imaginary tours) the Sultan of Turkey bow-string with his own hands one of his wives who had uncovered her face in public. I have seen a man in Nashville tear up his theatre tickets because his wife was going out with her face covered – with rice powder. In San Francisco's

Chinatown I saw the slave girl Sing Yee dipped slowly, inch by inch, in boiling almond oil to make her swear she would never see her American lover again. She gave in when the boiling oil had reached three inches above her knee. At a euchre party in East Nashville the other night I saw Kitty Morgan cut dead by seven of her schoolmates and lifelong friends because she had married a house painter. The boiling oil was sizzling as high as her heart; but I wish you could have seen the fine little smile that she carried from table to table. Oh yes, it is a humdrum town. Just a few miles of red-brick houses and mud and stores and lumber yards.'

Someone knocked hollowly at the back of the house. Azalea Adair breathed a soft apology and went to investigate the sound. She came back in three minutes with brightened eyes, a faint flush on her cheeks, and ten years lifted from her shoulders.

'You must have a cup of tea before you go,' she said, 'and a sugar cake.'

She reached and shook a little iron bell. In shuffled a small negro girl about twelve, bare-foot, not very tidy, glowering at me with thumb in mouth and bulging eyes.

Azalea Adair opened a tiny, worn purse and drew out a dollar bill, a dollar bill with the upper right-hand corner missing, torn in two pieces and pasted together again with a strip of blue tissue-paper. It was one of the bills I had given the piratical negro – there was no doubt of it.

'Go up to Mr Baker's store on the corner, Impy,' she said, handing the girl the dollar bill, 'and get a quarter of a pound of tea – the kind he always sends me – and ten cents' worth of sugar cakes. Now, hurry. The supply of tea in the house happens to be exhausted,' she explained to me.

Impy left by the back way. Before the scrape of her hard, bare feet had died away on the back porch, a wild shriek – I was sure it was hers – filled the hollow house. Then the deep, gruff tones of an angry man's voice mingled with the girl's further squeals and unintelligible words.

Azalea Adair rose without surprise or emotion and disappeared. For two minutes I heard the hoarse rumble of the man's voice; then something like an oath and a light scuffle, and she returned calmly to her chair.

'This is a roomy house,' she said, 'and I have a tenant for part of it. I am sorry to have to rescind my invitation to tea. It was impossible to get the kind I always use at the store. Perhaps tomorrow Mr Baker will be able to supply me.'

I was sure that Impy had not had time to leave the house. I inquired concerning street-car lines and took my leave. After I was well on my way I remembered that I had not learned Azalea Adair's name. But to-morrow would do.

That same day I started in on the course of iniquity that this uneventful city forced upon me. I was in the town only two days, but in that time I managed to lie shamelessly by telegraph, and to be an accomplice – after the fact, if that is the correct legal term – to a murder.

As I rounded the corner nearest my hotel the Afrite coachman of the polychromatic, nonpareil coat seized me, swung open the dungeony door of his peripatetic sarcophagus, flirted with his feather duster and began his ritual: 'Step right in, boss. Carriage is clean – jus' got back from a funeral. Fifty cents to any –'

And then he knew me and grinned broadly. ''Scuse me, boss; you is de gen'l'man what rid out with me dis mawnin'. Thank you kindly, suh.'

'I am going out to 861 again to-morrow afternoon at three,' said I, 'and if you will be here, I'll let you drive me. So you know Miss Adair?' I concluded, thinking of my dollar bill.

'I belonged to her father, Judge Adair, suh,' he replied.

'I judge that she is pretty poor,' I said. 'She hasn't much money to speak of, has she?'

For an instant I looked again at the fierce countenance of King Cetewayo, and then he changed back to an extortionate old negro hack-driver.

'She a'n't gwine to starve, suh,' he said slowly. 'She has reso'ces, suh; she has reso'ces.'

'I shall pay you fifty cents for the trip,' said I.

'Dat is puffickly correct, suh,' he answered humbly. 'I jus' *had* to have dat two dollars dis mawnin', boss.'

I went to the hotel and lied by electricity. I wired the magazine: 'A. Adair holds out for eight cents a word.'

The answer that came back was: 'Give it to her quick, you duffer.'

Just before dinner 'Major' Wentworth Caswell bore down upon me with the greetings of a long-lost friend. I have seen few men whom I have so instantaneously hated, and of whom it was so difficult to be rid. I was standing at the bar when he invaded me; therefore I could not wave the white ribbon in his face. I would have paid gladly for the drinks, hoping thereby to escape another; but he was one of those despicable, roaring, advertising bibbers who must have brass bands and fireworks attend upon every cent that they waste in their follies.

With an air of producing millions he drew two one-dollar bills from a pocket and dashed one of them upon the bar. I looked once more at the dollar bill with the upper right-hand corner missing, torn through the middle, and patched with a strip of blue tissue-paper. It was my dollar bill again. It could have been no other.

I went up to my room. The drizzle and the monotony of a dreary, eventless Southern town had made me tired and listless. I remember that just before I went to bed I mentally disposed of the mysterious dollar bill (which might have formed the clue to a tremendously fine detective story of San Francisco) by saying to myself sleepily: 'Seems as if a lot of people here own stock in the Hack-Driver's Trust. Pays dividends promptly, too. Wonder if –' Then I fell asleep.

King Cetewayo was at his post the next day, and rattled my bones over the stones out to 861. He was to wait and rattle me back again when I was ready.

Azalea Adair looked paler and cleaner and frailer than she had looked on the day before. After she had signed the contract at eight cents per word she grew still paler and began to slip out of her chair. Without much trouble I managed to get her up on the antediluvian horsehair sofa and then I ran out to the sidewalk and yelled to the coffee-coloured Pirate to bring a doctor. With a wisdom that I had not suspected in him, he abandoned his team and struck off up the street afoot, realizing the value of speed. In ten minutes he returned with a grave, grey-haired and capable man of medicine. In a few words (worth much less than eight cents each) I explained to him my presence in the hollow house of mystery. He bowed with stately understanding, and turned to the old negro.

'Uncle Cæsar,' he said calmly, 'run up to my house and ask Miss Lucy to give you a cream pitcher full of fresh milk and half a tumbler of port wine. And hurry back. Don't drive – run. I want you to get back some time this week.'

It occurred to me that Dr Merriman also felt a distrust as to the speeding powers of the land-pirate's steeds. After Uncle Cæsar was gone, lumbering, but swiftly, up the street, the doctor looked me over with great politeness and as much careful calculation until he had decided that I might do.

'It is only a case of insufficient nutrition,' he said. 'In other words, the result of poverty, pride, and starvation. Mrs Caswell has many devoted friends who would be glad to aid her, but she will accept nothing except from that old negro, Uncle Cæsar, who was once owned by her family.'

'Mrs Caswell!' said I, in surprise. And then I looked at the contract and saw that she had signed it 'Azalea Adair Caswell.'

'I thought she was Miss Adair,' I said.

'Married to a drunken, worthless loafer, sir,' said the doctor. 'It is said that he robs her even of the small sums that her old servant contributes toward her support.'

When the milk and wine had been brought, the doctor soon revived Azalea Adair. She sat up and talked of the beauty of the autumn leaves that were then in season, and their height of colour. She referred lightly to her fainting seizure as the outcome of an old palpitation of the heart. Impy fanned her as she lay on the sofa. The doctor was due elsewhere, and I followed him to the door. I told him that it was within my power and intentions to make a reasonable advance of money to Azalea Adair on future contributions to the magazine, and he seemed pleased.

'By the way,' he said, 'perhaps you would like to know that you have had royalty for a coachman. Old Cæsar's grandfather was a king in Congo. Cæsar himself has royal ways, as you may have observed.'

As the doctor was moving off I heard Uncle Cæsar's voice inside: 'Did he git bofe of dem two dollars from you, Mis' Zalea?'

'Yes, Cæsar,' I heard Azalea Adair answer weakly. And then I went in and concluded business negotiations with our contributor. I assumed the responsibility of advancing fifty dollars, putting it as a necessary formality in binding our bargain. And then Uncle Cæsar drove me back to the hotel.

Here ends all the story as far as I can testify as a witness. The rest must be only bare statements of facts.

At about six o'clock I went out for a stroll. Uncle Cæsar was at his corner. He threw open the door of his carriage, flourished his duster and began his depressing formula: 'Step right in, suh. Fifty cents to anywhere in the city – hack's puffickly clean, suh – jus' got back from a funeral –'

And then he recognized me. I think his eyesight was getting bad. His coat had taken on a few more faded shades of colour, the twine strings were more frayed and ragged, the last remaining button – the button of yellow horn – was gone. A motley descendant of kings was Uncle Cæsar.

About two hours later I saw an excited crowd besieging the front of a drug store. In a desert where nothing happens this was manna; so I edged my way inside. On an extemporized couch of empty boxes and chairs was stretched the mortal corporeality of Major Wentworth Caswell. A doctor was testing him for the immortal ingredient. His decision was that it was conspicuous by its absence.

The erstwhile Major had been found dead on a dark street and brought by curious and ennuied citizens to the drug store. The late human being had been engaged in terrific battle – the details showed that. Loafer and reprobate though he had been, he had been also a warrior. But he had lost. His hands were yet clenched so tightly that his fingers would not be opened. The gentle citizens who had known him stood about and searched their vocabularies to find some good words, if it were possible, to speak of him. One kind-looking man said, after much thought: 'When "Cas" was about fo'teen he was one of the best spellers in school.'

While I stood there the fingers of the right hand of 'the man that was,' which hung down the side of a white pine box, relaxed, and dropped something at my feet. I covered it with one foot quietly, and a little later on I picked it up and pocketed it. I reasoned that in his last struggle his hand must have seized that object unwittingly and held it in a death-grip.

At the hotel that night the main topic of conversation, with the possible exceptions of politics and prohibition, was the demise of Major Caswell. I heard one man say to a group of listeners:

'In my opinion, gentlemen, Caswell was murdered by some of these no-account niggers for his money. He had fifty dollars this afternoon which he showed to several gentlemen in the hotel. When he was found the money was not on his person.'

I left the city the next morning at nine, and as the train was crossing the bridge over the Cumberland River I took out of my pocket a yellow, horn, overcoat button the size of a fifty-cent piece, with frayed ends of coarse twine hanging from it, and cast it out of the window into the slow, muddy waters below.

I wonder what's doing in Buffalo!

SUGGESTIONS FOR FURTHER READING

Arnett, Ethel Stephens, *O. Henry from Polecat Creek*. Piedmont Press, 1962. A lively and anecdotal biography.

Brooks, Van Wyck, *The Confident Years: 1885–1915*. Dutton, 1952. A wide-ranging study of the determinant period of American literary realism which includes a good account of O. Henry's New York stories.

Current–Garcia, Eugene, *O. Henry*. Twayne, 1965. A volume in the useful 'Twayne's United States Authors' series which combines pertinent, though brief, biographical information and analysis of the works. While O. Henry's characterization is criticized as depending too heavily on 'conventionalized types', his word-play and 'surprise' endings are found to be important developments in the short story form.

Davis, Robert H. & Arthur B. Maurice, *The Caliph of Bagdad*. D. Appleton, 1931. The last sustained appreciation of O. Henry prior to the decline of his reputation and popularity during the 1930s.

Gallegly, Joseph, *From Alamo Plaza to Jack Harris's Saloon: O. Henry and the Southwest He Knew*. Mouton, 1970. A vivid account of the region which, in conjunction with New York, attracted most of O. Henry's attention.

Langford, Gerald, *Alias O. Henry. A Biography of William Sidney Porter*. Macmillan, 1957. Arguably the most perceptive and sensitive study of O. Henry.

Long, E. Hudson, *O. Henry. The Man and His Work*. University of Pennsylvania Press, 1949. Particularly good on O. Henry's use of locale (especially in the stories with a western setting) and attends well to the 'compassion' which underwrites all his work.

O'Connor, Richard, *O. Henry: The Legendary Life of William S. Porter*. Doubleday, 1970. Stern on what are perceived as O. Henry's 'weaknesses' (sentimentality, etc.).

Smith, C. Alphonso, *O. Henry. A Biography*. Hodder & Stoughton, 1916. The first biography of its subject, published during the height of O. Henry's reputation, and keen to stress O. Henry's expansions of the thematic preoccupations of the short story form.

Stuart, David, *O. Henry. A Biography Of William Sidney Porter*. Stein and Day, 1987. The most recent and most fully documented account of O. Henry's life.

Williams, William Walsh, *The Quiet Lodger Of Irving Place*. Dutton, 1936. An expressive and impressionistic study which concentrates upon O. Henry's years in New York.

SHORT STORY COLLECTIONS
IN EVERYMAN

A SELECTION

The Secret Self
Short Stories by Women
'A superb collection' *Guardian* **£4.99**

Selected Short Stories
and Poems
THOMAS HARDY
The best of Hardy's Wessex in a
unique selection **£4.99**

The Best of
Sherlock Holmes
ARTHUR CONAN DOYLE
All the favourite adventures in one
volume **£4.99**

Great Tales of Detection
Nineteen Stories
Chosen by Dorothy L. Sayers **£3.99**

Short Stories
KATHERINE MANSFIELD
A selection displaying the
remarkable range of Mansfield's
writing **£3.99**

Selected Stories
RUDYARD KIPLING
Includes stories chosen to reveal the
'other' Kipling **£4.50**

The Strange Case of
Dr Jekyll and Mr Hyde
and Other Stories
R. L. STEVENSON
An exciting selection of gripping
tales from a master of suspense **£3.99**

Modern Short Stories 2:
1940-1980
Thirty-one stories from the greatest
modern writers **£3.50**

The Day of Silence and
Other Stories
GEORGE GISSING
Gissing's finest stories, available for
the first time in one volume **£4.99**

Selected Tales
HENRY JAMES
Stories portraying the tensions
between private life and the outside
world **£5.99**

£4.99

£6.99

AVAILABILITY

All books are available from your local bookshop or direct from
**Littlehampton Book Services Cash Sales, 14 Eldon Way, LinesideEstate,
Littlehampton, West Sussex BN17 7HE.** PRICES ARE SUBJECT TO CHANGE.

To order any of the books, please enclose a cheque (in £ sterling) made payable to
Littlehampton Book Services, or phone your order through with credit card details (Access,
Visa or Mastercard) on 0903 721596 (24 hour answering service) stating card number and
expiry date. Please add £1.25 for package and postage to the total value of your order.